Beast in Shining Armor

A Kinda Fairytale

Cassandra Gannon

Text copyright © 2013 Cassandra Gannon
Cover Image copyright © 2013 Cassandra Gannon
All Rights Reserved

Published by Star Turtle Publishing

Visit Cassandra Gannon at starturtlepublishing.com or on the Star Turtle Publishing Facebook page for news on upcoming books and promotions!

Email Star Turtle Publishing directly:
starturtlepublishing@gmail.com

We'd love to hear from you!

Also by Cassandra Gannon

The Elemental Phases Series
Warrior from the Shadowland
Guardian of the Earth House
Exile in the Water Kingdom
Treasure of the Fire Kingdom
Queen of the Magnetland
Magic of the Wood House
Coming Soon: *Destiny of the Time House*

A Kinda Fairytale Series
Wicked Ugly Bad
Beast in Shining Armor
The Kingpin of Camelot
Coming Soon: *Happily Ever Witch*

Other Books
Love in the Time of Zombies
Not Another Vampire Book
Vampire Charming
Cowboy from the Future
Once Upon a Caveman
Ghost Walk

You may also enjoy books by Cassandra's sister, Elizabeth Gannon.

The Consortium of Chaos series
Yesterday's Heroes
The Son of Sun and Sand
The Guy Your Friends Warned You About
Electrical Hazard
The Only Fish in the Sea

Coming Soon: Not Currently Evil

The Mad Scientist's Guide to Dating

<u>Other books</u>
The Snow Queen
Travels with a Fairytale Monster
Everyone Hates Fairytale Pirates
Captive of a Fairytale Barbarian
Coming... Eventually: The Man Who Beat-Up Prince Charming

For Daddy
Who barely winced at all when I dropped out of law school to write romance novels.

Prologue

Once Upon a Time...

    When Avenant was born, the Northlands wept.
    His mother was inconsolable, sealing herself in her room and refusing to see the child who'd just ruined her life. The court doctors spoke in hushed tones, terrified that they would be blamed for this disaster. The citizens, sensing the gloom that had settled over the palace, postponed their celebrations and peered through their drapes, waiting for news. As a thick snow fell over the landscape, the kingdom was engulfed in despair.
    The heir they had longed for was Bad.
    His father took it the hardest. Prince Vincent told the servants to take the boy into the wilderness and leave him to the elements. Forty generations of the royal family wouldn't be tainted with a beast. Some unworthy, unlovable mistake of nature. It would humiliate the prince to claim a dirty animal as his own.
    While the staff quickly prepared to erase all trace of the child, the infant was left alone in an unused laundry closet. His unanswered cries echoed off the walls of the small room. A royal nursery had been prepared for the long awaited prince, but no one wanted to sully it with this monster. One day there would be a worthy heir. Someone Good and noble to wear the crown. The carefully furnished bedroom, filled with toys and books, would wait for him.
    Except that boy would never come to claim it.
    In the cruelest twist yet, the princess began to

bleed heavily in the hours after the birth. Surgeons saved her life, but the cost was enormous. There would be no more royal children. If Prince Vincent's line was to remain unbroken, the Beast was his only hope.

Weeping at the injustice, the staff wheeled the baby into the throne room. Prince Vincent was waiting there, a man defeated. He couldn't bear to look at the monster who'd been born in place of his son. Instead, he stared at the pictures of his ancestors on the snow-colored wall and debated his options.

Everything in the palace was decorated in the cold blues and whites of the Northlands. The castle was a reflection of the wintery kingdom, with no bright colors to draw the eyes. No warmth to distract people from their duties. The temperature inside was precisely calculated to chill the air and inspire activity, without causing needless hypodermic deaths.

Through the power of magic, the gigantic Icen Throne stayed forever frozen, though. Even inside the palace, the frosty surface remained hard and unyielding. According to legend, the throne of the Northlands would never melt, so long as their royal line remained strong.

Prince Vincent sat down on it, as if to assure himself that it hadn't turned back into a puddle of water. "Is there any possibility that we're wrong about... it?" He asked, waving a disgusted hand towards the basinet. "Perhaps, it merely *looks* Bad. Perhaps it's Good underneath and we can perform some spell to make it physically presentable."

"I'm sorry, sire." The head wizard shook his head, hating that he had to crush Vincent's final hope. "The boy is Bad all the way through. All the tests confirm it."

Vincent sighed, having already known the answer. "We'll have to go through with the plan to execute it, then. Better to have no son at all, than that *thing*. I would be the laughingstock of the Four Kingdoms if anyone saw it."

The Four Kingdoms was made up of the Northlands, Southlands, Eastlands and Westlands. There were other lands beyond the borders of each, but they were nothing compared to the glory of these realms. Everyone in the Four Kingdoms agreed on that. And of the four, the Northlands was the most forbidding. Their frigid strength inspired fear and awe. No misshapen child would threaten that powerful reputation. He would have to die.

Pride demanded it.

"There is one thing you need to see before you get rid of him, sire." An elven nursemaid piped up.

Vincent's jaw ticked. It annoyed him whenever servants spoke. "What do I *need* to see?" He mocked. "What could *you* possibly know that *I* don't?"

The woman looked down, intimidated by his scathing tone. "The prince no longer looks like a beast." She murmured. "He looks... normal."

Vincent's eyebrows drew together. He stalked over to glower down at the child, the counsel of wizards clustering around him.

The uppity nursemaid was right. The baby appeared *normal*. A soft down of blond hair covered his head, his body soft and pink. His eyes no longer glowed that horrible electric-blue. Instead, they blinked up at Vincent in the same icy hue that he saw in the mirror every morning. Obviously, something wicked was afoot, but there was no denying that it was an improvement over the way he'd looked before.

Vincent glared over at the wizards for an explanation. "Well?"

The head wizard cleared his throat, thinking things over. "It could be that the Beast is," he made a vague gesture with one hand, "merely a *part* of the prince. The boy might be able to suppress it and appear normal." He hesitated. "He's still wholly Bad, of course. But, the physical manifestations of the..."

Vincent cut him off. "He can hold the Beast back? That's what you're saying?"

"So it would seem, sire. That doesn't change the legal ramifications, though. A Bad folk cannot inherit the crown."

Good folk were the only people who mattered. The only ones who were protected under the law. Bad folk were abominations. Genetically inferior and universally evil, they had to be kept in check for fear of their villainy spreading. They were fit for mindless physical tasks like cleaning stables or digging a wishing well, but they couldn't be a prince. A prince needed to be Good. He needed to be *important*.

The wizard gave his head a sad shake. "The Icen Throne will have to pass to your cousin's son Lancelot."

Vincent's eyes narrowed. "That little turd? The boy is five and still in diapers. You think I'd hand over my kingdom to a moron like *him?*"

"There isn't a choice, sire."

"There's always a choice when you're a prince!" Vincent scowled at the baby who'd caused him all this trouble. As long as it didn't *look* like a monster, he might be able to make do with this freak. What else *could* he do? Let his cousin's boy steal the Northlands? Let the royal line break? Let himself be humiliated?

Let someone else *win?*

The thought of this hated creature carrying on his legacy was abhorrent, but not as abhorrent as losing.

Vincent would never surrender and he'd teach his beast of a son to do the same. Fuck the law. No one would steal the Icen Throne from him. Vincent was a *prince*. He could do whatever he wanted. He'd train his son to hold onto the kingdom through force and guile. The boy was Bad, after all. It was in his makeup to be a villain. Why not use his twisted DNA to the family's advantage? Maybe the boy could learn to control the Beast. Maybe he could use it to increase the family's power. If the little monster was here, it might as well make itself useful.

    Vincent gave a cold smile. "Put it in the nursery." He decided and looked over at the nursemaid. "I don't think I'll kill it today."

Chapter One

Do you think a beast has to be ugly?
We citizens of the Northlands certainly know better and that's why we're here today.
Our prince is as handsome as any knight in shining armor.
...But he has the heart of a monster.

Opening Statement for the Prosecution- *The People of the Northlands v. Prince Avenant*

Scarlett Riding-Wolf could talk smart people into doing dumb things.

It was the main reason that Avenant, *rightful* Prince of the Northlands, had hired her to be his lawyer.

Well, "lawyer" was perhaps the wrong word, as Letty wasn't technically an attorney. She was a do-Gooding ugly stepsister who'd taken over the Enchanted Forest and was busily making it into a fifth kingdom for the world's outcasts. And "hire" was perhaps the wrong word, too, as he certainly wasn't going to *pay* Letty. They were supposed to be "friends," after all.

But, Avenant knew if anyone could help him reclaim the Icen Throne it was that pushy redhead. He'd been there when Scarlett masterminded a prison break, and convinced most of the Four Kingdoms to begin granting Bad folk the same rights as Good, and overthrew that bitch Cinderella.

If Letty could do all that, surely she could convince one little tribunal of wizards that Avenant wasn't a beast.

A trial had taken his crown away and a trial would get it back. Eight months before, Avenant had been arrested for crimes against his people, deposed as their prince, and incarcerated in the Wicked, Ugly and Bad Mental Health Treatment Center and Maximum Security Prison. He'd been humiliated in the WUB Club. Locked-up by peasants and fools. Half-starved with their rancid food. Forced into group therapy. It had been a waking nightmare.

But he'd never surrendered.

Not even for a second.

He'd always known that this day would come. The day when he took everything back again. The day when he resumed his rightful place on the throne. The day when he *won*. Today, the moronic judges in front of him would rule in his favor.

It was inevitable.

To aid the cause, Avenant did his best to look as innocuous as possible. He folded his hands on the desk and tried to radiate Good intentions. Which was difficult, considering he planned to make this whole kingdom pay for what they'd done to him, but what better place than a courtroom for theatrics and lies?

He even managed a smile.

Letty paced back and forth in front of the judges. "All we're asking for is justice. We haven't come here for war or fighting. All we want is for you to see the truth." She gestured towards Avenant. "Prince Avenant had his kingdom stolen from him. His enemies wanted to claim the Northlands as their own and were willing to exploit every loophole to do it. He was deposed because he was born Bad. That's the only reason. But, if you would just look past your prejudice to see the need for change..."

"That's *not* the only reason!" Honorary Princess Rosabella Aria Ashman was on her feet again, looking furious. "He's a tyrant! Why do you think we call him the

Beast of the Northlands? He terrifies the entire kingdom."

Belle was kidding herself if she thought he'd earned the nickname because of his administrative techniques. She had never seen the real Beast. Few people had, although most of them sensed the darkness lurking inside of him. All his life, Avenant had worked to control the monster. He had a wall in his mind, keeping it contained. But, it was getting harder and harder to hold it at bay. The Beast was breaking free. He could feel it stirring inside his mind, wanting to emerge.

And its biggest trigger was Belle. Whenever Avenant looked at her, he could feel two sets of eyes focusing.

Wanting.

"He embezzled a mountain of gold from the royal treasury." Belle continued. "*That's* why we finally overthrew him and *that's* why he was sent to prison. Where he would *still* be if he hadn't escaped, which was *also* a crime! It all came out at the first trial!" She waved a hand at the judges. "How can you *listen* to this garbage?"

Avenant's mouth curved as the head wizard banged his gavel for silence. Belle's lawyer tried to keep her seated and quiet, but the woman was too furious to listen. Her outbursts were irritating the judges and only helping Avenant's cause. Belle was passionate. She always had been. But, ice cold logic would rule the day. *Avenant* would rule the day.

They could both feel it coming.

In any contest, momentum built as one side pulled into the lead. Avenant knew victory was swinging his way. So did Belle. After so many years of competition, the two of them could read the signs.

Whether it was over first place at the middle school science fair or for the crown of the Northlands, Belle and Avenant had been locked in a never-ending war for supremacy since childhood. She was his greatest opponent and she'd thought her last victory had been their final battle. That he'd finally been defeated.

She'd been so wrong. He would never stay away from what was his, even if it meant enduring this farce of a trial.

Avenant sent her a bland look.

Belle glowered back like she wanted to incinerate him with the force of her temper. On the surface, she looked like the straight A student she'd always been. The interesting little oddball who held charity poetry readings at her cluttered bookstore. The Good girl who did her best to stay far, far away from the Beast. But underneath the conservative yellow suit and the conservative cut of her dark hair and the conservative make-up on her beautiful face… the woman could be a raging *bitch*.

That was so damn appealing.

"You're trying to twist this all around, as usual." Belle's brown eyes blazed at him. "When your parents died, you seized the throne even though you weren't Good and it was illegal for you to rule. Did I try to overthrow you, then? *No*. It wasn't until later that I rebelled and you know it." She jabbed a finger at him. "So, you being locked-up had *nothing* to do with you being Bad. It had to do with you stealing from our kingdom, you ass!"

Avenant knew she'd see the smirk that he kept hidden from the others. Knew it would just make her angrier. Avenant knew Belle better than anyone.

Or so he'd once thought.

"Your honors, this blatant antagonism is exactly

what I was talking about." Letty put in. "Prince Avenant never received a fair trial for his alleged crimes, because all the evidence was collected and presented by the very people who wanted to steal the Icen Throne. All the financial records of this so-called 'embezzlement' are tainted by the greed and self-interest of Rosabella Aria Ashman and her group of extremist friends. Prince Avenant was deposed thanks to the lies of *that* woman," she pointed at Belle, "who has fanatically persecuted my poor client for years."

Belle gasped in outrage. "That's not true!" She looked over at Avenant like she expected him to suddenly switch sides and back her up. "You know I didn't lie about *any* of that. *I'm* not the liar here."

Avenant's jaw ticked.

"He was officially pardoned by Prince Charming of the Westlands." Letty pressed on. "He'd be welcomed in the Enchanted Forest, if he wished to stay there. Instead, he's risked *everything* to come back here. *This* is his home." She moved towards the long bench, her expression open and persuasive. "This tribunal was called to determine the true ruler of the Northlands in a peaceful and fair way. In fact, it was Prince Avenant's idea to convene you here and he is committed to respecting your decision."

Avenant nodded as if he actually recognized the authority of these morons to determine his fate. He didn't. In fact, amusing as it was to watch Belle fume, he was regretting this whole silly misadventure. It made him look weak to just sit here, when he could be freezing these insipid wizards into ice and claiming what was his through open war. There was a reason he'd banned all lawyers from his lands before he'd been overthrown.

Letty had been the one who'd championed the

use of legal strategies to reclaim the Northlands. The woman was so depressingly *Good*. Avenant had been willing to go along with her plan, though, because it offered something a battlefield couldn't. If he won this trial, he would actually *see* Belle's face when he took back his throne. He'd be in the room with her when she realized she'd lost. That possibility seemed worth all the extra paperwork.

Unfortunately, it was turning out to be a discouragingly easy triumph. He didn't just want to win. He wanted to defeat *Belle*. He wanted it to be her and him, struggling for victory. And when he emerged on top, he wanted her to know that *he'd* done it. Just him. The lawyers and the judges were spoiling the whole contest.

"I submit that Prince Avenant coming here, at such personal risk, proves that *he* should be wearing the crown." Letty continued. "His heart is forever with the welfare of the Northlands. He has been supportive and open throughout this process. He's shown deference to the wisdom of the court and has only the deepest concern for his citizens."

Belle gave an audible scoff.

Even Avenant had to squint a little at Letty's hyperbolic sentimentality. But, the three ancient judges seemed moved by the idea and that was all that mattered.

"All we want is fairness." Letty concluded. "This is about Prince Avenant's legacy. The palace she took from him?" Another gesture towards Belle. "That was the place where he was born. Where his parents lived and died. Where he should have been allowed to rule, as his ancestors have for centuries." She sadly shook her head. "This case is really about bigotry. He was driven out because he was labeled Bad and Bad folk can't rule according to these antiquated laws."

There were Good folk and Bad folk in the Four Kingdoms. The Good were in charge. They always had been. Assured of their moral superiority, they smugly waited for their happily-ever-afters and relished the fact that they were genetically blessed. For so long, they'd believed they would always be in control.

But now the Bad folk were fighting back. They outnumbered the Good and they were beginning to assert their power. Social change was sweeping the Four Kingdoms. These ancient wizards were terrified of what might happen if they tried to keep Avenant from the Icen Throne. The protests would be all over the news. Bad folk would shut down the Northlands with strikes and picket lines. Letty would make sure of it. And the more violent factions might take things even further. The judges didn't want radical trolls and goblins firebombing their houses.

Avenant was about to be the first Bad folk in history legally granted a crown. After a lifetime of being told he wasn't Good enough, it was finally going to happen. His parents would've been shocked. They'd weaned him on the idea that he'd have to hold the Northlands by force in order to sustain the family legacy. That was all they cared about. Keeping the line intact. Maintaining power. They'd expected him to rule through pain and fear and tyranny. It was how they'd trained him. What they'd hardened him for, through countless insults and beatings.

And closets.

Avenant's hand clenched against the table. Remembering his parents was always a bad idea. The Beast snarled in agreement.

"Prince Avenant had his whole life stripped

away." Scarlett insisted. "He was called a beast and plotted against. Because of prejudice, he was driven from his lands. He's the *victim* in the story."

Belle opened her mouth to argue that point, but her lawyer quickly clamped a palm on her arm, urging her to keep silent.

"For so many years, we've branded people Good and Bad, without really seeing into their hearts." Letty said passionately. "All that's changing, now. We're finally realizing that everyone is born both Good *and* Bad. We can all live in equality and peace, if we can just move on from the past. Maybe Prince Avenant has made mistakes, but he's paid for them. He's forgiven everyone who plotted his downfall and we ask that they forgive him in return. All he wants to do is come back to the Northlands." She placed a hand over her heart. "Please. Let him come *home*." Letty headed back over to sit beside him at their table.

The courtroom was a cavernous space, with white stone walls and a gallery of busts depicting dead judges lining the perimeter. Through the windows, Avenant could see snow falling and blanketing the kingdom in another foot of frost. His homeland wasn't called the "Northlands" because of its sunny climate. He absently used his powers to create patterns on the chilly glass. Controlling the ice always calmed him. He wished he was standing in the cleansing blizzard, rather than stuck in some depressing little room.

Claustrophobia was a personal weakness that he worked tirelessly to hide from the world.

"Passable job, counselor." Avenant lowered his voice so only Scarlett could hear. "Your speech got a tad melodramatic at the end, but I think they were dumb enough to buy most of it."

"Shut-up and keep looking un-beastly." Letty whispered back. "God, it's a lucky thing this is a private hearing and they made Marrok stay outside. No way could he have kept a straight face, listening to me praise you so *effusively*."

"The wolf wants me out of the Enchanted Forest." Scarlett's True Love had made his position crystal clear on that front. "He'd be a character witness, testifying that I volunteered in soup kitchens and had donated both my kidneys to needy kittens, if that's what it took to get me back to the Northlands."

"Well, it would help your popularity if you weren't always such a conceited jerk. Remember how you promised that, if I helped you, you'd work on being nicer? When is that going to start happening?"

"I don't know how to be nice." Avenant glanced to the other side of the courtroom where Belle and her attorney conferred in heated tones. He felt a surge of satisfaction. "She's going to blow it for herself." He predicted. "She's too angry to think rationally. It's always been her downfall."

"I just hope you know what you're doing by antagonizing Belle." Letty fixed him with a pointed look. "Even if you win the case, it doesn't mean you win *her*. I've told you, there are much better ways to get a girl to pay attention then by pulling on her pigtails."

"I'm after my kingdom, not that fucking usurper."

"Right." Scarlett rolled her eyes. "Attorney client privilege, Avenant. Just admit that you're doing all this because Belle is your True Love. You want the woman, not some chilly throne."

"Once I reclaim the Northlands, you're invited to that treacherous librarian's public execution on the castle steps. Then, you can see me get what I really want."

He watched as Belle pushed her shiny brown hair behind her ears with a graceful sweep of her hands. She only did that when she was agitated. Even from across the room, he could sense the heat of her emotions. Warmth pooled in his lower body as he remembered the last time they were in this courthouse together. The sounds she'd made and the feel of her.

He told her there'd be a next time.

"I don't believe in most of the distinctions between Good and Bad folk." Scarlett murmured from beside him. "You know that. But, Good folk never recognize their True Loves as quickly as Bad folk do. Maybe it's just an outcome of environment or maybe it's a biological thing, but we both know it's true. Marrok knew me right from the beginning. He said he looked at me and he just *knew*."

Of course, the wolf had known. Avenant didn't doubt that for a minute. A True Love was the ultimate prize. The one person you were destined for. If you found them, you'd won the game of life and Bad folk were never supposed to win. Traditionally, they were pariahs, excluded and oppressed. No one would ever *give* them a mate. Bad folk had to fight to claim what was theirs. As a survival mechanism, they'd developed a sixth sense when it came to identifying their True Love. Their instincts took over where faith left off.

They saw their other half and just... knew.

"Belle's Good. She has no idea of your connection and you're not giving her many reasons to discover it." Letty pressed. "You're mad at her for ignoring something she doesn't even know is there."

"I'm mad at her for a lot of reasons."

"I'm telling you, this is the wrong way to win her over." Letty made a face. "Better than a *war* would've been, granted, but still a terrible idea. Why don't you try being *nice* to the girl?"

"She framed me, stole my kingdom, and had me sent to prison. Why should I even attempt to be nice?"

"Because... you *long* for Belle. I see it every time you look at her."

Avenant ignored that. His gaze stayed locked on Belle even when she turned and caught him staring. Chocolate brown eyes met blue for a long moment, as if they were the only two people in the courtroom. As far as Avenant was concerned, they *were*. All the ceremony and spectators were just extraneous pieces on the board. It was always him versus Belle in their endless game.

"Don't." Belle hissed, leaning closer to him over the aisle. "Just don't do this."

"Give me a reason not to."

Her mouth thinned into a tight line. "What do you want?" Just the fact that she asked for terms told him she knew she was losing.

"Surrender." It was what he'd *always* wanted from her.

"Not. happening."

He arched a brow. "Think of the good of the kingdom. We could both live here in peace, if you just give in to the inevitable."

"I will go live with the ogres under a bridge before I surrender to you." She snarled.

She'd sounded the exact same way at their senior prom. Belle had been seventeen when she'd shoved him away and told him it would always and forever be *no*. Seventeen when she'd won the most important round. Everything since was bullshit.

Everything until *now*.

This was their ultimate showdown and he was

going to walk away the champion.

Belle's moronic lawyer was jabbering, again. The elf had created a poster of Avenant's crimes and set it up on an easel, emphatically highlighting each charge with his laser pointer. Avenant was annoyed at the list. He could've filled up at least three of those boards. This entire enterprise was a farce.

In fact, Avenant was growing more and more certain that this strategy had been a mistake. Inside of him, the Beast paced restlessly. They both knew the victory would be hollow if he couldn't defeat Belle one-on-one. It *had* to be just the two of them. Otherwise, she would never admit that he'd won. She'd keep fighting and fighting and fighting. Slipping through his fingers and refusing to surrender. She might even move away from the Northlands and then…

The door to the courtroom burst open and Lancelot swept in.

Dressed in a full suit of armor, the idiot looked like an idiot. His idiot blond hair and idiot chiseled jawline further contributed to his idiocy. The idiot cleft in his too pretty face and the idiot swagger to his too swaggering walk proclaimed to anyone watching that he was the biggest idiot in the kingdom. And, given the Northlands was full to bursting with idiots, that was quite a feat of idiotosity.

Avenant's eyes rolled towards the ceiling. Just what he fucking needed. "Oh, here we go…"

"Do you know that very shiny man?" Scarlett whispered.

"Sadly, yes." Avenant's gaze slid over to Belle, who looked almost as appalled as he felt. "This is your fault." He told her.

"He's *your* cousin." She hissed back.

"I object to these proceedings!" Lancelot proclaimed, the overhead lights bouncing off his helmet and causing half the room to squint against the glare. "Avenant is not fit to lead our glorious lands and this woman," he swept a gauntleted hand at Belle, "is a pretender to the throne. As the next in line and a man among men, *I* should be granted the crown of the Northlands."

Scarlett leapt to her feet. "Your honors, this is a private hearing. This person has no standing in…"

"Do we want someone Bad ruling us?" Lancelot interrupted passionately. The presumptuous ass strolled passed the gate at the front of the room like he had every right to be heard. "Do we want some book-selling female in charge of our lands?"

Belle's mouth dropped open. "I have helped this kingdom achieve fiscal solvency for the first time in…"

"No!" Lancelot answered his own question, talking right over Belle's outrage. "We need a *man*. Someone to take back our land from the women and the beasts." He banged a fist against Avenant's table. "A man born and bred for the hard task of being a monarch. A man with refinement and valor and innate Goodness, who will live in that castle and *inspire* our people to greatness." He paused for dramatic effect. "And that man… is right here, gentlemen." He spread his arms and waited for the applause.

Avenant sighed. He *definitely* should've skipped the lawsuit and gone with the bloodshed option.

"If I wasn't supposed to be ruling the Northlands, why hasn't the Icen Throne melted?" Belle challenged. "Obviously, the kingdom is still strong."

There was a very simple reason why the Icen Throne accepted Belle as part of the royal line. Avenant could've explained it to her, but she wasn't in the mood to listen. She had *never* been in the mood to listen.

"This is ridiculous." Scarlett glowered at Lancelot. "I'm sure there are hundreds of random people in this kingdom who'd like to be king, but they're *not* and they never will be. Are we supposed to listen to this...?"

"Actually, there are twenty-four." One of the judges piped-up. "The court has received *twenty-four* separate petitions from citizens detailing why they believe they are the rightful heir to the Northlands."

Avenant arched a brow at that news.

"My client is the rightful heir!" Scarlett insisted.

Belle jumped up again. "I ousted Avenant from the Northlands, fair and square. It's *mine* by right of conquest! The last judge ruled it, right from where you're sitting."

"That ruling was a travesty!" Lancelot raged. "I am the last Good member of the royal family! I'm a knight and a hero. Plus, I'm the only one here with his own action figure. *I* deserve to be enthroned."

"Nobody even bought that action figure!" Belle snapped. "They couldn't give them away at the store."

"They're collectors' items!"

The courtroom descended into chaos, everyone shouting over each other.

Avenant put his chin in his palm and considered his options. Lancelot's arrival was actually a lucky break for him. A throne contested by *many* people allowed him more possibilities for victory. Once they opened that door, the judges couldn't award the crown without hearing all their competing claims. Unless...

"We should have a contest of valor." Avenant put in lazily. "That's the traditional solution when the kingdom is in dispute. Who are we to question the wisdom of our ancestors?" He paused. "*My* ancestors."

Scarlett's head whipped around to gape at him. "What?" She sputtered. "Are you out of your mind?"

Avenant ignored her.

The judges' ruling meant exactly nothing to him and Lancelot mattered even less than that. Avenant had no conscience and magical powers. He could've taken this land by force weeks ago if that's all he desired. He could kill his cousin where he stood and smile as the social-climbing idiot bled out on the floor. He could walk out of the dreary courtroom the undisputed ruler of the Northlands.

But, he wanted so much more.

Belle's chocolate eyes narrowed in his direction. They were the exact shade of warm cocoa. "You arrogant son of a bitch. It's never enough just to win, is it?"

Avenant glanced over at her. "Or maybe I just never tire of beating you."

"I support this plan." Lancelot volunteered in a loud tone. "Contests of valor are the way of men. They prove who is the strongest and the most fit to lead the women and other lesser folk."

Scarlett stabbed a finger at him. "You shut-up. You too, Avenant." She whirled back to face him. "They're about to rule our way, dumbass! Why do you want to give them some crazy, obsolete alternative?"

"I'm magnanimous even in total victory." His eyes stayed on Belle. "I propose we settle this once and for all. The winner will take everything and the loser will surrender... everything." He arched a brow. "Unless you're scared."

Belle glared back at him. "Really? Are we challenging each other on the playground, again? You *really* think goading me will work?"

Of course he did. The woman could never resist a dare. "I think I'm going to have everything that's mine." He told her truthfully. "It's inevitable."

"The last time you thought that you wound up in a cell and I wound up in charge of the kingdom."

Avenant's teeth ground together at the reminder. "That only happened because I underestimated how far you'd go to win."

She threw her hands up. "How in the *world* can you still blame me for what happened? Huh? It's *not* my fault you were sent to prison."

"Of *course* it's your fault." It infuriated him to remember how Belle had screwed him over. He never thought she'd go so far. She'd set him up. Even if she didn't like him, she'd never deliberately hurt him before. He *wasn't* hurt. Obviously. Nothing could hurt him. But, it did piss him off. "You cheated."

"That's preposterous. I wasn't the one caught embezzling."

"If I'd been embezzling, I wouldn't have gotten caught." He felt the Beast yanking at its leash and fought to hold it back. It was getting more difficult to stay in control. It worried Avenant what might happen when the monster finally got free and that only made him sharper. "*You're* the one who changed the rules and made this into a blood sport, Belle. So fine. We'll do it *your* way. From now on, we play the game full out."

No matter what she did, Avenant would triumph. He knew that. It really was inevitable. Until now, his utter certainty in the eventual outcome had kept him sanguine about the back-and-forth nature of their encounters. Some days she won a skirmish and sometimes he did. But, in the end, he knew he'd have everything he wanted. Avenant was a patient man.

However, being sent to jail for eight months made him seriously reconsider his timeline for victory.

Before, he'd been savoring the challenge. Now he just wanted his prize.

Deep inside, the Beast gave a low growl, its sights fixed on Belle.

Belle scowled at him, oblivious to the danger. "You've *always* played full out! What, I'm supposed to believe that you've been ruining my life all these years because you're such a nice guy?"

"You have no idea what it means to have your life ruined." Avenant snapped, remembering all she'd done. Maybe he did belong at the WUB Club, because the woman drove him insane. "I never took away everything you had. I never locked you in a cage. I never left you at the mercy of those goddamn doctors and prison guards."

"That wasn't my fault! I never intended…"

"You fucking betrayed me!" Avenant roared.

"You betrayed *me!*" Cocoa-colored eyes suddenly glittered with suppressed tears. "I asked you if you were stealing that money from the treasury and you said no. You *lied*. And when I figured out the truth, you had me taken away in the night. Right from my *bed*. How could you do that?"

Avenant squinted. What the hell was she talking about?

Scarlett leaned closer to him, looking suspicious. "For someone who you *swear* framed you, Belle seems pretty sincere in thinking you're guilty."

His attention stayed on Belle as she wiped at her cheeks. "She's acting. She has to be." Taking her *from* a bed was the last thing he'd ever do.

"She doesn't *look* like she's acting."

Avenant gave his head a shake, trying to focus.

He had no idea what Belle's game was with this new tactic, but it didn't matter. At the moment, the important thing was getting her to agree to the contest of valor. "I have always gone easy on you, Bella. Do you think you'd *ever* beat me unless I allowed it?"

"Oh my God. Are you *really* going to try that bullshit? Really?"

Avenant gave an expansive shrug. "It's a court of law. I've sworn to tell the truth."

"You wouldn't know the truth if it hit you in your lying face!"

"I also go easy on women in battle." Lancelot chimed in. "Any real man does. They're fragile beings, so it's ungentlemanly to beat them *too* badly."

Scarlett and Belle both shot the chauvinist asshole looks of death.

"Thank you, cousin." Avenant said sincerely.

"I will agree to a contest of valor against you *and* him *and* anyone else." Belle told Lancelot through clenched teeth, her temper getting the better of her sense. "I've been fighting you for the crown ever since Avenant was sent away and I've been fighting him about *everything* since kindergarten. I'm not frightened of *either* of you assholes." She jabbed a finger at the knight. "We'll do this no-holds-barred and we'll see who wins. Alright? We'll just *see*."

Lancelot backed up a step under her fury.

Avenant couldn't quite control his triumphant smirk. "Agree to it." He ordered Scarlett and gestured towards the judges who looked overwhelmed by all the pandemonium going on. "Tell them to set up the contest."

"Avenant, there hasn't been a contest of valor in a century, because they always kill everyone. You could get the Northlands back without all this..."

He cut her off. "Just agree to it, before she changes her mind."

Letty swore under her breath. "*Or* you could just ask Belle on a date and not risk your kingdom and your life. Wouldn't that be simpler?"

"There isn't a risk."

"Yes, there *is*. Belle's smart. She could *win*. Have you even stopped to consider that?"

"I know what I'm doing."

Letty's eyes narrowed at his confident tone. "Whatever horrible trick you have up your sleeve, I'm advising you against it. If you insist on turning this into a cut-throat competition, it's going to backfire. You'll lose Belle or the Northlands or --most likely-- *both*."

Avenant gave a slow smile. "I never lose."

Chapter Two

Prince Avenant has done many terrible things. We all know that.
Yes, he condemned the library. And the orphanage. And everyone's favorite teddy bear shop.
Yes, he fired the entire cast of Mother Goose's TV show, because the rhyming games annoyed him.
Yes, he outlawed candy.
But ladies and gentlemen of the jury, it's not his fault that he's a villain. Avenant can't help that he was born Bad.

Opening Statement for the Defense- *The People of the Northlands v. Prince Avenant*

Rosabella Aria Ashman was not the most beautiful girl in the kingdom.

She wasn't the smartest or the most charming or the highest born. By the time she was six, she'd been labeled an oddball by everyone who knew her. As an adult, she spent most of her days with her nose buried in a book, running her small business, or thinking up ways to improve the Northlands. From the outside, she was just a boring woman who needed to date more.

But Belle *was* the only person who'd ever had the guts to stand up to the Beast. In the Northlands that made her a legend… And now she was going to die because she never knew when to give in.

Since childhood, she'd been fighting back against Avenant's arrogance and tyranny and effortless accomplishments. He'd had thoroughbreds at his tenth birthday party instead of ponies and he hadn't let any of the other kids ride them. He'd won the Sophomore Spring Showcase by strolling out on stage and throwing gold coins to the audience as his "talent." He'd scored exactly one point higher than her on the college entrance exam. One goddamn point. And he hadn't even *studied* for it.

That was the part that really pissed her off.

Avenant didn't have to *try*. Belle spent her whole life trying. Sometimes it felt like she had to work twice as hard just to keep pace. Avenant was naturally gifted at everything. He had the soul of a beast, but his external façade was unbelievably gorgeous. He was charismatic and brilliant. When he walked into a room, everyone took notice. Anything he'd ever wanted was handed to him… and, if it wasn't, he just took it. Greedy and mean, he ruthlessly crushed anyone who opposed him.

He was going to beat her.

It was inevitable.

Belle blew out a long breath and tried to calm her racing pulse. Every time she had to compete against Avenant the same doubts plagued her. He would win and laugh at her. Everyone was going to see that she was a complete fraud. She'd break before the contest even started and surrender without a fight. She wasn't up to this kind of challenge.

She should call this off. Pretend to break an ankle and slink home to hide. Leave the Northlands and never return. There was no way she could do this. It was too hard. No one could stand there, the walls of the labyrinth looming overhead, and not be overwhelmed by the magnitude of the task facing…

"Is that it?" Avenant adjusted his white leather gloves and studied the cavernous entrance to the maze. It was guarded by statues several stories tall, their icy eyes promising death to all who entered. "I expected it to be bigger. Didn't you expect it to be bigger?" He gave an unimpressed sigh, blue eyes rolling towards the gray sky. "Well, at least this charade will be over quickly. I imagine I'll have my victory by dinnertime."

That was all it took for Belle's anxiety to fade.

No matter what, she'd never surrender to this man. She would fight until she was dead and then come back as a ghost to fight some more.

She slowly turned to glare up at his perfect profile. Since he'd escaped prison, Avenant was back to dressing like a prince. A tacky prince. He favored ostentatious fashions that showed off his money and his masculine build. This was one of his favorite outfits, sort of a cross between a military uniform and a frying pan. His family's black insignia was emblazoned on the front on his chest plate. Unsurprisingly, it was a vicious, fanged monster.

Even decked out in his bedazzled gold and ivory regalia, he still looked… amazing.

White blond hair brushed his wide shoulders. His mouth looked like it had been sculpted from pornographic fantasies. He smelled fresher than fresh snow. From his calf-hugging boots, to his "I'm the best looking guy you'll ever gape at" face, to everything in between, he was just… amazing.

God, she hated him.

How could such a beast of a man be so beautiful?

"If the labyrinth is too simple for you, maybe you should just wait here and give the rest of us a head start." Belle suggested sweetly. "Make it sporting."

"Begging for mercy already?" He arched a brow. "I thought we'd agreed to compete with no quarter given. Or are you switching up the rules, again?"

"I thought we'd agreed there *are* no rules. Isn't that the way you like to play? Victory at any cost?"

He glanced down at her. "It depends on the prize."

She snorted. "Everything is a prize to you. You don't care about the welfare of this kingdom, or all the people depending on you, or your family's legacy. You don't care about anything but yourself and *winning*."

"My family's legacy *is* winning."

Belle hesitated, hearing the flat quality to his voice. A lifetime of sparring with Avenant made her the world's leading expert in his tones and she knew her words affected him. For whatever reason, she instantly regretted what she'd said. She knew better than anyone how touchy Avenant was about his parents.

"That came out wrong. I meant more --like-- your royal ancestors in a general sense..."

He cut her off. "It's *fine*. Say whatever you want. We're playing hardball, remember?"

Belle bit her lower lip. "I'm sorry." She said simply.

The old prince and princess had been merciless in their pursuit for perfection. It was no wonder Avenant was such a competitive jackass, given his upbringing. Winning really *was* his family's legacy and they'd been determined that their only child continue their quest for total domination of... everything. Failure was met with disapproval and pain. They'd never had a kind word for anyone, especially not their son. *Especially* not on the rare occasions when he lost some t-ball game.

Or spelling bee.

Belle knew what it was like to be a disappointment to your parents. She felt like she and Avenant had that in common. Every time she tried to reach out to him, though, he came back at her like a wounded bear. Their entire relationship was based on his refusal to just be nice.

Blue eyes flicked to hers and she saw that her apology had irritated him. "How in the hell did someone so soft ever take over my kingdom?" He asked contemptuously. "Do you really think you could ever claim the Northlands when you can't even argue without crumpling?"

Belle had no idea why she bothered.

Avenant was quiet for a beat, watching her from the corner of his eye. When she didn't snap some insult back, he sighed. "A ruler can never be perceived as weak. Not that you'll *be* a ruler much longer, but it's a lesson you should've learned by now." He gestured for a servant to rush forward with a hot drink. "Power only comes from strength." He handed her a tankard of coffee, then reached back to take one for himself. "Cold, hard strength."

"I don't believe that."

"Which is why you'll never win this game."

She almost dumped her coffee on his stupid blond head. "Why do you *care* if you win back the kingdom?" Belle liked ruling, but it took a lot of work to get it right. Avenant seemed to put all his energy into getting it *wrong*. "Aside from people bowing at you, what do you get out of being a prince?"

"Never underestimate the bowing." He paused. "Wait, you didn't get rid of the bowing, did you? I know you want to rule with equality and Good works, but we *do* still have the bowing, right?"

"I've been trying to drag this kingdom out of the dark ages and my approval rating is *quintuple* what yours was." Belle informed him smugly.

He sighed. "That's a 'no' to the bowing, isn't it?"

"I hate you." She brooded for a moment. "What

are you planning to do if you reclaim the Icen Throne? At least, I enjoy the job. I don't think you do, at all. I don't think I've ever seen you enjoy *anything*."

"I'm going to enjoy seeing all my loyal subjects again." He smirked. "We have so much to catch up on."

Belle's eyes widened, envisioning the snows of the Northlands stained red with blood. She knew the Beast too well to think he'd get over his ousting without elaborate and savage retribution. Avenant's present calm façade didn't fool her one bit. Given the wide berth everyone else was giving him, it wasn't fooling *anybody*. They were all braced for his revenge.

"*I'm* the one who overthrew you last year." She told him swiftly. "If you want to behead anyone it should be me."

"Don't worry. You're still at the head of that line." Avenant arched a brow. "No pun intended."

"Avenant, I led the rebellion against you. It was all my fault."

"I know." His voice was flat again. "No one else in this kingdom would have the balls to frame me."

"Frame you? Really?" Belle rolled her eyes. "Asshole." Sometimes he said such idiotic things, she didn't even feel like arguing with him. Especially not when she had bigger problems. She turned her attention back to the gigantic maze in front of them.

It was impossible to know for sure how big the labyrinth was because parts of it were built into the mountains. The hundred foot walls were constructed of solid ice and stretched off for miles in either direction before meeting up with jagged rock. Its length and width and depth were a geometry problem with too many missing variables.

Belle had always hated geometry.

"They say it's impossible to get through that thing." She told him after a long moment, wrapping her hands around the coffee cup for warmth. This far north, snow always fell. Within hours of entering the maze it would erase any trace that they'd been there at all. "They say that the labyrinth is endless."

"'They' say a lot of things."

"You're seriously not worried about this?" She gestured around. "There are dozens of other people here vying for the crown and an impenetrable labyrinth promising certain death to everyone who enters it. The odds don't look good for either of us."

"Eight months ago, I was sentenced to life plus a century in prison, yet here I am. Odds don't matter when something's inevitable. And me beating these peasants and reclaiming my crown is pretty fucking inevitable."

She frowned in irritation. "We could just call off this whole thing. You could give up and let me stay in charge of the kingdom. It would be the safest option for everyone."

Avenant sent her an amused smile. "I'll certainly consider your offer." He drawled.

He was *such* an asshole.

Belle snuggled deeper in her favorite yellow coat and resigned herself to going through with this stupid competition. "If I die, at least I'll die fighting you." She muttered.

"That's the spirit. Don't worry. I'll tell everyone how brave you were at the end."

An old wizard mounted the podium set-up in front of the crowd. He tapped the microphone imperiously, getting ready to start the proceedings. Half the Four Kingdoms had gathered to watch this spectacle. Grisly deaths were quite the sightseeing draw, even in this remote corner of the world. Belle was almost pleased that the Northlands was receiving such a huge influx of tourist money.

Almost.

"Today, we begin the first contest of valor in a century." The wizard said in a rasping voice. "Contenders for the Icen Throne have gathered here in agreement with the ancient ways. They will face the mysteries of the labyrinth, searching for the most sacred object in the Northlands... Excalibur. It lies hidden within these walls, awaiting the one who will free it."

Avenant shook his head in disgust. "Such a stupid name for a sword."

"Whoever returns with Excalibur is destined to be our greatest ruler." The wizard continued. "Our true prince."

"Or princess." Belle called. "Sexist jackass."

The corner of Avenant's mouth quirked.

Everybody else ignored her. "No one alive knows who forged the blade. No one alive knows the scope of the tunnels and corridors before us." The wizard gestured towards the impossibly high ramparts. "They tower above the ground and circle below, filled with unknown creatures and unknown dangers, twisting into infinity. Legends tell us that the labyrinth moves, forever keeping the unworthy from what they desire."

"It can try." Avenant muttered.

"Our legends also speak of the day Excalibur will find the one it seeks. One who will lead through his example of love."

Avenant snorted in derision. For once Belle agreed with him. Why were legends always so melodramatic?

"We've awaited that person for generations. But,

only someone with the warmest heart and noblest intentions can solve the riddles contained within these walls. No one has ever entered the maze and emerged alive." The wizard paused for dramatic effect. "They weren't chosen by the sword and their hubris ruined them."

Belle very much doubted she was the one person in the history of time to prove worthy of Excalibur. This contest would probably kill her. It would probably kill all of them. She looked up at Avenant's bored face, not sure what to say to him, but knowing they should end this madness. They were going to destroy themselves, because they were too stubborn to back down.

He glanced at her, feeling her gaze. "We can stop this, Bella." He murmured in his most persuasive voice. He was the only one who ever called her that and it always made her insides dip. "Even if they go through with the contest of valor, none of the others will find the sword. Let them march in there and vanish forever. You and I will stay right here and find better ways to spend our time." His eyes locked on hers. "Just *surrender*."

She swallowed. "No."

"You're simply postponing the inevitable. Give in now and save us both the trouble."

"I'll die before I surrender to you."

"Suit yourself." His jaw ticked. "Either way I'll win."

"You could at least *try* to not be a beast."

He slanted her an unreadable look. "I've never been given a reason to try."

The wizard raised his hands over his head in dramatic welcome. "Let all those courageous enough to face death step forward."

Lancelot shoved his way to the front. The crowd

cheered for him. He heroically posed at the entrance while cameras flashed. He lifted a palm in conceited acknowledgement, soaking in the adoration.

"I dislike your cousin almost as much as I dislike you." Belle informed Avenant sourly. "Maybe more." Lancelot had been on her shit-list since seventh grade. More recently, he'd been trying to claim the crown ever since Avenant was arrested. Clearly the whole family was filled with dickheads.

Avenant looked surprised. "You dislike someone more than me? I'm a little bit hurt by that."

Belle refused to be provoked. She watched as more competitors joined Lancelot and began filing into the labyrinth. "I don't even recognize most of these people." She gestured to some random guy swathed in a purple hood and cape. "If they're not *from* the Northlands, how can they possibly *rule* the Northlands?"

"These morons won't be ruling anything." Avenant helped himself to another coffee and took a leisurely sip. Apparently, he wasn't worried about the others getting a head start. "No one takes what's mine."

Belle wasn't feeling so confident.

There were goblins and Cheshire cats and fairies entering the maze. The cannibalistic pumpkin-headed Mr. Pumpkin-Eater. That psycho bitch Mary and her salivating attack lambs. An army of shoemaking elves loaded down with mallets. Dower, one of the wolves who'd escaped the WUB Club.

And a lot more. Too many more.

Pretty much everyone competing was Bad, which meant that they were twice as dangerous. Lots of dangerous people with supernatural abilities and deadly skills were all questing after the same thing. There was just no way this would end well. At least Avenant had powers. Belle didn't have anything except what she'd learned from her research. Somehow she doubted that was going to intimidate anybody.

She saw Bluebeard heading inside and knew a moment of genuine fear. His turquoise facial hair and his citrus colored pirate outfit made him a pretty distinctive figure. So did the fact that he wore a necklace with six gold rings hanging from it, one for each of his "missing" wives. There was a double-bladed axe in his hand and he gave it a practiced twirl, like he was already anticipating the feel of it hacking through bone.

It was going to be a bloodbath in there.

"Give it up, Avenant." Jack B. Nimble called out, heading for the maze. His red hair always flickered like a candle, a trait which had created quite the fashion sensation in the Four Kingdoms. …And caused a lot of stupid people to light their heads on fire. "The Northlands will never be yours. Bad folk have no right to possess lands that Good folk need. You aren't civilized. You don't have the capacity to rule. We have no choice but to…"

Avenant moved his fingers and the would-be fashion model was frozen in a solid block of ice. The smug look on Jack's face stayed visible through the blue-ish frost, his eyes open and his mouth gaping. His trademark hair winked out, leaving nothing but blackened stubble on his charcoaled skull.

Half the crowd jumped back in panic. Teenage girls shrieked in horror at Jack's bristly baldness. Other people gasped at the massive ice cube surrounding him. Avenant gave them all an imperious wave, mocking his cousin. Unlike with Lancelot, no one took his picture.

Belle's lips thinned. Jack was a bigoted idiot with bad hair, but Avenant really wasn't helping Bad folk's reputations by doing things like that. Or his own. The Beast of the Northlands had terrified people from childhood because he never hesitated to show his claws.

"Is Jack going to thaw out?"

Avenant cast a thoughtful glance at the position of the shrouded sun. "I guess it depends on how soon summer comes."

Considering summer only lasted for about six hours in this region of the kingdom, that wasn't very reassuring. Belle made a frustrated sound. Avenant was so gifted and so incapable of using his gifts for anything positive. If he tried helping his people, instead of keeping them in line through fear and intimidation, the Northlands would be a far better place.

"Why can't you ever use your powers to do something Good?"

"Because I'm *not* Good, obviously."

"Isn't Scarlett's whole message that the distinctions between Good and Bad don't exist? That we're all the same."

"Scarlett is a very nice girl." He made it sound like a mental impairment. "Like you, she believes she can rule with friendship and hugs. My management style is a little different."

"Such as scaring your citizens shitless?"

"Such as scaring my citizens shitless." He concurred. "They should know by now to cower in silence. I don't ask for them to be smart --God knows, most of them couldn't figure out which side of a cow is up, in two tries-- But, they should at least be awed and obedient in my presence."

"And you wonder why you were overthrown."

"People know what they'll unleash when they cross me." He nodded towards the Jacksicle. "It's not like

I'm subtle about dealing with my enemies. You might be soft, but..." He trailed off in consideration. "It's actually *your* fault that the runt's been cryo-frozen, now that I think about it."

"*My* fault?"

"You're a bad example to the others. You make them think I'll tolerate insubordination from peasants. If I'd dealt with you the way I should have, B. Nimble would've been too fearful to do anything but tremble before me. In fact, *none* of this rabble would be rising up to oppose my rule. They'd be too frightened."

Belle looked up at him. "Why *didn't* you fight back when I came to arrest you?" Avenant hadn't even tried to use his powers against her. He'd *never* used his powers on her, as a matter of fact. Physically, he'd never hurt her, at all. Not even when they were children and she'd hit him first.

Avenant gave a dismissive shrug. "I think I was laughing too hard to strike out at you."

"No, you weren't. I'll bet you've never laughed hard at anything. It would mean you had to feel something and you're emotionally constipated. So, what's the real reason?"

For months, that question had plagued her. Why wouldn't he crush her rebels before they had a chance to take the castle? Belle could've taken him down. She believed that. But, not *that* easily. It was like Avenant had seen her and surrendered rather than lash out. Avenant would *never* surrender, so there *had* to be some ulterior motive.

His gaze flicked down to her face. "The real reason I didn't freeze you solid for defying me?" He shrugged. "I wouldn't use force to beat you. There's no victory in that. Just be glad I'm not my father."

She still felt like she was missing something. "Meaning what?"

"Meaning you have no idea what a beast really is."

"Avenant." Scarlett Riding-Wolf came marching over with a black backpack in her hand. "Here." She thrust the bag at his chest. "If you're determined to go through with this idiocy, I packed you some stuff. Water, toothbrush, a flashlight... Everyone else seems to have supplies, but clearly you weren't smart enough to bring anything silly like food on your death march."

"Why bother? You've seen my opponents." Avenant gave an indifferent shrug. "Winning this will be embarrassingly simple. I'm not going to be gone long enough to get hungry."

Belle's teeth ground together.

Scarlett's husband Marrok made a scoffing sound. "Good to know you'll die just like you lived, Avenant. An arrogant dick."

The Big Bad Wolf was the only guy in the world who even came close to matching Avenant's looks. Marrok was a tawny Adonis of a man, with a muscular body and topaz eyes that seemed permanently fixed on his wife. As stunning as he was, that was the part that impressed Belle the most. Marrok was clearly and unabashedly head-over-heels for Scarlett. She was his True Love. The most important thing in his universe.

Belle couldn't imagine that kind of devotion.

She'd never been important to anyone.

Avenant slung the knapsack over his shoulder. "Pray I don't return with the sword, Wolf. If I do, I plan to stab you with it and mount your head on my castle wall."

"Just add some more chrome to that outfit and I'll burn to death from the shine."

"Both of you stop it." Scarlett ordered. "Avenant, pay attention. I also packed you some medicines and a flare gun and a deck of cards."

"Oh thank God. Playing cards. I'm saved."

She disregarded the sarcasm. "My grandmother bet five hundred gold pieces that you're going to win this thing, you know."

"Is that all? Tell her to double it."

"I have a vested interest in your survival, wiseass. And I was thinking about how the walls in the labyrinth move..."

"That's just a story told by idiots." Avenant assured her. "This whole stupid maze was built by my grandmother's great-great-great grandfather Adam who was, according to the stories, an insane drunk. I'd be shocked if it leads to anything but a barrel of whiskey. The corridors probably dead-end fifteen yards that way." He gestured off to the left with a dismissive flick of his wrist.

Scarlett kept talking. "...and I think it would be a lot safer if you go in as a pair. Like when mountain climbers clip themselves together. So I had the fairies in the Enchanted Forrest whip this up for you." She held up a bizarre gizmo shaped like a fishing reel.

"I have no idea what that is." Avenant didn't sound very interested in finding out, either.

"It doesn't really have a name, but it works like a really big ball of string." Scarlett moved forward to clip said string to his belt. "It unravels as you go, so, if you're fastened to someone, you can always find your way back to them. If you use this, when one of you gets into trouble, the other person can help." She smiled like it all made perfect sense. "I know it's a competition, but you have to *survive* before you can win, right? Working together is a logical safety precaution."

"Who is he going to work with?" Belle demanded, shooting Avenant a frown. "You have a partner?" For some reason, that annoyed her more than anything else he'd done lately. "Who? Nobody even likes you."

Avenant glared back at her. "Many people adore me."

Marrok laughed outright at that lie.

"*You're* his partner, Belle." Scarlett put in, as if it was obvious. "Who else?"

Belle frowned. "Me?"

"Of course." Scarlett fastened the other end of the gizmo to Belle's coat. "You two know each other, so it's the best choice. Besides who else would look after the big dummy?"

"Hang on." Belle protested, uncomfortable with this idea. "I didn't agree to work with *him*. He'll break my neck and leave me for dead before the first turn."

"I promise to hold out until the second." Avenant assured her. "Or at least to *try*."

"He's just teasing." Scarlett said. "Don't worry. There's plenty of lead to the string, so you can have some privacy. This is going to work out for both of you. You'll see."

"Letty is a genius when it comes to planning." Marrok agreed. "And she looks after her friends... Even when the arrogant dicks don't deserve her help."

Avenant studied the thin filament connecting him to Belle and then glanced at Scarlett. "I asked you not to meddle in this." He intoned. "I told you I could handle it."

"Just say thank you."

Avenant considered that for a beat. "Thank you."

He said quietly.

Scarlett winked at him.

Belle's eyebrows soared. She'd never heard Avenant thank anyone before. Maybe he was more worried about the labyrinth than he let on. The entrance was as black and ominous as a tomb, so it only made sense that he'd be wary. Avenant wasn't an idiot. Maybe he wanted the security of a partner, but he'd been too proud to ask for help. Belle understood that feeling. She didn't want to go in there alone, either. Not with Bluebeard and the others on the loose. Even being tethered to Avenant seemed like a better option. No one would dare mess with him, so sticking close made sense.

...But she still wasn't going along with this plan.

"I'm fine on my own." She declared with a firm nod.

"As am I." Avenant watched her intently. "The only way I'd agree to this arrangement would be if you could pull your own weight. And, honestly, I don't see that happening."

Belle glowered at him. "Of course I can pull my weight! In fact, I have more information than you do on what's waiting for us in there."

"You think so, huh?"

"I *know* so."

Avenant sighed. "Fine. Have it your way. We'll join forces, but I still don't think it'll work."

"It'll work." Belle snapped and then realized she'd just accidently agreed to team up with him. "Hang on..."

"But, we're not staying together for long." Avenant interrupted. "Just until we get rid of the others. Then, it will be you and me at the end, and we'll finally finish this game."

Belle swept her hair behind her ears, considering that proposal. He had a point, damn it. Their final showdown *should* be one-on-one. They both knew that. "Temporarily teaming up doesn't seem like the *worst* idea in the world." She allowed. "I guess we can try it. Temporarily."

The grudging agreement had Avenant's mouth curving. "Temporarily." He murmured.

Belle's eyes narrowed, not liking his tone.

"Can I talk to you for a sec, Belle?" Scarlett didn't wait for an answer. She just tugged Belle away from Avenant, the string unraveling for a dozen or so feet. "We don't really know each other yet, but we have a lot in common."

"We do?"

"Sure. We both know Avenant is a pain in the ass."

"Letty…" Avenant began.

"Oh, you know it's true." Scarlett made a face at Belle. "He's narcissistic and stuck-up and grouchy. I don't really recall him ever being pleasant to anyone. I'm never sure what he's thinking, because he doesn't share his actual feelings. It's all insults and snarking. He's no one's idea of a knight in shining armor. He's more like…."

"A beast." Marrok finished helpfully.

Scarlett nodded. "A beast."

"I know." Belle agreed. None of that was news to her, although it did annoy her a bit to hear other people saying it.

"Oh for God's sake." Avenant drew out in a long suffering tone. He didn't look insulted, just bored. Belle had no idea why she'd worried about hurting his feelings earlier. It was impossible to hurt the feelings of someone who had none. "Can we just go already?"

Scarlett ignored him and leaned closer to Belle. "There's a reason for him being a beast, though." She said quietly, so Avenant couldn't hear. "All his life, Avenant has been told that he's Bad. That he's evil and monstrous and that no one will ever love him. That kind of label is like being stuck in a small, lonely cage. He's trapped and he needs someone to set him free."

Belle's eyebrows drew together. "Well, that someone isn't me." She whispered back. "I'm his least favorite person in the whole world. He gets irritated just looking at me."

Scarlett shook her head. "That's not what I see. Give him a chance. I'm pretty sure that if you're nice to the beast, you will *own* the man. And there are worse fates in this world than owning a handsome prince with magical powers who thinks you're awesome."

Belle stared at her, not knowing what to say.

"Great! I'm glad we had this talk." Scarlett paused. "By the way, if you don't take super-good care of him, I'm going to send large men to kill you." She nodded liked it was all settled and turned back to Avenant who was frowning suspiciously. "Alright, on with the contest of valor!" She clapped him on the shoulder. "FYI, I met a guy who met a gnome who used to date one of the monsters in the labyrinth."

"Real monsters don't 'date.'"

"Real monsters do whatever they want." Scarlett assured him. "Stay focused. Now, the monsters in the maze are mostly minotaurs. I'm not real clear on the details of them, because they're rare as hell. But I know they're hard to kill."

"Are they hard to freeze? Because that's really all that matters to me."

"I have no idea, but I have it on good authority

that they like music." She gestured to the black bag. "Don't worry. I packed you a flute."

"I don't play the flute."

"I know. That's why I got you some help."

Chapter Three

Even as a child, he was rotten to the core.

Testimony of Mrs. Poppins, Royal Nanny- *The People of the Northlands v. Prince Avenant*

Twenty-One Years Ago

Avenant slammed into the library. "Spell 'inevitable.'" He ordered, enraged by what she'd done. "Come on. I dare you."

Belle glanced up from her book, her gaze defiant and wary. She was curled up on the window seat, her small body cuddled under a plaid blanket. Her smooth hair was twisted into two pigtails and tied off with yellow ribbons. Belle always wore yellow. The color was bright and warm, just like her. She always reminded Avenant of the short days of summer that turned the frigid Northlands green.

He couldn't let her prettiness distract him.

"What are you doing here?" Belle demanded, as if she was surprised to see him in her house. As if she had no idea what he was so angry about. As if the fourth grade spelling bee championship meant nothing at all.

"Spell 'inevitable.'" He ground out again.

"Why?"

"You know why."

She sighed like he was the one being annoying. "Fine. I-N-E-V-A..."

"Bullshit!" Avenant interrupted. "That is *bullshit*, Belle." He had the satisfaction of seeing her eyes widen in shock at the swearing.

She looked towards the door, making sure no adults overheard. "Avenant..."

"In.ev.it.able. You know how to spell that." He stomped closer to her. "So why did you miss the word in the last round? Huh?"

"I just got mixed-up. Everybody gets mixed-up sometimes."

"Bullshit." This time it was quieter. "You threw the contest."

"That's ridiculous." She studied her book, pretending that the ponies on the cover fascinated her. "Why would I do something like that?"

Avenant's lips pressed together. "You threw the contest because you heard my parents shouting at me." He said flatly. "You heard them say that I'd be locked in my closet for a week if I lost." Being locked in his bedroom so his parents didn't have to look at him was hard enough, but he dealt with that almost every day. The tight confines of the closet were far worse. The walls felt like they were always moving closer.

Chocolate brown eyes flicked to his and he saw compassion in them. "It was just a stupid spelling bee." Belle whispered and all his suspicions were confirmed.

He hadn't been able to confront her in front of all the parents and teachers, but he'd known from the moment it happened that she'd let him win. All afternoon he'd been stewing over it and now he was ready for a fight. He'd glared over at Belle as the principal gave him the first place ribbon and she'd been clapping for him. *Clapping*. That was the worst part of all, because it showed she didn't do it out of fear, or as part of some plan, or even to taunt him.

She did it because she felt *sorry* for him.

Betrayal and shame and fury filled him, so Avenant couldn't tell one from the other. "You *cheated*." He spat out. "How many other times have you done that?"

"Never! It wasn't even cheating. We're both good spellers. Either one of us could've been champ, depending on which words I got and which you got." She bit her lower lip. "What's the big deal?"

Of *course* it wasn't a big deal to her. Belle's parents didn't care if she won the spelling bee. They barely noticed her at all, except to buy her frilly yellow dresses and pat her head on their way to some party. She had no idea what it was like to be the son of a royal family. To *have* to win or face the consequences. Every night his mother would tell him stories of what happened to princes who failed in their duties.

"The big deal is *I'm* Prince of the Northlands." Avenant yelled. "I don't have to cheat to beat you. I'm *better* than you."

That was a lie. Belle was far better than him in every way. He'd always known that. She was so damn pretty and smart and Good. She was like sunshine in the dead of winter. Sometimes in school he just sat at his desk and stared at her when no one was watching.

If she ever stared back, it would be the happiest day of his life.

"I was trying to help you, you jerk." Belle snapped. "You could just say thanks, you know."

"I don't need your help! And I don't need this." Avenant threw the first place ribbon at her and headed for the door. "It's yours. Take it."

Belle swatted it away and got to her feet. "You're being a baby." She marched after him, her beautiful face fixed in a frown. "Why can't you ever be nice?"

Avenant didn't know how to be nice. His parents would've been horrified if he even tried. Princes should rule by fear, intimidation, and cold brutality. Especially when they were Bad. When they were beasts. Anything less was weakness. That absolute law had been drilled into his head since babyhood.

Now Belle was looking at him with sympathy and he *hated* it. She nursed wounded squirrels back to health and let every loser in school sit at her lunch table, for crying out loud. The girl always helped the helpless. But, Avenant wasn't one of her oddball projects. He was a *prince*. As long as she was fighting with him, she knew he was strong. When she deliberately lost the spelling bee, he'd wanted to curl up into a ball and die. He couldn't stand that Belle saw him as weak.

He wanted her to admire him. To *like* him.

Instead, she thought he was pathetic.

Avenant turned and jabbed a finger at her, trying not to cry. "Don't *ever* pity me. You're nobody. Just a commoner. I'm going to rule this whole kingdom someday. I live in a palace. *You* don't live in a palace." He waved a hand at the nouveau riche decorations of the library. Belle's family lived in a nice house, but they were basically just socialites who'd stumbled into cash. "I'm royalty. *You're* not royalty.

"I wouldn't *want* to live in a palace." Belle retorted. "And it seems horrible to be you, so I don't want that, either."

That just made him madder, because he knew she'd seen his parents yelling at him and she was pitying him, again. "Well, your parents didn't even *come* to the spelling bee. Just like they didn't come to the art show or your violin recital. It doesn't matter to them *what* you do. Everyone knows that." He was going too far, but he couldn't stop. "I'm *important*. Important to everyone and you're not important to anybody. If anything, I should feel sorry for *you*."

She wasn't looking at him with sympathy anymore. She wasn't looking at him, at all. Avenant thought he'd wanted that, but it just made everything worse. She didn't even answer him back and Belle *always* answered him back. He could hear his heart pounding in his ears, knowing he'd hurt her feelings and not knowing how to fix it.

Belle stared down at the rug and didn't say anything.

"I can have anything I want." Avenant continued in a more deflated tone. "And when I marry my princess, she can have anything *she* wants."

Belle's eyes were swimming with tears and it made his stomach hurt. Deep inside the Beast howled, knowing Belle was upset and blaming him for it. Usually Avenant tried to ignore the monster. His parents told him it was Bad, and wrong, and that he should lock it away. But *Avenant* was the one wrong, this time. He'd made Belle cry and the Beast knew he was wrong, wrong, *wrong*. Her tears were the last thing in the world either of them wanted. He tried to think of something that would make it better.

"I can even get her horses." Avenant gestured to the book she was reading. "I can buy my princess all the horses she asks for. Hundreds of them. We could ride them together. Or she could ride them alone. She probably won't want to ride with me. I know. But she would be *so important* to me that it wouldn't even matter, Belle, so long as she was happy and..."

"You're never going to find your True Love, because nobody likes you." She interrupted, wiping at her cheeks. "You're mean and horrible."

Avenant winced. "But, I'm a prince. Lots of girls would want to marry a prince."

"If you think that's True Love, I really do feel sorry for you."

"Because you know everything about True Love, right?" He retorted, stung by her words. "You don't know *anything*."

"I read books. I know what it is and I know you can't just buy it like a horse. *My* True Love is going to be a knight in shining armor."

Avenant didn't like hearing that. "He'll have to be blind, too." He muttered, just to make her mad.

Belle pointed towards the door. "Go home. I don't want you here. I'm sorry I tried to be friends, okay? It won't happen again. Just leave."

"Friends?" Hope filled him. Even the Beast was calmed by the idea. "Wait, you want to be friends? We can be friends."

"Are you crazy?!" She gaped at him. "I will *never* be your friend, now."

"Why not?" He demanded in disappointment. No one had ever asked him to be friends before, but he was *supposed* to be friends with Belle. It was what he wanted. To have her like him the way he liked her. For one gleaming second, Avenant even pictured them riding horses together. "We could at least *try*."

"I don't want to try. You're ungrateful and selfish and you're a bully." More tears fell, but now they were angry. "You don't care about anyone but yourself. I would never be friends with a beast like you."

Avenant's insides turned cold. His mind took her words and automatically filtered them through all the experiences of his short life. He didn't consider the fact that he'd just made her cry and that was why she was refusing to be friends. All he heard was that she didn't want to be around him because he was Bad. It was the same reason his parents hated to even look at him and why the kingdom whispered about him in disgust. Because, he wasn't Good.

He wasn't worthy.

Belle was too important for someone like him. Deep down he knew that and it made him insane.

"I don't want to be your friend, *anyway*." Avenant shouted. "I have a lot of friends already. Better friends than you. Interesting friends. And we do a lot of interesting things."

"So go bother them, Mr. Popular!"

"I *will*. I don't have time to hang out with someone so boring."

She swiped at her nose. "And don't come back!"

"I won't." Avenant slammed out the door and then stood in her hallway. He stared at the tacky gilt mirror across from him, breathing hard and hating what he saw. In that second, he knew Belle would never, ever be his friend.

He slowly slid down the wall, not wanting to see his reflection. Avenant sat there for a long moment feeling broken. The backs of his eyes burned and he pulled his knees up to his chest to hide his face. She would never, ever like him. Not *ever*. Because he wasn't Good enough. His parents were right. He was a beast. Belle saw it, too. She probably just wanted to pretend he didn't exist, now. To go through the rest of her life never, ever thinking about him, again.

Avenant's jaw tightened.

No. She wasn't going to ignore him. That would be worse than getting locked in the closet. Belle *had* to talk to him. Avenant wanted her to notice him and, no matter what it took, he was going to have her attention.

So, if she wouldn't like him... then he'd make sure she *hated* him.

Chapter Four

We had kind of a sick joke down at the station that Avenant didn't have an enemy in the world.
…At least not for long.

Testimony of Morgana Le Fey, Sheriff of the Northlands- *The People of the Northlands v. Prince Avenant*

Belle gazed around the icy interior of the labyrinth and let out a long breath. Enough light filtered through the ice that she could see around her. It looked like a temple, with massive columns supporting an arched roof. It was warmer inside than it had been out, but the scale of the place creeped her out. She felt very small in the vast space; every sound she made magnified and judged by whatever ancient beings still dwelled there.

No one else was in sight, which didn't surprise Belle considering she and Avenant were the last two people to enter the maze. It was only the first room and already six hallways went in six different directions, each one as long and frosty as the next. They all looked identical, with ominous symbols carved above each doorway.

Basically, she had no idea which way to choose, she was tethered to her mortal enemy, and she was currently tied for last place. All in all, this contest could be starting off *a lot* better.

She looked up at Avenant and decided to be decisive. "I'm going left." She informed him. Given his normal spirit of cooperation and the challenge in her tone, Belle expected him to instantly tell her that he was headed right.

Instead, he just shrugged. "Fine." He checked his gold watch. "Let's just get this over with, so I can go home. I have important things to do today."

"Hitting puppies with rocks or evicting the elderly?"

"Repopulating my dungeon. I'll probably have to expand it, too, given how many uppity peasants will need cells there."

"I got rid of the dungeon, when I took over the Northlands. It was an archaic pit of torture and sadness. We painted it yellow and now we use it as a daycare center for the children of the palace staff. We have a swing set and everything." She shot him a meaningful glare. "Not all of us get our kicks out of firing Mother Goose."

"That children's show was annoying. All they did was sing. Badly. I was right to cancel it."

"Well, when I get control of the kingdom again, I'm putting it back on the air. It promotes early reading skills."

"You're so fucking soft." He muttered. "It's a miracle you weren't killed off long ago."

"Well, I'm sure it's on your 'to do' list." Belle started down the left hallway, trying to act more confident than she felt. She was silent for a beat, but curiosity overcame her. "So what did Scarlett mean when she said she'd gotten help for you? Did she send someone else in here to lend a hand?"

"I have no idea." He gave a nonchalant shrug. "If she did, she shouldn't have bothered. I can do this just fine on my own."

"You really think you're going to just stroll in, find Excalibur, and be done with the whole contest in a couple of hours, huh?"

"That's my plan."

"That's a *terrible* plan." She waved a hand around them. "Look where we are." Already, new corridors were jutting off and twisting into infinity. They could literally spend months exploring them all. "Obviously, this is going to take a while to figure out."

He scoffed at that idea, because he truly was the most arrogant man ever born. "There has to be a trick to it. We just need to discover what it is and we'll be fine."

It annoyed her whenever she had to agree with him. "I know. And I researched this labyrinth, with that idea in mind." Belle nodded. "You're right. It was built by your grandmother's great-great-great grandfather, but Prince Adam wasn't a drunken lunatic. He was actually a very impressive man. Intelligent, inventive, kind to his people..." She glanced at Avenant. "I can only imagine his genes are recessive."

"I hope so, given he was a drunken lunatic."

"No, he wasn't. I'm telling you. I found his diary in the royal library and it was filled with so many amazing ideas. Way more interesting than the writings of your other relatives."

"No one's ever read those ponderous journals." Avenant peered off down a random hall, trying to see the end. "Dear God. I can't imagine anything duller. They weren't even *written* to be read. They were written to sit on shelves and look important."

"*I* read them. As soon as I took over the Northlands, I studied everything I could on how to rule a kingdom. I wanted to do a good job."

"And so you turned to *my* relatives for tips?" He rolled his eyes. "You poor girl."

"Adam was a brilliant man." Belle insisted.

Avenant grunted. "I'm feeling far less charitable towards the drunken lunatic. Especially since I'm standing in the middle of his ridiculous mousetrap." Avenant ran a finger over the blocks of ice that made up the wall.

Belle was beginning to rethink the idea that the ice was filtering daylight and causing the eerie illumination. The walls themselves seemed to glow.

"You know, if you really wanted to help the Northlands, you should've had this stupid maze closed down and left my dungeon alone." Avenant told her.

"I never even thought about the labyrinth before our court hearing." Belle had been focused on the parts of the Northlands with actual people in them. She hadn't paid any attention to some relic tucked away in the farthest corner of the kingdom. No one ventured up here unless they were stupid or desperate. "I don't think anyone remembered it existed, at all. Except you." She shot him a suspicious frown. "How did you come up with the idea of a contest of valor right off the top of your head, anyway?" Even her lawyer needed to look up what it meant.

"When you're an *actual* ruler and not a usurper, you intuitively know things."

"I intuitively know you're lying."

"You've always been a bitter person." He said sadly. "You should try to let go of the past and focus on your future. You have so little of it left. It only seems smart to make the most of the scant days that remain before your execution."

Belle stopped walking and turned to pin him with a serious look. "If we're going to be stuck with each other for a while, do you think you could stop sniping? Do you think you could *attempt* to make this partnership work?"

"Can you?"

Belle sighed. "I'll try not to kill you if you try not to kill me. Deal?"

He considered that. "Give me a reason."

"Simple. Unlike you, I didn't just leave Adam's journal sitting on its dusty shelf. I brought it along with me, because it has instructions on how to solve this maze." She dug the journal out of her coat pocket and held it up. All life's answers could be found in books. Belle believed that completely. "If you're civil, I'll share what I've figured out so far."

Avenant stared at her. "That's a good reason." He allowed.

"I thought you'd see it my way." Belle flipped to the section she'd marked. "Now, I read it all over and it seems like it's in a code. Like riddles only... not."

"Coded not-riddles written by a drunken lunatic." Avenant sighed. "I'm suddenly remembering why I hated those tedious stories my mother used to tell about my tedious ancestors. I should just turn everyone into an ice cube and win the contest by process of elimination."

Belle ignored that. "The journal talks about how the labyrinth was built as a test for princes. Solving it is supposed to prove their worth."

"Uh-huh." He checked his watch again.

"It has three different parts to it, all of them needing different skills. We're on the ice level. It's designed to test the first quality that every prince needs."

"Money?"

"No." She held up the page so he could see. "It says, 'A prince must burn through an icy heart and help those around him. By focusing beyond his own selfish desires, he shows he is worthy of victory.'"

He leaned closer to her. "Which means what exactly? Aside from the fact that Adam had real potential as a fortune cookie author."

Belle tried very hard not to notice his perfect profile. When she was this close to Avenant, it was hard to breathe. It just wasn't fair that he was so attractive, considering his true nature. You should be able to look at him and *see* he was a beast. His handsomeness was false advertising.

She swallowed hard. "I think it means I need to be helpful, if I'm going to find the sword."

"Helpful?" Avenant repeated skeptically. "Helpfulness is *not* a princely quality. Trust me. I've been one all my life and I've never helped anyone."

"Which is why I deposed you, remember?" She snapped the journal closed and arched a brow. "Maybe Adam expects better from the Northlands' true ruler. Which is what I plan to give him."

"*I* am the true ruler of the Northlands." He snarled. "And now is probably not the best time to discuss how you stole my crown. We're trying not to kill each other, remember?"

"I didn't steal anything. *You're* the one who stole. The royal treasury was ransacked, Avenant. It took me months to get enough gold together to pay the workers. Did you even think about them?"

He glowered down at her. "Even with just the two of us here, you still can't admit...?"

An agonized scream cut through their bickering. The horrible sound echoed off the hard walls, coming from a dozen directions at once. It was impossible to know who'd made it, but there was no mistaking the fact that somebody had just died in a lot of pain.

Belle glanced up at Avenant, her heart hammering. "I think it was ahead of us." She whispered.

He nodded. The hallway forked off in two new

directions about ten yards ahead. Both corridors glowed with the same otherworldly blue light. Avenant chose the one on the right and crouched down to examine the floor. His fingers brushed against the icy surface. "Someone came this way. They disrupted the frost." He stood up and brushed his hands together, heading back to her. "I don't think that path leads to anything good. Shall we try left?"

Belle's lips parted as she suddenly realized why he'd taken his time before entering the maze. "You let the others go first so they'd trigger any traps." She gasped. "So they'd warn you which way *not* to go."

"If they're going to be here, they might as well fulfill Grandpa Adam's wishes and be helpful."

"You are un*believable!*"

"I know." He nodded. "Wait until you see me naked."

Belle made an aggravated sound. "I can't believe I tried to work with you." She unfastened the string connecting them and marched down the corridor to the right, towards the source of the sound.

Avenant swore. "Where are you going?"

"I'm going to see if I can help whoever was hurt, you ass."

"Why?" He actually sounded confused. "*Why?*"

"Why would you want to help someone who's out to steal your crown?"

"Because I'm not a beast!" She shouted. "Look, you do whatever you want. I'm going this way."

He cursed and stalked after her. "This is a waste of time. Whoever screamed is already dead. You know that, Belle. You heard it."

"I need to be sure."

"Goddamn it." Avenant caught up with her. "You drive me insane. Do *not* take this off." He clipped the cord onto her belt again, reconnecting them. "I'll go first." He maneuvered his way ahead of her. "The last thing I need is for you to go down here and end up dead."

"As if you'd care."

"You have that stupid journal with the instructions, remember? I need you to find the sword and the sword to get my throne."

Well, that didn't make any sense. Avenant topped her by a foot and could freeze her solid with a wave of his hand. If he wanted the journal, he could just take it. Hell, it had been written by his ancestor and she'd tracked it down in the royal library, so it was sort of his, anyway. Belle frowned up at him, trying to figure out his game. She was used to spotting Avenant's tricks and angles, but this time there didn't seem to be any obvious benefit to his actions.

That made her nervous, because he was suddenly harder to predict.

"You've been different since you came back from that prison." Belle wasn't sure why she said it, but the words just sort of came out. "You seem so... different."

"Weren't you paying attention at the hearing? I'm rehabilitated thanks to all the drugs they forced on me in that hellhole."

Belle hesitated. "They gave you drugs in there?"

"What the fuck do you think?" He flashed her a glare. "That we played polo all day?"

"I don't know. I just..."

"There were drugs. There were iron bars. There were guards who beat us, and administrators who tried to molest us, and they almost killed me with a rocket launcher. And *you* sent me there."

Belle opened her mouth, even though she wasn't sure how she planned to respond. There didn't seem to be an answer she could give to that. She'd brought Avenant down. She had. But, she'd never, ever thought he'd go to prison. To be honest, she hadn't thought about the day *after* her victory, at all. She'd been so *angry* at Avenant and she'd just wanted to beat him.

It had all gotten out of control. Everything had gotten out of control.

"Why did you have me locked up?" Avenant demanded, cutting off whatever she might have said. "What did I do that was so terrible?"

"You've done a *million* terrible things."

"But, you never took my kingdom before!"

"You never had men break into my house and attack me before!"

He had the audacity to look insulted. "Are you out of your mind? I never sent anyone to your house." He flashed her a look over his shoulder. "*How* did they attack you? Are you alright?"

"I'm fine, no thanks to you."

"I'm telling you, I'm not the one who sent them."

Belle snorted. "Sure you're not."

"Damn it, if you'd..." He stopped short his attention on the ground. "Huh." He stepped back, checking the bottom of his foot and making a face. "Well, I found the source of your screaming."

Belle's eyes went wide as she took in the carnage. Someone had carved up Mr. Pumpkin-Eater. Stringing clumps of pumpkin guts and seeds covered the floor in a gruesome orange crime scene. His scarecrow body was crumpled at an unnatural angle and his jack-o-lantern head had been hacked open. Its gooey contents were spilled out on the icy ground like a Halloween party gone horribly wrong.

Belle cringed. He'd been a cannibal, eating his own kind after baking them into grotesque pies, but it was still a terrible way for someone to die. "Who could've done this?" She asked.

"Well, anybody who knew him had a motive." Avenant scraped some of Mr. Pumpkin-Eater off his shoe. "Narrowing the suspects, it looks like he was killed with something big and sharp. His head was hacked apart with a blade. Possibly that." He pointed to a meat cleaver on the floor. Mr. Pumpkin-Eater's hand was resting on it, so maybe he'd tried to wrestle it away from the assailant. "Or possibly an axe or a knife or a sword. I'm sure everybody except you brought at least fifty-six weapons with them today, so it's a toss-up."

"That makes me feel a lot better."

Avenant wasn't quite done with his CSI analysis, though. "I'm betting one of our more strategically-minded competitors plans to thin the herd and this jackass was just the first to go. It seems like a really focused hit. No other blood or clues." Avenant edged around the pumpkin slurry. "The killer probably wants to hide in plain sight. Then, he'll pick us off, one-by-one, until it's just him and Excalibur."

"Could you not sound like you admire him, please?"

"Well, it's a good plan. To be honest, I'm almost impressed."

"What are you doing?" Belle demanded as he made it to the other side of the mess. "Whoever did this must have gone that way, you idiot. Are you seriously planning to follow them?"

"Of course I am. I'd just as soon catch him now, rather than wait and let him catch *us* later."

"How do you know it's a 'he'? Maybe a woman is lying in wait to kill us."

"Nonsense. Women love me. Most of them, anyway." He held out a palm to her. "You're a notable exception, but I've crossed you off my suspect list. You have an ironclad alibi of aggravating me during the time of the murder." He arched a brow when she didn't take his hand and let him guide her passed the remains. "Coming?"

Belle hesitated. "I hate this idea." She told him, her gaze on the grisly hunks of pumpkin shell. She'd never been around this kind of violence. Heading off to look for the perpetrator seemed insane, but not as insane as getting closer to the gore. "I don't think I can do it. It's freaking me out to think about bits of Mr. Pumpkin-Eater touching me."

"You're too soft." Avenant muttered. "Just step over it."

"I *can't*. I'm telling you. I actually met this pumpkin and now he's all over the floor and I…" She trailed off with a shudder. "I just… can't."

He studied her for a beat and his expression softened. "Alright." Belle expected him to lob some more insults her way or simply walk away. Instead, Avenant edged back into the orange pulp and seized hold of her waist. "Close your eyes." He swept her up into his arms.

For once, Belle didn't argue with him. She squeezed her eyes shut as he lifted her over the slaughter. "Thank you." She whispered. Her arms wound around his neck and she felt his grip tighten.

"You're welcome, my love."

His voice was a warm whisper by her ear. It sent her heart pounding. When he called her that, it always brought Belle back to their senior prom and that was a night she tried not to think about very often. She didn't want to recall the sound of his voice or the way he tasted or the feel of his hands. Obviously, it was impossible to forget, though. As much as she detested this man, he was the only one she'd ever longed for.

Avenant deposited her on the other side and cleared his throat. "You okay to go on?" He adjusted her coat collar, not meeting her gaze.

Belle nodded, staring up at his beautiful face. Why was he suddenly acting more like a knight in shining armor than a beast? "Avenant?"

"Yes?"

"You were just helpful." She arched a brow. "How does it feel to try something new?"

"You probably don't want an honest assessment of my feelings. They'll just scare you."

Clearly, he didn't want to talk about it. Too bad for him, Belle *did*. "Why are you sticking with me?" She pressed. "Why didn't you leave me behind?"

"The journal..."

She cut him off. "Forget about the journal. Tell me the truth."

He hesitated. "You're the only one I will ever lose to." He finally said. "I *won't* lose, obviously. But, if I *did*, it would have to be to you. I want this contest to be you and me, right to the end. I want to beat you and for you to see that I did it honestly. That we played this whole game by the rules and that I *won*. And then, I want you to look at me and just... know."

"Know what?"

Avenant shrugged and turned away. "I guess you'll figure that part out when we get to the finish line." He started down the corridor. "Stay behind me, alright?"

Belle stared after him.

Avenant hadn't been the one who attacked her in her bed.

In that moment, it was so clear to her. Maybe a part of her had instinctively known that all along. Would she have literally tied herself to the man and come into this labyrinth with him if she thought he was capable of physically harming her? Avenant wasn't a cheater. He never had been. His tactics were often dirty and ruthless, but they were never violent. Never outside the boundaries of fair play. That was why she'd been so furious when she thought he'd sent men to abduct her. It ruined their whole game to take things to that level. It had been such a betrayal.

Except, Avenant hadn't done it. Which meant that someone else had targeted her.

Only Belle had no idea why.

Chapter Five

Little Boy Blue: He accused me of falling asleep on duty and threw me into the dungeon.
There's bugs down there, man! It was a total overreaction.

Defense: Overreaction? Weren't you hired to guard the royal cows and chickens?

Little Boy Blue: Well, yeah. But, really, I'm a musician. See, I just took the job because I knew it would be a snooze. No one would steal from Avenant. Everybody knows what the Beast will do if you touch what's his.
Who would be that stupid?

Mr. Little Boy Blue- *The People of the Northlands v. Prince Avenant*

The maze circled around in circles upon circles.
 Avenant wasn't clear on where they were within its corridors. Since rocks were beginning to appear beside the ice wall, he could only guess they were somewhere near the mountains. Not that it mattered. After hours of walking down identical frozen hallways, he was resigned to the fact that Belle had been right. This was going to take a while.
 Fucking Grandpa Adam.
 The domed roof overhead made it impossible to see the sky, but a quick check of his watch said it was close to five o'clock in the evening. They'd been walking all afternoon and nothing had been accomplished towards his goal. Clearly, it was time to regroup.
 "This looks like a good place for dinner." Avenant decided and casually dropped his backpack. It was the first halfway reasonable resting spot he'd found. The hall

was angled so he could see anyone approaching and the flat rocks provided a makeshift bench. Given the circumstances, it was the best he could do.

Belle had been unusually quiet ever since they found the dead pumpkin. She actually jumped at the sound of Avenant's voice, like she'd been lost in her own thoughts. "What?" She looked around as if she had no idea where they were. "Wait, you want to eat here?"

"No, I *want* to be eating lobster amandine in the grand dining hall of my palace. Since you've gotten me lost in a labyrinth, though, I'm making do." He sat down on a rock and unzipped his pack. "Scarlett better have packed me something palatable, because I'm starving."

Eight months of tepid jailhouse porridge left Avenant in an almost constant state of hunger. He let out an annoyed sigh when he saw the stack of protein bars. Was chocolate really so much to ask? Yes, he'd outlawed candy in the Northlands because those damn oompa-whatevers started fucking him over on the tariffs, but he'd made sure that chocolate bars were excluded from the crackdown. Avenant craved the stuff. When he was locked-up chocolate was what he'd missed the most.

Well, there was *one* thing he missed more.

"Do you think it's safe here?" Belle asked, still not looking convinced they should stop. "We haven't found who murdered Mr. Pumpkin-Eater, yet. What if they sneak up on us?"

"Then, I'll kill them." It seemed like a fairly obvious solution. Avenant grudgingly tore open the least offensive looking healthy snack Scarlett had provided. It was some kind of granola thing with dried fruit and bits of solidified yogurt. Actually, it wasn't *so* terrible. He upended the whole bag of crumbly bits into his mouth and opened another. "Eat something."

"Shouldn't we be focused on the maze?"

"What's to focus on? There are hallways and we follow them. It's hardly turning lead into gold or something that takes actual skill." He snorted. "Until we figure out what the riddle about being helpful means, we're just spinning our wheels."

"It means we have to be *helpful,* obviously."

"And what? The labyrinth will see that and reward us?"

"I don't know." She paused. "Maybe."

Avenant rolled his eyes at the idea that the maze was somehow conscious of them. "You *definitely* need to take a break."

Belle frowned. "The others are getting farther ahead of us." She warned, but she picked up an apple.

"I'm not worried about the others."

"What if they're all off doing helpful things? What if they find Excalibur first?"

Another simple question. "Then, I'll take it from them."

"You can't cheat in a contest of valor!"

"Did you see a rule book?" He asked archly. "I didn't. Whoever leaves here with the sword wins. That's it. No one said anything about how we *get* the sword, in the first place." He fished a bottle of water from the bag and held it out to her. "Besides, none of these idiots will solve this maze before I do, so there's nothing to worry about."

Belle's lips pressed together in annoyance. "You're such an arrogant prick." She snatched the drink from his hand and sat down on the far side of the rock.

"There's a difference between confidence and arrogance."

"Yes, there certainly *is*." She agreed. "You know,

you're a smart person. You could've been a wonderful ruler if you weren't always so hateful to all your citizens."

"My citizens are always hateful to me. I'm just returning the favor."

"Maybe if you'd shown them you could be a reasonable, compassionate man, they would've given you a chance. As it was, you came in and immediately started oppressing the entire Northlands. It's like you assumed they wouldn't accept you and so you did everything possible to make sure it was a self-fulfilling prophesy."

The woman would never understand what it took to maintain real power. "You might have quintupled my approval rating as ruler, but *I'm* the one they feared. I had their respect, which is something your hand holding method of leadership never accomplished. Otherwise, they wouldn't have been so ready to give me back the kingdom in that courtroom. They were terrified about what I'd do if they denied me. They *knew* they could fuck you over, though. You're too soft."

"You're too hard!" She snapped back and chewed on her apple in fuming silence.

Avenant felt his mouth twitch upward.

"What?" Belle demanded, not appreciating his smile.

"This is the first dinner we've ever shared together. It's not going how I imagined it."

Cocoa-colored eyes flicked over to him. "You imagined having dinner with me?"

"I imagine *a lot* of things about you." He took the apple from her hands and bit deeper into the same spot she had. "You never think about me?"

"I try not to."

"Not even about that time in the courthouse?"

Belle stared at him.

Avenant smirked and passed the apple back to her. He leaned forward to see what else was stuffed into his bag. "Do you want to play cards while we eat?"

"What?" She gave her head a shake. "Cards? You want to play *cards?*"

"Yeah." He held up the deck Scarlett had packed. "Strip poker can be a lot of fun." He gave the pack an enticing waggle.

"I'm not playing strip poker with you, Avenant."

"We can play for something else, then."

Her eyes narrowed. The woman loved competition. "Money?"

"What money?" He scoffed. "You don't have any money. I'd win just by sitting here."

"Fine. We'll play for the joy of beating each other, then." She scowled at him. "And maybe right *now* I'm broke, but when I'm the one and only princess of the Northlands I will have *lots* of money. The coffers are filled again, thanks to *my* management."

Avenant peeled the cellophane off the cards and shuffled them. "The one and only princess of the Northlands will have whatever she wants." He agreed quietly. "I'll make sure of it."

Belle was quiet for a long moment. "Are you planning to get married?" She finally asked. "Like to someone in particular?"

He shrugged. "Aren't most marriages to someone in particular?"

Belle apparently took that as confirmation. "Who is she?" She demanded.

"I'm not going to tell you about my love life. You'll just try to ruin it for me." He began dealing the cards between them.

"No, I wouldn't!" She sounded insulted. "I never

76

bothered your girlfriends. You were always the one who did stuff like that..." She stopped short, her eyes slashing over to his.

Avenant raised a brow, knowing they were both remembering their prom.

Belle cleared her throat. "You could at least tell me this girl's name." She muttered. "Do I know her? God, she's not someone you met in prison, is she? She could be a criminal, Avenant! How well do you know this woman?"

"I know her so well it irritates us both. Just leave it alone and play cards." Avenant examined his hand. Two aces, two eights, and a red nine. Dead Man's Hand. Wasn't that just typical?

Belle wasn't willing to let it drop. "Why are you marrying her? It's part of some nefarious scheme, isn't it?"

That was the easiest answer of all. "I'm marrying her because she's my True Love."

His words drew Belle up short. "Oh." She dropped her gaze to her cards, but she didn't seem to be seeing them. "Well, I'm happy for you, then." She didn't *sound* happy for him. She swiped her hair behind her ears in agitation. "Is she beautiful? I bet she's beautiful."

Avenant's eyes traced over her angry face. "She's beautiful. Especially her eyes."

"Very poetic." Belle muttered. "She's probably dumb as a post, though, knowing your usual type."

"She's brilliant. She's the only one in the world who can outsmart me."

"She can't be *that* smart if she's engaged to you."
"We're not engaged."

Belle's beautiful eyes snapped back to his. "Why not? Didn't you tell her she was your True Love?"

"She doesn't care." He discarded the nine and selected the queen of hearts. It seemed fitting, given the conversation. "She thinks I'm a beast."

"She said that?"

"Yes."

"After you told her how you felt?"

"Yes."

"Well, that's... horrible." Belle decided. "She sounds like a very heartless person to have just dismissed you like that. Maybe she's *not* your True Love."

"She's not heartless. If anything, she feels too much. It's not her fault that nobody could ever want a beast..."

Belle cut him off, not even listening. "Don't defend her! It was cruel of her to say that to you and it's certainly not the first time you've made a huge mistake. You could have gotten your signals crossed and she's not your destined princess, after all." She gave an encouraging nod. "If this girl doesn't want you, you should just forget about her and move on."

"Have you ever known me to give up what's mine?"

Belle ignored that. "I think you're just freaking out because you were in prison for so long. That's what this is about. But, look at you!" She gestured to his face. "You could have *ton*s of girls, even being a total jackass. It's not like you to moon over just one."

Avenant snorted at that. All his life, he'd been mooning over just one. Unfortunately, she was the one who most clearly saw the animal behind the prince's mask. The Four Kingdoms had many success stories of hideous creatures discovering their inner Goodness. Frogs could turn into princes and ducks could become swans. Avenant's case was just the opposite. He was a monster who looked like a man. Behind the handsome façade, there was something Bad struggling for control. Something very, *very* Bad.

And it grew stronger all the time.

His parents had known it and they'd warned him to keep the Beast locked away. If it escaped its cage, Avenant had no idea what would happen. But the chains were weaker than they'd ever been. Sooner or later it would get free and Belle would see him for what he really was. The Beast wouldn't hurt her. Its need for Belle went as deep as his own. But, Belle would look into its eyes and she would know that she'd been right about him all along.

He was Bad all the way through.

"Are you going to stay with that hand or draw?" Avenant prompted, finishing off another package of granola. He'd lost his appetite, but he needed the fuel.

"I'm serious. You should just *completely* forget about the whole idea of getting married." Belle randomly picked one of her cards, tossed it down, and grabbed another. "I mean, I haven't even thought about getting married, yet."

"Haven't you?"

She shook her head. "There's so much else we have to focus on. We have to get through this labyrinth and one of us will take over the kingdom and," she hesitated, "there's also the *other* thing."

"What other thing?"

Belle bit down on her lower lip, which just wasn't fair to his sanity. "I have a straight flush." She laid it on the rock in front of her.

"Two pair." Avenant showed her his cards. "You win." For once, losing didn't bother him. This wasn't the real game. He waited for her to talk to him. Belle wasn't one to keep things bottled up. She'd been brooding about this "other thing" all day. He wanted to know what it was and she wanted to tell him. One of the best parts about being mixed-up with someone Good was they were lousy at keeping secrets.

Belle hesitated. "I've been trying to figure something out, but…" She shook her head. "Any way I figure it, I come up with the same conclusion: Someone set me up to go after you."

Avenant frowned. "What?"

"About a year ago, I was lying in my bed and I heard a noise downstairs."

Even though her tone wasn't an accusation, Avenant felt the need to defend himself. "I didn't have anything to do with someone attacking you, Belle. I would *never*…"

"Just shut-up and listen." She interrupted, sweeping her hair back. "I was in my bed and I heard a noise, so I got up and went to investigate. You know how the upstairs balcony in my house sort of overlooks the foyer?" She didn't bother to wait for an answer. "Well, I saw three big guys, dressed in black, coming through my front door."

Avenant's jaw ticked.

"They saw me, too." She continued. "I ran back to my room, but they were right behind me. I have pepper spray on my nightstand, because I live alone. So, I was going for that. It was the only thing I could think of."

"You should have thought of getting out of the fucking house."

"I told you to shut-up." She reminded him. "I didn't get to the pepper spray. Obviously. The biggest guy caught me and he threw me onto the mattress, with his hand over my mouth."

"Christ." Avenant sincerely hoped that man wasn't dead. *He* wanted to be the one to kill the bastard. It was like a physical *need* inside of him. The Beast howled and struggled to get free. Any threat to Belle set it off. Avenant had to fight for control, although he suddenly wondered why he bothered. He wanted the monster to ravage the men who'd attacked Belle.

No one touched what was his and lived.

"He pinned me down on the bed." Belle went on. "And he said so clearly, 'Prince Avenant says to stop digging into the missing money or next time you won't wake up.' Those were his exact words."

A fury like he'd never known boiled up inside of him.

Belle kept going with her story. "Then, he hit me and I guess I passed out. When I came to, I was tied to a tree five miles from home. It took me hours to get free. Then, I had to walk through the snow barefoot and in my pajamas. And the whole time I was freezing my ass off, all I could think about was how you'd sent men to threaten and kidnap me. And *that* is when I decided to take your crown." She let out a long breath. "I'm sorry."

Avenant squinted. "*You're* sorry?"

"It wasn't you who did it. I see that now. They wanted me to believe it was and to go after you." She pinched the bridge of her nose. "At the time, though, I was just so *mad* that I wasn't thinking straight. I'd never imagined you'd hurt me. All of our fights and you'd never raised a hand to me. Not *ever*."

Of course he hadn't. Not even the Beast would unleash its strength on Belle. It went against every instinct in his body. Avenant and the monster both treasured the woman.

When she'd outsmarted him for the final time

and come to arrest him, he'd known he had to defend himself or be chained. But, even then Avenant had refused to use force against Belle. Instead, he'd raised his palms and let himself be taken. The Beast had subsided with a cornered snarl, not even trying to seize control. There hadn't been a choice for either of them.

He'd sworn he could hear his father screaming from beyond the grave that day.

Belle sighed. "I felt so *betrayed* when it seemed like you'd sent those guys to attack me, just to protect your stolen money." She gave an awkward shrug. "I don't know why I felt that..."

He cut her off. "You felt betrayed, because you know what's between us is more important than gold. You expect me to know it, too. And I *do*, Bella." He knew it better than she did.

"I'm sorry." She said again.

Whatever resentment he'd been clinging to faded away. He could never look at her and stay mad. Sitting in jail had pissed him off, but it didn't do a damn thing to alter his need for her. He'd tried hating her for setting him up with that embezzlement bullshit. Tried telling himself that he'd been wrong about their connection. Tried forgetting about her and freezing the emotions right out of his chest. But it was like trying to shut off the sun. His feelings for Belle were indestructible.

No matter how cold he got, he always felt her warmth.

"It's alright." Avenant heard himself say. "Just so you know I would *never* send men to terrorize you." He shifted closer to her. "Not for any reason. Do you believe me?"

Chocolate brown eyes stayed on his. All his life, the color had soothed him. "I believe you." Belle whispered. "Do you believe me? About the rest of it, I mean."

"Yes."

"Good." She exhaled in relief. "Because, it's the truth. There were men in my house saying *you* sent them. I have no idea why, but I think we should find out."

"Oh, I intend to track them down and discuss all sorts of things. Don't you worry about that." It wasn't even the framing him part that pissed him off. Everyone Avenant knew hated him. It was only to be expected. But, *nobody* came at him through Belle and survived.

She hesitated. "So you're going to do something beastly to these guys?"

"Absolutely." The Beast purred at the very idea.

Belle's mouth slowly curved.

Her small grin dulled the raw edges of his rage. "You don't like it when I'm Bad." He reminded her. "You want a knight in shining armor."

"I just love the idea of letting you loose on someone who actually earned the pain." Belle wrinkled her nose. "That's probably really hypocritical, but I don't care. They deserve anything you do to them." She let out another shaky breath and glanced away. "They scared me." She admitted like she was ashamed of that fact.

"Anyone would've been scared, Belle."

"*You* wouldn't have. You could've just waved your hand and they would've been frozen forever."

He wouldn't have been scared for himself, but he was completely terrified of someone harming Belle. It had always been his greatest fear. She was so soft and without her in his life… "I would've been scared." Avenant murmured.

She gave him another small smile. "You're nice to say that."

"I don't know how to be nice." He assured her. "Listen, those guys who terrorized you? They don't know what fear really is." He dipped his head so his eyes could meet hers. "They will." It was a vow.

Belle bit her lower lip, again. "Thank you."

Avenant managed a nod, his mind already planning three executions.

Actually *four*.

Someone had sent those assholes to attack Belle. Someone had told them to hit her. To kidnap her. To pin her down and put a hand over her mouth, so she was unable to cry for help. Belle was Good straight down to her soul. She couldn't even bear to look at that asshole Pumpkin-Eater's cracked gourd. She was no match for three armed men. Someone had ordered those guys to overpower and frighten her, because they thought she was defenseless. Someone had preyed on her vulnerability.

And that someone was going to die screaming.

Rosabella Aria Ashman might be hopelessly, frustratingly, beguilingly soft... but she had a goddamn beast guarding her. Avenant would shred anyone who harmed Belle, without a drop of remorse. Everyone in the kingdom knew that and, if they didn't, they were about to learn.

Graphically.

"I mean it." She pressed when he didn't say anything. "Thank you for wanting to help me, despite everything."

He closed the last distance between them, his body brushing against hers. "You're welcome, my love." He murmured.

She never had to thank him for protecting her, though. The drive went deeper than anything else inside of him. The woman drove him insane, but Belle was a part of him. She was the heart he hadn't been born with, beating outside of his body. Avenant smoothed her hair back from her cheek, his eyes on hers.

Belle blinked up at him like she was in a trance. "It's a bad idea." She got out breathlessly.

"Probably." Avenant agreed and lowered his head towards hers. "But, I'm a Bad guy."

Belle didn't move away from him, her eyes going wide. Every time they got this far she looked panicked, but she never ran. On some level, she knew they were inevitable. "What about the other girl?" She blurted out.

He almost sighed at how completely blind she was to the truth. Being Good must be like living with your head in a box. "What other girl?"

"Well, I mean, I know I told you it would be smart to give her up, but..." Those incredible eyes met his, looking apprehensive. "Are you sure you *can?* I've never known you to just forget about something you want."

He tried not to smile. Belle was right. He would *never* forget his True Love. She would be the last thought he had in this world and the first one he had in the next. "You're the only woman I can ever remember." Belle had been his entire universe from the second he first spotted her across the kindergarten classroom. Avenant had looked at her studious little face and he'd just... known. "Bella..."

"*Move!*" Esmeralda the wicked witch came tearing around the corner at a dead run. Her curly black hair was in a wild disarray, her green skin pale. "Avenant, we gotta go!"

Belle jumped to her feet like she'd been caught doing something wrong.

Avenant bit back an oath. "What the hell are you

doing here, Ez?" He demanded in frustration.

"Saving your ass!" She shrieked. "Except the music just pissed him off and I think he's immune to magic!"

"Do you know that woman?" Belle asked in confusion. "What's she talking about?"

"I have no idea what she's ranting about, but that's Esmeralda. She was locked-up with me in the WUB Club."

Esmeralda had been part of the prison break, too, so it didn't take a genius to figure out that she was the one Scarlett had sent into the labyrinth to "help." Avenant could've flipped opened the phone book, pointed at the first name he came across, and come up with a better person to be his backup. The witch was annoying on the level of flesh eating viruses and electroshocks to the eyeball.

And she had the worse fucking timing in the world.

Why did these interruptions always happen to him?

"Can we catch up later?" Esmeralda shouted. "He's right behind me!"

"Goddamn it, I was right in the middle of something important..." Avenant's words were cut off by the explosion. A fireball the size of a refrigerator blasted a hole in the an ice wall further down the corridor. "Holy shit!" Chunks of ice and gallons of water sprayed through the air at supersonic speeds. "What was that?" He roared.

"A really pissed off minotaur." Esmeralda sprinted passed them. "Time to *run,* people."

Chapter Six

Belle was a sweet little girl.
A bit of an oddball, but a very Good student.
She tried hard to be a proper young lady.
It was always the Beast who pushed her into those terrible fights.

Testimony of Old Mother Hubbard, Seventh Grade Teacher - *The People of the Northlands v. Prince Avenant*

Sixteen Years Ago

On the day she turned fourteen, Belle stormed up the marble steps of the castle with one birthday wish in her heart.

A uniformed guard opened the huge door for her as she approached. She wasn't sure if it was simply royal protocol or if Avenant had told them to expect her. Probably the later.

He *knew* she'd be showing up.

She slammed straight through the cold, ornate rooms of the palace and into the courtyard. It was one of the Northland's rare days of summer and dozens of partygoers were taking advantage of the warm weather. A huge waterslide had been set up, along with several massive inflatable pools. Water guns sprayed and people laughed and three barbeques grilled up hotdogs for a line of kids in swimsuits.

Tears burned her eyes. Avenant had done this just to spite her.

"Hey, Belle." Peter Piper came dashing over, his bathing trunks a vivid shade of purple. If Northlands High was a movie, Peter would've played the computer nerd. He was a pudgy boy with a talent for math and an addiction to pickled peppers. "I didn't expect to see you here." He had the grace to look slightly abashed. "Um… Happy birthday."

"Thanks." She said dully.

"I was going to come to your party, too." Peter nodded. "Really. Like maybe in half-an-hour or so. I just wanted to check this one out first." He gestured over his shoulder. "Avenant's paying some guy just to make *water balloons*. I didn't know there *were* professional water balloon makers. It's unreal." He hesitated, spotting the gallon-sized cardboard cylinder she was carrying. "Hey, is that ice cream?"

Belle ignored him, her eyes scanning the crowd. The crowd who should've been at *her* party, except Avenant had high-jacked them. Her parents had hired a DJ, and decorated the house with miles of sparkly streamers, and bought her a cake five layers high to share with all her friends. Only no one had shown up.

Not one single person.

Her parents were baffled. Nothing like this had ever happened to *them*. They threw parties all the time and *everyone* came. They'd patted her head and told her the invitations must have gotten lost, but she'd seen the pity in their eyes. They all knew the truth. Belle's party hadn't been important to anybody, because *Belle* wasn't important to anybody. Not even her parents, since they'd gone out to some art show opening and left her alone with fifteen gallons of melting ice cream.

It didn't matter. Belle's sights were fixed on vengeance, not self-pity.

Right from the beginning, she'd known Avenant must have sabotaged her birthday. Whenever anything went wrong, she always suspected he was behind it and she was always right. Two minutes of investigating her email had revealed that he'd invited the entire school to an impromptu pool party at the palace that morning. Obviously, RSVPs to Belle's birthday meant nothing compared to a wave machine.

She didn't really blame the others. It was hard for Belle to make friends. She was kind of an oddball, who liked reading far more than gossiping on a telephone about boys. Most of the people she knew were acquaintances. She was nice to people, but she wasn't particularly close with anyone. Of course, a huge reason for that was Avenant. People would much rather be his friend and everyone knew he hated her. They tended to steer clear, afraid of being caught in the crossfire.

"Belle." The Prince of Darkness must have been waiting for her. He came loping over, shirtless and wet and disgustingly chipper. And handsome. Lately she'd been noticing how damn handsome he was and that made her even angrier. "There you are." He looked her up and down, taking in her yellow party dress. "You look pretty." He had the audacity to smile at her.

She despised him. "I got your invitation." She bit off.

"Good. I thought maybe there was a breakdown in communication between our houses or something." He gave a mock frown. "People have been telling me that *you* were having a party today, too. But I knew that couldn't be true, because *I* didn't get an invitation. You couldn't have invited *everyone else* in the school and not me."

"Yes, I could." Belle assured him. "In fact, I *did*. I'd gladly have no party at all before I let you come to it."

Whatever Avenant had been expecting her to say,

that wasn't it. His smirk faded.

"I got the invitations to both parties." Peter piped up.

Avenant slanted Peter a look and Belle realized the other boy was still standing beside her. Avenant's gaze went back and forth between them, his face growing hostile. "What are you doing hanging around, Piper?" He demanded.

"Talking to Belle. I'm just here for another half-hour or so. Then, I'm going to her party."

"My party is over." Belle told him flatly.

"Really?" Peter blinked. "'Cause, I got you a gift."

"She doesn't want it." Avenant growled and glowered over at Belle. "You had *him* on the guest list and not me?"

"I *like* him and not you."

"You like me?" Peter sounded awed. "Wow. I totally like you too, Belle! I think you're the most beautiful..."

"Get lost." Avenant's voice went dark and Belle could've sworn his eyes glowed electric-blue for a beat. "*Now*, while you can still walk."

Peter's eyes widened at the deadly tone. The Beast of the Northlands was on a very short leash and everyone knew what would happen when it snapped. He'd ruin lives without a drop of remorse. It was why they'd come to his stupid party, just as much as the gigantic water cannon. If you defied Avenant you were lucky if you lived to regret it.

"We can talk later, Belle." Peter went scurrying off.

Avenant scowled after him. "Fucking little toad better enjoy this party, because it's the last one he'll ever attend."

Belle glared at him. "Peter's harmless. Leave him alone. This is between you and me."

"It's not my fault he just committed social suicide. I never even *noticed* that twerp before he went and said that to you right in front of me."

"You've got *everybody* else on your side." She waved a hand at all Avenant's guests. "*Everybody* here wants to be your friend. You can't even let me have Peter?"

"Friends?" He scoffed. "Please. Like I'd ever be friends with these peasants." He arched a brow. "Your precious Peter is here because he's weak. He skipped *your* party to come to *mine*, because he knows what'll happen if he crosses me. *That's* how much he likes you. You *really* think he's your friend?"

Avenant was right. She knew that. Honestly, she didn't even like Peter that much. The boy was just her study-buddy in math class. That really wasn't the point, though. "Peter's the only one who's wished me happy birthday today." She said. "So, right now, I think he's probably the best friend I have." It was depressing, but true.

Avenant's jaw ticked. "He's not your friend. You invited all these people to your birthday and they didn't come. If *I* was your friend, *I* would be at your party and not here."

"Except you're *not* my friend. You're the one who threw *this* party."

He shrugged. "You didn't give me a reason not to."

"How about the fact that it's my birthday and you spoiled it for no reason, at all? My parents think I'm a loser, thanks to you!" She didn't want to give him the satisfaction of showing him how upset she was, but the words burst free. "Even the caterer felt sorry for me, Avenant. He told them there wouldn't be a charge and I could tell they were embarrassed to even know me. We *never* bring parents into this." That was one of the unwritten rules of their war. It had been ever since the spelling bee.

Avenant frowned. "I didn't really think about your parents..."

"Of course you didn't!" She interrupted. "You never think about anything but yourself!"

"Hey, *you're* the one who turned these parties into weapons. I invited you to mine, didn't I? But, you thought it was fine to snub *me*. This is all on you, Belle."

"I didn't invite you, because I knew you'd ruin everything! Which you *have,* just like you *always* do. You're a selfish, mean jerk and I wish I'd never met you!"

Pushed to the brink, she hefted the carton of ice cream she still carried and threw it at him. She'd been planning to do it all along, but the result was even better than she could've imagined. The entire gallon of Strawberry Delight had melted into a thick pink liquid. When the cardboard cylinder slammed into his chest, it detonated like one of those professionally-made water balloons. Ice cream exploded all over him.

For a moment there was nothing but silence. It seemed like even the music blasting from the poolside speakers went quiet. Everyone gaped at Belle and Avenant in horror.

Waiting.

Even Belle was a little shocked by what she'd done. She'd just doused the prince with ice cream in his own palace. No way was he going to let this go. People had disappeared forever for doing less. Her heart was pounding so hard everyone could probably hear it in the eerie stillness.

Avenant looked down at the sticky goo covering him and very slowly raised his eyes back to hers. "Get out."

Belle swallowed. She wasn't backing down, but she *was* willing to declare victory and leave the field before the battle got even more intense. "Gladly."

"Not you. *Them.*" Avenant's glare swept over the dozens of guests. "Everybody *out.*"

There was a stampede for the door. Under other circumstances it would've been almost comical. Avenant told them to show up at his party and they were all too intimidated to refuse. He told them to leave the party and they were all too intimidated to stay. Everyone in the whole kingdom kowtowed to the bastard, but not because they wanted to. They were just terrified. In that moment, Belle didn't even blame them.

Avenant's gaze stayed locked on Belle as the courtyard emptied out. It only took a matter of minutes to find themselves alone.

Belle kept her attention on the cruel angles of his face, refusing to be intimidated. "I'm not sorry." She told him, braced for all sorts of Badness. "And I'm not scared of you."

"I know you're not." He gave his hand a shake, trying to clear the ice cream from his fingers. "You're not smart enough to be scared."

"Not smart enough?! My GPA is two-tenths of a point higher than yours, so... *Hey!*" Her retort ended in a yelp as Avenant picked her up and tossed her in the pool. "You maniac!" She sputtered, coming to the surface. "What if I couldn't swim? Did you even think of that?"

"Then, I'd jump in to save you." To illustrate his point, he hopped into the water beside her. His eyes swept over her soaked form, lingering on the front of her dress. The wet fabric was clinging to her body. "That's more like it." He grinned like he'd somehow gotten exactly what he wanted. "This party idea is working out better than I thought."

Belle crossed her arms over her chest, although she didn't know why she bothered. She wasn't well-endowed enough for him to see much of interest. "I hate you so much, I can't even think of anything mean enough to say."

Avenant casually rinsed the ice cream from his skin. "Oh, I'm pretty sure you can come up with something. You always do."

For the good of science, some doctor should cut Avenant open and figure out what had gotten twisted inside of him to make him such a despicable person. "If I had powers, I would drown you, right now." She headed for the edge of the pool.

"If you had powers, you would've killed me years ago." He paddled over to her. "Come on, don't be a sore loser. You just got here. We have a whole barbeque thing going on and you have to eat. It might as well be with me."

"I'd rather eat beside a rabid dog."

"I'll take you to see the stables, then. We have twenty-six horses. You can have one as a birthday gift and we'll forget all about how you tried to screw me over today."

"*Me* screw *you* over?!" She kept wading towards the ladder. "You're insane, you know that?"

Annoyed that she wasn't going to hang around for more torture, Avenant got between Belle and the exit. "Damn it, why can't you just be normal? Every other girl in this whole kingdom would accept the horse from me.

They would thank me. They would *want* me at their party. I'm the fucking prince!"

"They wouldn't *want* you at their party. They'd just be too afraid not to invite you, because you're a bully." Belle retorted. "You think *I* don't have friends? Well you don't either. No one *likes* you, Avenant."

"I don't care if anyone likes me. Just so they fear me."

She splashed water at him in frustration. "That's why you're always coming after me like this. I'm the only one who won't back down from you and you can't stand it."

"You don't understand anything."

"Don't I? You think you can just buy and threaten people to get your own way." She shook her head. "But you can't. Not always."

Avenant's mouth thinned. "Seems like I did this time, though." He gestured around the remnants of his improvised celebration. "My party was way bigger than yours."

"Only because you sabotaged me."

"So what? I still won."

"You can't 'win' a birthday." She snapped, even though he clearly *had*.

"Liar. You tried to exclude me from the guest list and you're pissed that it didn't work. Admit it."

Belle's eyes narrowed. "It *did* work. You weren't invited. You won't *ever* be welcomed at my birthday, no matter what you try. I'll have a party every year from now on and you'll *never* be invited and there's *nothing* you can do about it."

Avenant looked away. "So what?" He repeated bitterly. "I got you to come to this party and that's what matters today."

"Well, now I'm *leaving* this party." She tried to go around him, but he shifted into her path.

"Bella, no. Stay."

Unprepared for the way he blocked her, Belle's body slammed into his...

...And she felt their whole relationship shift.

Her eyes flashed up to his and she saw Avenant's expression go taut. Belle hadn't been so close to him since she'd shoved him off the stage in the middle of their fifth grade play. It had felt great to send him careening into the audience during his big scene. This felt even better. Her body got all tingly and warm. Avenant's hands went to her waist, holding her against him. She could feel his breath coming faster. So was hers. For a second, neither of them moved. They just stood in the water, staring at each other.

"Stay with me." He whispered.

He was so amazingly beautiful that it was almost hypnotic.

"Well, fuck." A male voice sang out, breaking the spell. "A *real* man would've had her naked by now, cousin."

Belle jerked away from Avenant, her mind whirling.

"Son of a *bitch*." Avenant's head snapped around to pin Lancelot with a deadly look. "You have two seconds to leave before I have you executed."

"Hey, the palace is my home, too." Lancelot retorted. He was a few years older than them, on leave from the Knight Academy. Warm weather was so rare in the Northlands that most everyone used this time of year as a vacation. "I can't help it if I come into the courtyard and I see you making out with some floozy in a pool." He took a sip from the beer in his hand.

Belle's mouth dropped open. "Floozy?"

Avenant moved in front of her, his eyes narrowing at his cousin. "No, it's *not* your home. Everything here belongs to *me*. You're the poor relation who shows up on holidays to pretend like you matter."

"I'm going to be a knight!" Lancelot roared back. He sounded like he'd been drinking away the afternoon. "That's something you'll *never* be, Avenant! Bad folk aren't allowed to become knights, because it's the most important job in the kingdom and you're not fit for it. All the men want to be us and all the girls want to fuck us."

There was some truth buried in that gibberish. The knights were the superstars of the Northlands. Even Belle admired them. She had pictures of the greatest warriors taped to her bedroom walls and the whole set of their novelized adventures on her bookshelf. But, Lancelot was hardly their poster boy. He was only accepted into the training program because his father was the cousin of Prince Vincent. Everyone knew that.

Belle shoved her way up beside Avenant. "Being the *ruler* of the kingdom is obviously the most important job in the kingdom." She heard herself say. "And, for your information, girls can be knights *too*, you Neanderthal. We don't just marry them."

"It's a job for men." Lancelot insisted, most of his attention on his cousin. "Women disgrace the sacred armor." He arched a brow at Avenant and took another drink. "By the way, Bad folk aren't allowed to be *princes*, either. Your parents can't force this kingdom to accept you, no matter how many people they throw in the dungeon. No one wants a beast in charge. One day, you'll be kicked out of this palace and I'll take it *all* from you."

Belle felt the pool water getting colder and she

knew it was from Avenant's powers. She instinctively opened her mouth to warn Lancelot, but it was too late. At least a ton of snow dumped from the clear summer sky... right onto Lancelot's head. He hit the ground, dazed and buried in a mountain of frost. Even wearing that stupid metal helmet, he was going to be feeling the impact of the avalanche for days.

Belle didn't feel too sorry for him.

Avenant calmly surveyed the damage. "No one takes what's mine." He looked over at Belle and gave a slow smile. "And hey, don't worry. *I* don't think you're a floozy."

Belle fulfilled her birthday wish and punched him right in the nose.

Chapter Seven

Prince Charming: I wouldn't call it a duel, exactly. Avenant just tried to kill me.

Prince Avenant: If I tried to kill you, you'd be dead, you simpering idiot.

Judge: Silence in my courtroom! One more outburst and I'll have your client removed, Counselor.

Defense: We apologize, your honor. But, he *does* have a point about this questionable testimony. Prince Avenant has never once been accused of *attempted* murder.

Testimony of Prince Charming- *The People of the Northlands vs. Prince Avenant*

"Explain why a minotaur is chasing us." Belle got out when they finally stopped running. "I thought that's why Letty gave us that damn flute. Because they were -- like-- charmed by the melody or something."

"I told you, the music thing isn't working." Esmeralda bent forward with her hands braced on her knees, trying to catch her breath. "The flute just got him all grouchy."

Avenant snorted. "Maybe you just suck at playing it."

"Maybe you should shut-up, wiseass." Esmeralda slanted him a glare. "I'm only here to help you save your stupid frozen kingdom, you know."

"I didn't ask for your help."

"No, you asked for Letty's help and *Letty* asked for my help. Tuesday share circle sticks together, ass-wipe."

Avenant sighed, but he stopped arguing.

Belle's gaze cut between them, sensing their bond. Was this girl his True Love?

Ever since Avenant had hinted at his forthcoming marriage, Belle had been on edge. She hadn't really considered him finding a wife before. The idea troubled her on some deep level. So much so that she'd frantically tried to talk him out of the whole idea, which had probably made her sound like a lunatic.

Avenant wasn't stupid. He wasn't just going to walk away from his one True Love.

Now Esmeralda had shown up and Belle couldn't stop thinking that maybe she was the woman he'd been talking about. Ez was certainly beautiful and, like most witches, favored as little clothing as possible. Even at these frigid temperatures, she was showing off her ample cleavage in a way that had Belle's teeth grinding together. Worse, Avenant wasn't killing her for being such a pain in the ass, so he had to *like* the witch. Maybe she was the one he wanted. Why *wouldn't* he want her?

Belle's stomach tightened in dismay. "What's Tuesday share circle?" She demanded, hating the fact they had some kind of private code.

"It was our therapy group back in prison." Avenant explained. "Marrok, Letty, Me, Ez, and a couple of others. We had to meet every Tuesday and share our feelings about being Bad."

Belle couldn't imagine Avenant doing anything even remotely like that. He was the most emotionally unavailable person she'd ever met. "You shared your *feelings?*"

"Hell, no." Esmeralda scoffed. "He just sat there and complained about the rest of us. Oh and about *you*."

Yeah, that made more sense.

"The usurper stole the Northlands." Esmeralda mocked in her best Avenant impression. "The usurper framed me for embezzling. The usurper didn't go to prom with me."

Belle looked at Avenant. "You told them about prom?"

"Of course not."

"He completely did." Esmeralda assured her. "I think you really hurt Avenant's feelings when you dated that other guy instead of him."

Belle glanced over at Avenant, who was glowering at Esmeralda. "You didn't even *ask* me to prom." She snapped, outraged that somehow he'd cast her as the villain in that mess. "Everything that happened was *your* fault."

"I don't remember it that way."

The man was insane. "How else is there to remember it?!" She demanded. "It's what *happened*. You were an obnoxious, lying jackass. I called you on it and you got pissed."

"I got pissed because you refused to listen to the truth." He snapped. "You were trying to break me and it didn't work. It *won't* work. I will keep fighting until I win."

Esmeralda leaned closer to Belle and lowered her voice conspiratorially. "Avenant's kind of sensitive under all the bullshit snarking. Dr. Ramona, our counselor, said he builds walls around his feelings."

"Ignore the witch." Avenant told Belle. "She has no idea what she's talking about."

Esmeralda rolled her eyes. "Fine. How about we focus on the giant minotaur out to flambé us, then? I mean, you two didn't see this thing. He's *huge*, with horns and a lousy sense of humor."

"Horned creatures are notoriously moody." Avenant agreed. "I've always said that. I tried deporting all of them from my kingdom, but *someone* started whining about monsters' rights and blocked the eviction." He looked pointedly at Belle.

She disregarded that. "Does he really have the head of a bull?" She asked Esmeralda, interested despite herself. So little was known about minotaurs. Every book she'd researched had been filled with speculation and unanswered questions.

"Let's just say, he's not the handsomest guy in the Four Kingdoms. We need to keep going."

"Where?" Avenant gestured to the maze of corridors. "We have no idea which direction is safest, Ez. For all we know, we're circling back to him."

"Or towards whoever killed Mr. Pumpkin-Eater." Belle reminded him, sitting down on a rock. The floor was slippery in this section of the maze, as if the ground was mostly ice. It felt good to stop sliding around for a minute. She dug into her own pack to grab a bottle of water and twisted the top off.

Avenant slanted Esmeralda a suspicious glare. "Wait a minute... Did *you* lobotomize that jack-o-lantern guy?"

"What? *No.*" She promptly frowned, reconsidering her automatic denial. "Well... wait. Let me think about it." Her crimson eyes narrowed, like she was trying to recall the specifics of all her crimes. "Was he a skinny dude living with his plus-sized wife in a pumpkin shell? Because, that was *totally* an accident."

"No, he was the scarecrow looking cannibal trying to steal my crown." Avenant told her calmly.

"Oh, awesome! *That* guy's dead?"

Belle shook her head in frustration and leaned

back against the wall. "How did you find us, Esmeralda?" She demanded, passing her water bottle to Avenant.

Esmeralda shrugged. "I'm a witch. I did a spell." She made a face. "I would've found you sooner, but --I mean-- it *is* a maze. I was trying to stay kind of undercover and I ended up just getting lost." She snorted. "This thing is a stupid fucking way to run a kingdom, if you ask me." She waved a hand around the labyrinth.

"Tell me about it." Avenant took a sip of Belle's water. "Trust me. As soon as I'm back in charge, it's all getting torn down."

"It was nice of Esmeralda to come all this way to help you." Belle pushed her hair behind her ears and tried to look casual as she steered the conversation back towards their relationship. "You guys are... close?"

"Well, doing hard time together has a way of bonding people." Avenant's lips quirked at Esmeralda. "Even when they hate each other's guts."

She winked at him.

The sick feeling got worse. "You usually don't 'bond' with anyone." Belle said weakly. He was too busy calling them peasants or oppressing them. "You two must have a very special relationship."

"Special?" Esmeralda tilted her head. "Hang on... Are you trying to figure out if we've had sex?" She sounded amused.

Avenant choked on the water he was drinking.

"No." Belle snapped. She scowled up at Avenant. "...Have you?"

"Fuck no."

She frowned over at Esmeralda for confirmation. "So, you're not his True Love?" The relief that filled her was almost dizzying.

"Not unless there's something he isn't telling me." The witch smirked at Avenant. "Dude, if you're planning to pop the question, the diamond had better be the size of a small planet. No way will I put up with you for less than…"

"Clear the path!" Lancelot came dashing up, interrupting her. "Stay out of my way, pointless citizens. You will just hinder my quest." He posed, hands on his hips. "I hunt a minotaur."

Esmeralda looked over at Avenant. "For real?" She deadpanned.

"I know. The helmet cuts off his oxygen." Avenant heaved a longsuffering sigh. "Lancelot, I already have so many reasons to kill you. Why do you always have to add *more?*"

"You only want me dead because you know I am going to win this contest of valor, Beast."

"And because you're a dickhead." Belle muttered. God, the man was a disgrace to knights everywhere. "Ever since Avenant's been in jail, you've been trying to steal the Icen Throne. But, it won't work."

Lancelot scowled over at her. "I'm trying to save the Northlands."

"From what? An economic upswing? Environmental responsibility? Social programs that have improved the literacy of thousands? Because, I did *all* that." Belle liked running the Northlands and she was good at it. Anyone could see that. "I have been the best ruler this kingdom has ever had."

"What would a woman know about being a prince?" Lancelot scoffed. "Save your breath. Your feminine wiles won't work on me the way they do with my pussy-whipped cousin." He swept a dismissive palm towards Avenant.

Avenant made a considering face. "Belle is a wily one." He allowed. "Of course, she's also the only other person in the world I'd ever allow to sit on my throne. Even temporarily. She cares about the kingdom more than herself, which is something no one in the royal bloodline has ever been able to say."

Belle shot him a surprised look.

"Worry not, for justice will finally prevail." Lancelot continued, not hearing anything except his own voice. He raised his fist in triumph. "I'm going to force the minotaur to give me Excalibur and win the crown for my own."

"If the minotaur knew where the sword was, why doesn't he just go get it?" Esmeralda demanded.

"Because minotaurs are enspelled, witch. They live and die within these walls, forever guarding the maze. They cannot leave this labyrinth until the rightful prince comes to claim the blade." Lancelot paused. "Which is *me*."

Ez arched a brow. "And you know about minotaurs because...?" Her voice trailed off skeptically.

"I went to the Knight Academy." Lancelot explained with a superior sniff. "They made us watch many filmstrips as we prepared to be heroes."

"He's right." Belle glanced at Esmeralda. "About the minotaurs, anyway. They're trapped in here until someone frees Excalibur. Avenant's ancestor wrote about it in his journal."

"Well, I think that sucks." Esmeralda glowered over at Avenant like it was his fault. "You can't keep people caged up for no reason. That's why we escaped the WUB Club."

"Don't look at me. My grandmother's great-great-great grandfather Adam sealed them in here. That drunken lunatic is presently my least favorite relative." Avenant hesitated and then glanced over at Lancelot. "Not counting you, anyway."

Lancelot missed the insult, still scowling at Belle. He'd been furious at her ever since she claimed the Northlands and he clearly saw this as his opportunity to vent. "I have been slaying miscellaneous monsters all my life. Do you really think you have a chance to beat me in this maze? No one can match my skill with a sword or…"

He never got a chance to finish that boast. The minotaur cut him off by lobbing another fireball at them.

Avenant reacted before Belle could even process what was happening. He tackled her out of the way, dragging her to the ground and covering her. The fiery impact happened right where Belle had been sitting, turning the rock to gravel. Avenant's arms came up to shield her head from the falling debris. Flaming sparks and ice shards and chunks of granite rained down on them, but none of them touched her. Not a single piece.

Avenant lifted his face far enough to meet her eyes. "Are you alright?"

Belle nodded, gazing at him in wonder. Avenant had just saved her life.

Without even thinking about it, she leaned up to press her lips against his. Avenant drew in a surprised breath as her mouth slid over his. It was the first time she'd ever initiated anything between them and he seemed stunned. His eyes stayed locked on hers as she gently kissed him. His lips parted, responding with the softest caress imaginable. As usual, Avenant touched her like he was afraid of frightening her away. The tenderness had her whole body clenching with desire and wanting more.

The kiss only lasted a second, but that was long

enough to feel the heat beckoning her deeper. If they kept going it would be even better than it had been the last time. Belle felt the barely suppressed passion and it made her pull back in alarm. Getting close to the Beast of the Northlands would be a huge mistake.

No matter how much Belle longed for him, she would never be important to Avenant.

Belle jerked away from him, feeling dazed. "Thanks." She blurted out, because what else could she say?

Avenant stared at her, his chest heaving. "You drive me insane." He whispered and gave his head a sharp shake. "Come on." He got to his feet, dragging her with him. "Stay behind me."

Belle looked around and realized the fireball had seared its way straight through four walls, revealing the monster on the far side of the holes. The guy didn't look exactly like a bull, but he sure didn't look normal. The horns Esmeralda had talked about jutted out from the sides of his head like curved spears. His massive chest was covered in chainmail and bloody spikes. Best of all, he was absolutely, positively *ginormous*. Like patting-giants-on-the-head-as-he-stomped-past *ginormous*.

"I hate witches." He growled, his yellow eyes fixed on Esmeralda.

"This witch isn't real fond of you either, buddy." Ez retorted. "Watch it with the ice melting stuff, huh? Water and my kind don't mix."

Avenant raised a hand and tried to freeze the minotaur with his powers, but the frost seemed to melt before it touched his *ginormous* body.

"Immune to magic." Esmeralda snapped. "Pretty sure I mentioned that."

Lancelot let out a panicked curse and ran away as

fast as his armored legs could carry him.

The minotaur kept coming. He must have been used to creating shortcuts through the labyrinth with his fireworks. He casually climbed through the large holes he'd blazed for himself as if he had all the time in the world. "Christ, the trespassers get dumber every century." He muttered to himself.

"Fucking hell." Avenant grabbed hold of Belle's arm. "Move."

Chapter Eight

Then, Avenant foreclosed on my shoe.

Testimony of the Old Woman who (Formerly) Lived in a Shoe- *The People of the Northlands v. Prince Avenant*

Avenant, Lancelot, and Belle raced down the icy corridor.

"Want me to try the flute again?" Esmeralda asked, dashing along after them. "I can play the first seven notes of *The Alphabet Song* and the first six of *Twinkle, Twinkle Little Star*."

"They're the same goddamn tune!" Avenant roared. "No wonder the minotaur wants to kill you." Avenant really did detest children's songs. Mother Goose would never get her show back, if he had his way.

Esmeralda rolled her eyes. "Hey, the minotaur wants to kill you, *too*, buddy."

"Maybe we can try talking to him." Belle suggested. "He seems like an intelligent... *Jesus!*" She plowed into Lancelot's back as he skidded to a stop. "What are you doing?" She touched her nose, making sure she hadn't broken it on his armor.

"I shall not run, anymore. Cowards flee from danger." Lancelot hefted his sword. "Men face it, eager for death."

"We're all eager for your death." Avenant assured him.

Lancelot slanted him a glare. "I'm about to win the kingdom from you, Beast. Look on in awe as I force the minotaur to reveal the location of Excalibur. Neither you nor this woman will sit on the Icen Throne a moment longer." He waved a contemptuous hand at Belle. "In fact, it should have melted long ago with you two claiming it."

"But, it *didn't*." Belle shot back. "Both Avenant and I were accepted as rightful rulers by the throne. Weren't we, Avenant?"

"Of course we were. You might be a usurper, but at least you're legitimately part of the royal line."

Belle frowned, not understanding that calm statement.

Lancelot didn't care enough to even listen. "Now is the time to claim my due." He was fixated on his kamikaze mission, psyching himself up to do something stupid. Which, honestly, didn't take too much psyching. "DIE MONSTERRRRR!" He screamed as he barreled towards the minotaur, his helmet gleaming in the eerie light. "Now you face a *man!*"

Avenant shook his head in disgust.

Esmeralda's eyebrows soared as Lancelot rushed off. "Should we go after him?"

"No." Avenant intoned.

"I think he's about to get slaughtered, though."

"It's fine. I'm his next of kin." Avenant assured her. "Being a distraction is probably the pinnacle of his abilities, so let's just celebrate his brief moment of purpose. I'll buy him a nice memorial statue after we get out of here."

Belle hesitated. She wasn't Lancelot's biggest fan. Still... "We can't just let him get fried, Avenant."

"Sure, we can."

"No, we *can't*."

"Why not? He's an asshole." Avenant sounded

confused by this entire argument. "You *know* he is, Belle. He called you a floozy."

"That was like sixteen years ago!"

"What does that matter?" Avenant crossed his arms over his chest, refusing to budge. "He still said it."

Belle made an aggravated sound. "But, this is a perfect opportunity to help someone." She pointed out. "The journal said that's how we're going to get through this level of the labyrinth, remember? Princes should be *helpful*."

"This prince doesn't do 'helpful.'" He retorted. "This prince enjoys *not* helping the assholes around me. Everyone knows that. You testified to it at my trial, as I recall. In excruciating and perjurious detail."

"I did." She allowed, staring up at him. "But, I dare you to prove me wrong."

Avenant's gaze snapped to hers.

Belle smiled at him… And that was all it took to win.

"Son of a *bitch*." Avenant turned back the way they'd come. "Wait here."

"Okay." Esmeralda agreed readily. "Hey, if you die, is it okay if I try to claim your kingdom for real? I think I'd make an awesome princess."

Belle ignored that. She also ignored Avenant's command to stay put. "What are we going to do?" She asked, hurrying after him. "We can't fight the minotaur with our bare hands."

"I know." He sifted in his backpack to pull out the flare gun. "God, this is *such* a bad idea. If I'm alive when the encounter's over, I'm getting a much longer kiss, understand? You owe me."

Belle's insides took a pleasurable dip, even though she knew it was a huge mistake. "How long?"

"*Long.*" Avenant put up an arm to halt her progress as the sounds of a fight reached them. "Wait here." This time his voice was firmer.

Belle had no idea why he thought it would work. She'd never listened to him before and she wasn't about to start now. When Avenant stepped into the minotaur's sights she was right behind him.

The monster had Lancelot's unconscious body lifted over his head, preparing to heave him through a wall. Avenant's cousin was a big man, but the minotaur hefted him like he weighed nothing at all. Yellow eyes narrowed as he spotted Avenant and Belle.

"I'm going to have to ask you to put that asshole down." Avenant requested in a long suffering tone. "Apparently, it's important, for some reason."

"You're all trespassers." The minotaur growled angrily. "You deserve punishment."

"Technically, this land belongs to the crown and the crown belongs to me." Avenant argued. "*You're* the trespasser."

The minotaur wasn't interested in the finer points of property law. "If you're the prince of these lands, then it was your ancestor who put my kind in this maze." He threw Lancelot's limp body at them. "You know what happens to those who enter my home!"

Belle ducked to the side as Lancelot flew overhead and went careening down the hall like a rock skipping on a lake. He was definitely going to wake up with a headache. At least, he was still alive, though.

Avenant let out a sigh. "Alright, let's try this another way." He pointed the flare gun at the minotaur and fired.

The red projectile zoomed towards the monster's *ginormous* chest. It arced through the air, a trail of red sparks igniting as it soared along its path. The minotaur reared back, but it was too late. Nothing could stop the collision. The flare slammed into him…

…And promptly bounced right off, again.

The red tube plopped onto the icy floor, still burning. All three of them stared down at it for a beat.

"Well, that didn't work." Belle said. The minotaur looked healthier than ever, only now he was even more eager to kill them.

Avenant shrugged. "I told you it was a bad idea."

"You shoot flames at me, I shoot flames at you!" The monster pulled back a *ginormous* palm, preparing to blast them with one of his fireballs.

"Fucking hell." Avenant muttered again and glanced at Belle. "Close your eyes, I'm about to do something insane and I don't want you to see me change."

That didn't sound good. Ignoring this order, too, she took a deep breath and stepped forward. "Hi! I'm Rosabella Aria Ashman." She told the minotaur, moving on to Plan C. "Honorary Princess of the Northlands. And you are?"

"I am *pissed*." He retorted, but he didn't blast them into ashes. Instead, he watched her warily. Apparently, not many victims took the time to introduce themselves.

Avenant cursed and grabbed for her, but Belle shook him off.

"And you have every right to be pissed." She assured the minotaur. "I completely understand how upsetting it must be to have people wander into your house like this. To be honest, I don't blame you for wanting us gone."

"Good. Then you'll leave."

"Absolutely we will. And I truly apologize for the inconvenience we've caused you." She nodded. "But, we're in a contest of valor. So, we really *can't* go anywhere until we find this magical sword. We have to track it down before we can get out of here. I don't think the labyrinth will let us just quit. It's like a whole ritual deal-y."

The minotaur's eyes narrowed, his gaze cutting between Belle's encouraging expression and Avenant's tight features. "You seek Excalibur?"

"Yes. Have you seen it?"

The minotaur didn't answer that. His attention locked on Avenant. "Does your woman speak the truth?"

"Always." Avenant said simply.

Belle shot him a surprised look, touched by the compliment.

Of course, then he went and ruined it. "Honesty is one of Belle's most irritating habits." His hand gripped her tight, preventing her from getting any closer to the minotaur. "The little oddball has *a lot* of others, though. She talks too much. She never fucking listens. She has even worse ideas than I do." Avenant dragged her behind him. "She's hopelessly and irredeemably Good."

Belle made a face.

"You are not Good." The minotaur told Avenant with utter certainty.

"No." Avenant allowed. "I'm not. I'm exactly like you. I'm a beast. If I could think of a way to kill you without frightening the woman, you'd already be dead. See that sword?" He nodded towards Lancelot's fallen weapon, which had landed a few yards away. "I am currently running scenarios on how to get it and stab you in the eye."

The minotaur's head tilted, intrigued now. He

slowly lowered his hand and the flames that had been building between his fingers flickered out. "Others have tried to kill me." He gave a smirk. "My kind don't die easily."

Avenant didn't look impressed. "A lot of monsters have told me that, right before they died."

"You are just terrible at diplomacy." Belle lamented. She tried to take control, again. Left to his own devices, Avenant would be cooked to a cinder in no time. "Look, Mr. Minotaur. All we want to do is find Excalibur. You should really be helping us. If we free the sword, we free you, right?"

The minotaur no longer looked angry. Now, he looked amused. It was somehow worse. "You won't free the sword, woman. You are destined to lose everything. Both of you. You aren't fit for this challenge. You don't even understand what it's testing."

Belle felt a chill.

"So far it mainly seems to be testing my goddamn patience." Avenant snapped.

The minotaur shook his head. "Others have come seeking the sword over the years. All have failed, because none of you see the truth. To possess Excalibur means *surrender*. When you enter this labyrinth, you must surrender yourself. All you thought. All you wanted. All you *were*. You must begin anew."

Avenant rolled his eyes. "Let's skip the Zen shit and just get back to the killing each other part."

The minotaur chuckled, the sound echoing off the ice walls. "Oh, I never bother to kill those who seek Excalibur. The labyrinth will do it for me and with much greater... imagination." He stepped back from them. "The sword lays two levels below us, trapped in stone. I look forward to seeing you try to claim it. Really. You questing morons are my only real source of entertainment, so I'm hoping you don't perish *too* quickly."

"Thanks." Belle deadpanned. "Hey, one more thing. Can you *not* kill that witch who was with us, either? She's not really questing for Excalibur, but she's harmless."

Avenant slanted her a sideways look.

"Fine. *Mostly* harmless." Belle allowed.

"I will spare the witch if she stops that God-awful music." The minotaur's gaze met Belle's, again. "You truly aren't like the others who come here, are you? None of them have ever asked mercy for another. Why did you enter this place?"

"Honestly? I just wanted to beat him." She pointed at Avenant.

The minotaur gave a snort of surprised amusement. "That's actually a good reason." He allowed. "The first I've ever heard."

"I thought so, too."

"I am Knoss." The minotaur told her. "You interest me. You'll die on this journey, of course, but at least it'll be *interesting*. That counts for a lot when all I see in here are the same endless walls." He nodded as if coming to a decision. "I think you'll go farther than most, Rosabella Aria Ashman. If you survive long enough, I'll find you at the water."

"Okay." Belle said, looking baffled.

Knoss looked back at Avenant. "If I were you, I'd give up this quest and realize what is truly valuable. A real beast knows when he already holds the prize." He turned and vanished down one of the endless halls.

Belle let out a shaky breath. "Okay. That was weird."

116

"Well, you came out of it okay. Seems like you have a date lined up for later." Avenant scowled over at her. "You kiss me and then you flirt with him. Admit it. It's an actual *plan* to drive me insane, isn't it?"

"I wasn't flirting, you ass. I was being *nice* to him and it worked. I told you we should try talking first." She hesitated. "And I didn't kiss you. At least, not on purpose. It was an accident."

"Oh for fuck's sake..."

"It just accidently happened." Belle insisted. "I didn't *plan* for it to happen. I didn't *want* it to happen. It was just a heat-of-the-moment, accidental thing that sort of," she made a vague gesture, "*happened.*"

"Well, it's about to happen again, because we had a deal. If we survive, I get a kiss. And too bad for you, we survived."

"I never actually agreed to that deal." She informed him quickly.

"Don't be a welsher, Bella."

"I'm not." She swept her hair behind her ears. "I just don't think..."

"Good. Don't think." Avenant interrupted. He crooked a finger at her, his voice dipping lower. "Just come here and don't think about anything except how damn much I want you."

Belle chewed on her lower lip, debating. It was really, really hard to resist him when he stopped being a jerk and used that soft tone. Even knowing it was a mistake, she still found herself taking an instinctive step forward.

On the ground, the flare continued to burn. It must have melted enough of the ice to make the floor unstable in spots. As she edged towards Avenant, the block beneath her gave way and Belle toppled into nothing. It was some kind of shaft that dropped down to another level of the maze. Belle's hands scrabbled to find purchase on the slick walls, but there was nothing to hold onto. She went freefalling through the darkness and landed at the bottom, hard enough to drive the air from her lungs.

"*No.*" Avenant roared. "Belle!"

She gave a wheezing cough, unable to gather enough oxygen to answer him.

It wouldn't have mattered, anyway. Avenant was already following her. The filament clipped to their belts still connected them, but that wasn't what pulled him down. He jumped after her. "*Belle!*" He dropped into the room a lot more gracefully than she did. "Belle, look at me." He crouched down beside her, scanning for injuries. "Are you okay? Are you hurt?"

She shook her head, trying to sit up. "I'm alright. I just got the breath knocked out of me."

His hand found the side of her face. "Are you sure?" He seemed more shaken than she felt. His beautiful eyes glowed electric-blue. She'd seen that happen before, but she was never sure what it meant. "You fell pretty far, my love."

"No kidding." She looked up at the passage they'd come through. "Good thing Excalibur is this way, because I don't think we're getting back up there."

For better or worse, they'd made it to the second level of the labyrinth.

Chapter Nine

Wee Willie Winkie: And do you have any idea how many times he made fun of my name? I was fucking scarred for *life*.

Prince Avenant: How is it my fault that his name sounds like low-grade pornography? Blame his dumbass parents.

Prosecution: Objection! The defendant is out of order. *Again*.

Testimony of Mr. Wee Willie Winkie- The People of the Northlands v. Prince Avenant

"The journal has another passage about this level of the maze." Belle followed behind Avenant, flipping through the pages of that stupid book. "It says, 'A prince must have faith in those around him and not in a mirror. Otherwise, he will be lost in the darkness for all time.'"

Avenant rolled to his eyes. No wonder Belle was so enamored of Grandpa Adam. They were both too soft. "I hate mirrors." He muttered. "Does he say anything about how princes should carry machetes?"

The ice walls had given way to a jungle. The subterranean world must have worked like a biosphere, keeping this part of the labyrinth safe from the cold. It was warm enough here that Avenant and Belle had taken off their coats. The forested humidity pressed down on them as they walked through the tight corridor.

Thick tangles of brush and vines grew straight to the ceiling, creating the walls of the maze. The foliage blocked out most of the available light, so Avenant and Belle had to use flashlights as they made their way along the path. It was dark and oppressive and sticky with heat.

Avenant didn't like it.

Someone had planted the dense vegetation in organized rows, but there were far fewer passages here than there had been upstairs. Once you chose a direction, this level forced travelers to stay on course. There was no way to go except forward or back. It felt like the labyrinth was herding them into a trap.

"If we leave the path, I think we're just going to get lost." Belle slipped the journal back into her pack.

"We're already lost."

"I mean *more* lost. I know you want to start hacking down the plant life and heading off for parts unknown, but let's just do this the easy way, alright?"

"We're not going to be the only ones who find our way down here, you know." He shook his head. "As stupid as the others are, they're not *that* stupid. They'll bumble their way onto this level eventually. If we stay on the only path, we're vulnerable to an ambush."

"So you've said. Repeatedly. But if we leave the path, we're vulnerable to whatever's lurking on the other side of those trees." She gestured to the thicket of brambles and grasping branches. Something moved beyond those green walls. They could both hear it.

"I don't like this." Avenant muttered, but he kept going. "Ez is still upstairs. She has no idea where we are." There was no way to get back up to the ice level, though, so they really didn't have much of a choice but to go on. He just wanted to get through this section as quickly as possible.

The Beast agreed, pacing in agitation.

"Are you okay?" Belle asked.

Avenant shined his flashlight overhead, searching for a way out. "I'm fine."

"You don't sound fine."

"I *said*, I'm fine."

That was a lie. He wasn't fine. He'd been able to keep his claustrophobia under control in the cavernous ice level, but this narrow path was getting to him. It felt like there wasn't enough air. Everything was closing in on him. He scraped a hand through his hair and tried to stay in control.

Belle stopped walking. "Alright, that's it. You've been snapping at me for an hour." She crossed her arms over her chest. "What's going on?"

"I'm always snapping at you. Why would anything be wrong this time?"

"Because, I know the tones of your snapping and this time is different. What's wrong?"

Fuck.

"I don't like this." He repeated grudgingly.

"I don't like it, either. But..."

Avenant cut her off. "No, I mean," he struggled to find the right words, "the walls are too close here. I can't..." He trailed off and ran another hand through his hair, feeling like an idiot. She was going to laugh at him. He could feel it coming. "Just give me a minute."

Belle's jaw dropped. "You're claustrophobic?" She sounded stunned. "Jesus, Avenant! Why would you come into a labyrinth if you're freaked out by small spaces?"

"I'm not freaked out!" The claustrophobia was a personal failing. One that he could deal with, as soon as the tiny pathway stopped shrinking. "I came in here because I knew I could handle it and I *am*."

That was a lie, too. He came in here because it was the only way he could win.

Belle chewed her lower lip. "What can I do?"

"Nothing." He told himself he wasn't suffocating. It was all in his head. "I'm *fine.*"

"Avenant, shut-up and let me help you." Her hand came out and took hold of his. "Please."

Aw, fuck.

He let out a long breath as her fingers tightened around his. He couldn't stand being weak. Not in front of her. But he still gripped her palm like it was the only real thing in the darkness. He knew it was crazy, but the panicked feeling in his chest eased. The Beast whimpered, wanting to be closer to her. Needing her comfort. It felt the claustrophobia even more than Avenant did. It was locked away inside of him all the time, unable to get free.

"How did you get through eight months in jail if you're claustrophobic?" Belle asked.

"When you're in jail, you don't really have much of a choice." His thumb traced over the back of her hand, amazed at how soft she was. He could feel his heart rate slowing as he focused on Belle and not the smothering sensation of the confined space. "Besides, it got progressively worse the longer I was in there. It was bad when I was a kid and my parents..."

"Used to lock you in closets." Belle finished for him when he stopped short.

He hated that she knew that. That she saw him as pathetic. Avenant squeezed his eyes shut. "The closets were only for special occasions. They locked me in my room just about every day, though. Whenever they were home, I was confined. They didn't like looking at me."

"Jesus." She sounded appalled. "Avenant, you should've told someone."

"Who? My father was the Prince and I was Bad." He shook his head. "No one cared. No one ever tried to help me."

Except Belle.

She'd once lost a spelling bee so he'd be safe. As much as it had pissed him off, he'd never forgotten that. The do-Gooding little oddball was the only one who'd ever done anything nice for him. Even if he knew that she'd never love him, at least he could pretend she cared.

Until last year, anyway.

"The claustrophobia mostly faded when I got older, but then *you* framed me for embezzlement and sent me to a tiny little cell. Then, it started coming back." He muttered, angry at her for seeing him like this and for stealing what little warmth he'd ever known when she'd set him up.

Belle pulled her palm away from his.

Fuck.

"I'm sorry." He automatically reached for her, wanting her fingers intertwined with his, again. She'd never held his hand before. He didn't want to lose the connection. "I'm over that. I am. It wasn't your fault that the WUB Club was such a pit. Please don't..."

She cut him off. "You really think I framed you." She seemed astonished by that revelation, even though he'd been saying it for almost a year. "Don't you?"

"You *did* frame me." She'd been part of the stupid independent audit of the kingdom's finances and she'd used her position to make him look like a thief. A child could've seen it. He forgave her, though. He would forgive Belle anything. Nothing she could do would ever make him turn on her.

"Avenant," she met his eyes, "you know me. You *know* I would never cheat like that."

"What I *know* is that I didn't steal any money, but somehow there was a slush fund leading straight back to me. Then, you used the computer trail it left as evidence to depose me and takeover the kingdom." In his calmer moments, he almost admired the audaciousness of the plan. "Look, it doesn't even matter, anymore. You thought I'd sent men to attack you, so you had a right to..."

"I didn't frame you." She interrupted firmly. "You just got through telling the minotaur that I don't lie, so pay attention. If you were set up, it *wasn't* by me. I swear."

Avenant hesitated, studying her earnest face in the dim light. "You didn't frame me?" His voice was less steady than he would've liked, as a terrible hope filled him.

"No, you moron. I don't do things like that. I play rough, but I follow the rules of our game. You *know* that."

He *did* know that. Avenant's mind raced, the truth dawning on him.

Belle hadn't betrayed him.

She couldn't have. The woman was incurably Good. She wouldn't do anything that was morally wrong, no matter how far she was pushed. It was why Avenant would beat her in the end. Because he would do whatever it took to have victory and Belle was trapped by ethics. Relief flooded Avenant's system as he realized he'd been an idiot. Belle was innocent.

The Beast howled with satisfaction.

"I believe you." Avenant got out.

She hadn't betrayed him. Of course she hadn't. The girl was too soft to do anything so underhanded. The oppressive claustrophobia faded away and all Avenant could feel was an overwhelming sense of happiness. Belle hadn't left him in that prison to die. Everything she'd said to the judge before they dragged him off to jail had been the truth.

He hadn't realized how much he'd *needed* it to be the truth until this moment.

"Why *wouldn't* you believe me?" Belle looked annoyed that it was even a question. "When have I ever lied to you? How could you accuse me of...?" She stopped short, suddenly realizing the deeper ramifications of the argument. "Hang on. You didn't take that money? Really? All this time you've been saying someone framed you, someone *actually* framed you?"

"Yes."

"Holy shit." She blurted out. "But, there was so much evidence against you."

"That's the whole problem with being framed: There's evidence that *frames you*."

Chocolate brown eyes blinked up at him. "Oh God..." She was horrified. "Avenant. I am so *sorry*. I didn't know. I swear. I overthrew you because I thought..."

He cut her off. "I don't care that you overthrew me." That was just part of the game. "It was the rest of it that pissed me off. It felt like betrayal. Like it must have felt to you when you thought I'd sent those men to attack you."

Belle swallowed. "Neither of us betrayed the other."

"I know."

"But someone wanted us to *think* we did." She swept her hair back. "It has to be someone who hates *you*. I'm not important enough for anybody to target."

Avenant frowned, unsure which of them she'd just slighted.

"Whoever sent those men to my house knew it would start a chain reaction and that I'd come after you."

Belle continued. "That I'd find the evidence they planted and use it to depose you." She shook her head. "But, why would someone go through all that trouble to set you up?" She paused. "Besides the fact that you're a terrible ruler and a Bad person, I mean."

Avenant disregarded that last part. "Did you ever find the embezzled money?"

Her eyebrows drew together. "Some of it."

"Whatever's missing is part of the reason, then."

Not all of it, though. Someone had wanted him to suffer. Whoever was behind this had used Belle to come after Avenant, knowing that would hurt him the most. Knowing it would gut him to lose her. Knowing he wouldn't harm her, even if it meant he allowed her stupid rebels to chain him. Someone saw that she was his biggest weakness and they'd exploited that.

This was a personal attack. They didn't want him dead. They wanted him disgraced and locked away. They wanted to keep him from Belle. They wanted to steal away everything that mattered to him.

The Beast thudded against the thinning wall, wanting vengeance.

Avenant's jaw clenched.

"I still can't believe you thought I'd framed you." Belle muttered. "It's kind of insulting."

"You thought I'd ripped off my own kingdom. That's *more* insulting. Face it, we've both made mistakes."

She still looked miffed. "Maybe, but you've made *more*. I wouldn't have suspected you, if you didn't do such Bad things."

"But, I do them *well*. If I'd embezzled the money, it wouldn't have been such a sloppy crime."

Rolling her eyes, Belle started walking away. "My

God, that is the worse excuse... *Shit!*" Her complaint ended in a yelp as she tripped over something in the dark. Belle toppled forward right on top of a dead body.

Her scream of panic probably told everyone in the maze exactly where they were.

Fuck.

"Belle." Avenant grabbed her, his flashlight briefly illuminating the corpse.

It looked like it had once been a Cheshire cat. They were supposed to be the prophets of the Four Kingdoms, but this one must have misread her Tarot cards. Her tall, thin body was splayed at a grisly angle, her pink fur matted with gore. A blood-covered knife was in her hand. Had she been trying to defend herself and slashed her attacker? If so, why weren't there any blood trails leading away from the scene?

Avenant checked her frozen face and recognized that it was Cleo. The woman was an assassin, using her psychic abilities to plan intricate murders-for-hire. She was accustomed to being on her guard. Whoever had gotten the drop on her must have created one hell of an ambush to catch her unaware. But how had she been ambushed on this thin path? And couldn't Cheshire cats do that vanishing thing? Why didn't she zap out of there after the first strike?

"Goddamn it." Avenant tugged Belle away from the body and shone the beam down the corridor, looking for the killer. He didn't see anyone. Cleo's blood was still fresh, though, so the perpetrator had to be close.

"Who's doing this?" Belle whispered.

"I doubt it's your friend Knoss the Minotaur, given the lack of cremation. So, the smart money's on Bluebeard." What was one more body to that psychotic bastard? "Or possibly Dower."

"The wolf?"

"He was in prison with me. I don't think the rehabilitation took." That was a massive understatement. Wolves could savage a victim in seconds and Dower was more violent than most. That would certainly explain the grisly crime scene. Avenant's jaw ticked. "Stay here." He stepped over Cleo's corpse and started down the path at a faster pace. Whoever was behind this had to die. If Avenant could find the guy and stop him, Belle would be safer.

"Wait!" Belle followed him, cringing as she edged around the pool of blood. "We should stay together."

"We're *tied* together." He reminded her, gesturing to the clip on his belt. "Don't worry. I'm not going far. I just have to go kill someone real quick and I don't think you want to watch."

"I don't want you to kill someone, *that's* what I don't want." She retorted. "Let's go back the other way."

"And wait for this son of a bitch to pick us off next? No, I'm going to stop him, *now*." Avenant played offense. It was the only way to win. "Who knows how many other contestants he's killed, Belle. These are just the two we've come across, but there might be dozens more. He could be taking out everyone."

"But, it's not smart to incite…" She trailed off. "Avenant?"

"What?"

"Where are you?"

He turned back, shining the flashlight towards her so she'd see... Except she wasn't there. He stared at the empty path, his heart hammering in his chest. "Belle?" He swept the beam around and didn't spot her familiar form. She was gone. She was just *gone*. The claustrophobia was nothing compared to the panic that washed over him. "Belle!"

The Beast howled in fury and alarm.

Avenant's control slipped and, for a second, he processed the world through the monster's heightened senses. Belle was still alive. He could feel her. Dizzy with relief, Avenant and the Beast quickly focused their combined energies on reaching her.

"*Belle.*" His voice was a dark roar.

"Avenant!" Her call was faint, but at least it was there. "The labyrinth shifted. I think that was the rustling noise we were hearing in the brush. The walls change position on their own."

Fuck!

"Don't move!" He shouted. "I'm coming to you." He seized hold of the line connecting them and followed it.

The cord seemed to lead straight through an impenetrable mass of black roses and jagged thorns. It disappeared into the thicket, taunting him with the promise of Belle connected to the opposite end. No way could someone Avenant's size get through that wall. Maybe that was the point. Did this maze really think it could keep him from her?

He looked around, suddenly seeing the labyrinth as a sentient being. "Nice try, jackass, but it's not going to work. She and I are inevitable."

Avenant slammed a hand straight into the sharp barbs, his powers surging out. The roses hardened like they'd been dipped in liquid nitrogen, their petals becoming brittle and snapping away. The vines grew so cold that the air around them chilled into a cloudy vapor. The thorns cracked like glass, dropping to the ground.

Whoever had designed this trap hadn't been expecting someone with his abilities. You didn't send flowers up against a man who could manufacture winter with a twist of his fingers. Avenant shoved through the frozen vegetation, shattering it around him as he headed for Belle. His bleeding hand stayed locked around the string that connected them, using it to guide his way.

"Belle?" He shouted trying to gauge the distance. He'd been walking for ages and everything looked the same.

"I'm here. I can see you coming by the frost." Her voice was closer now. "The labyrinth isn't going to like you hurting its plants, you know."

"It can take me to court. Everybody else does." Avenant crunched passed the last frozen roses and finally spotted Belle. "There you are." He murmured in satisfaction. She looked safe and irritated and all was right in his world.

Mostly.

They'd found one edge of the maze. Belle was sitting on a rock in a small clearing. Behind her, there was a stone wall that seemed to mark the end of the labyrinth. It was lighter here, thanks to some small skylights build high on the granite barrier, but the added illumination didn't reveal much worth seeing.

Avenant spared a quick look around, scanning for a way out of the clearing. The other three sides of the space were covered in the twisting plants. The ceiling and skylights were far out of reach. It was a dead end; a small open space in a vast jungle. Behind him the flora was already regenerating, covering the route he'd traveled to find her. There was no way back to the path and no way to go forward.

This couldn't be good.

"Next time I tell you not to go kill someone, will you listen to me please?" Belle groused. "Now, we're never going to find our way out of here. I think we're stuck."

Avenant had to agree.

Right now, he had something more important on his mind, though. Dismissing the fact they were trapped, he stalked towards her. Losing Belle for that brief moment had brought back all the anxiety of the past eight months. Unable to see her... Unsure if she was safe... Fifty thousand crazed fantasies about what he would do when he got her back...

He *had* to make sure Belle never left him again. That they were tied together forever. He needed Belle's surrender and there was only one way to get it. It was so close to breaking the rules that even Avenant knew it was wrong, but he was going to do it anyway. He'd laid his heart bare on prom night and she hadn't cared. He'd promised her everything he had and it wasn't enough. Emotions and honesty didn't work, so he'd try a different tact.

"I'll take my kiss now." Avenant yanked her to her feet, his mouth finding hers.

For once, he and the Beast were of one mind: The only way to win was to cheat.

Chapter Ten

I hate him.

Testimony of Mr. Peter Piper- *The People of the Northlands v. Prince Avenant*

Twelve Years Before

Her prom date was a troll.

Not in the biological sense. He'd been born an elf. But, Peter Piper was *totally* a troll.

Belle had never noticed that before. He'd just seemed like a normal guy who was a little doofy and who used too much styling gel. She'd never forgotten that he'd been the only one who'd wished her happy birthday when she was fourteen, so she went out of her way to be nice to him.

Now she was seeing beneath the oily façade and straight into his inner troll-ness, though. Something about the position of Peter's nose and chin made her eyes cross when she looked at his face for too long. His overly blond hair smelled funny. His tux was an obnoxious shade of pickled pepper purple.

And, worst of all, he was making out with Jill Hill in Belle's seat.

Jill sat on his lap, her face suction-cupped to his. They were lost in their own little world of taffeta and groping, not even caring that they were in her chair. Or that she existed, at all.

The gym was festooned with white crêpe paper

streamers and blue balloons. Belle had helped string the decorations all afternoon and now they were a festive backdrop for her public embarrassment. No one in the school could possibly miss the fact that Belle's date had dumped her in the middle of prom.

It was all Avenant's fault.

Belle liked Peter, but she'd never *liked* the guy. Not in a romantic way. He was friendly enough and a hell of an asset to the Mathlete Squad, but mostly she'd just needed a date. He was the only one who asked, so she'd said yes. She was president of the dance committee and she wasn't going to show up alone. That would've just made Avenant's year. Peter had been a godsend. He'd approached her in the cafeteria and politely asked her out with everyone watching.

With *Avenant* watching.

Lounging at the cool kids' table, with his fan club of cheerleaders, Avenant looked like the pasha of Northlands High. He spent every lunch hour gazing down on the lesser beings as they genuflected passed. Belle knew that because she spent every lunch hour glaring at him from the not-so-cool table, willing him to choke on his food.

When Peter had asked her to prom, she'd seen Avenant's arctic-blue eyes narrow from twenty feet away. He hadn't expected anyone to approach her. Belle didn't get many dates, mostly because everyone was terrified of making Avenant's enemies list. You were either with Avenant or against him. Belle was "against," but most of the school preferred to stay on the handsome, popular, royal side of their war. She could see from Avenant's annoyingly perfect face that he was pissed when Peter decided to cross into hostile territory and join Team Belle.

So --obviously-- she'd agreed to the date.

Six hours in a push-up bra seemed like a small price to pay for an opportunity to irritate her nemesis. And Peter was tolerable enough. Usually.

She should've anticipated that Avenant would find a way to fight back, though. She *knew* he was behind this. Jill had never shown the least bit of interest in Peter before and now the girl was one love song away from unfastening his cummerbund with her teeth. Since Jill was part of Avenant's clique of evil, it didn't take a genius to piece together who was really behind this.

Damn if Belle was going to hang around and let him relish his victory. The looks of pity she was getting from the other students were bad enough. If she saw Avenant's smug smirk, she'd beat him to death with a mirror ball. Which, granted, he totally deserved, but which would probably not look so great on her permanent record.

She grabbed her coat and left Peter to his fun. As far as Belle was concerned, prom was *done*. Except, she was stuck there for at least another hour.

She couldn't go home yet.

Her parents would know something had gone terribly wrong and they'd been so *happy* when she'd told them she had a date. Her mother had helped her buy a poufy dress and her father had taken her picture. They were social people and their bookish daughter was a constant disappointment. Seeing her headed off to a dance had thrilled them. No way was Avenant going to spoil that.

So, Belle sat under the bleachers and plotted her revenge. Peter didn't matter. Belle couldn't even work up the energy to hate him. He was just a tool of the *true* mastermind. She was going to make Avenant pay. The Beast had no idea who he was messing with. She tried to think of something that would *really* hurt him. Something life-scarring and physically painful. Something that would haunt him for the rest of his pathetic, wasted days.

Something that would break him.

"*There* you are." Avenant sang out in his cheeriest tone. "I've been looking everywhere for you, Bella." He ducked under the bleacher's metal supports, heading towards her. A cardboard crown sat on his shiny hair, proclaiming him prom king. "I think Peter might like a dance."

Belle swiped at her eyes and hated him with the intensity of a thousand suns. "Peter's drunk. He has no idea where he *is*, let alone what he *wants*."

"Oh, I think he knows *exactly* what he wants. Presently, she's wearing a red spandex dress and has her hand down his pants." Avenant arched a brow when he saw she was upset. "Don't worry. Pete's not going to get a happy ending. Come Monday, Jill will forget he even exists and he'll be a laughingstock. I'll make sure of it."

"You must be very proud."

"Little bit." He agreed. "The guy's always been an asshole and now everyone will see it."

"*You're* the asshole. Peter is a nice guy and you're making a fool of him."

"*Nice?*" Avenant's voice lost its taunting quality. "He's tongue-fucking another girl in the middle of your date!"

"Peter's not usually like this. He's a Merit Scholar."

"He betrayed you! I just *showed* you that." Avenant looked confused. Actually, he looked… hurt. Like he was genuinely perplexed by her attitude. "Why are you defending him? How could you even go out with someone so weak?"

She got to her feet. "Peter was the only one in the school brave enough to ask me. *That's* why you're targeting him." She jabbed a finger at Avenant's chest. "You can't *stand* that someone would stand up to you. You can't *stand* that someone might not be intimidated by your stupid vendetta against me."

"I can't stand that you said yes to him!" Avenant loomed over her. "You only did it to piss me off and now you're surprised that it worked?"

"Oh, because everything is always about *you*, right? Why can't you ever take responsibility for being a jackass? You don't even feel guilty about it, do you?"

"No, I *don't* feel guilty. Peter knew I would destroy him if he came near you. *Everyone* knows that. What happened is on him. When he got between us, he became fair game. I should have finished him off that day at the pool."

"It was *your* fault, not his. Everything is *always* your fault, because you *always* go too far." She glowered up at him. "Do I attack your stick-figure girlfriends? *No.* I leave innocent people out of it, even when they're dumber than a pompom. Why can't you do the same?"

For some reason, Avenant grew even more agitated. "Peter isn't innocent. Neither is any other guy who asks you out. I will ruin *every* date you try to have with another man, I promise you."

"You are such a beast!"

"And I *know* you don't give a shit who I'm dating." He continued ruthlessly. "That's obvious. If you *were* pissed about any of them, I'd be thrilled and they'd be history."

Belle frowned. "You're *trying* to annoy me with...?"

He cut her off. "But I care about your social

calendar *a lot*. What did you think I was going to do tonight, huh? Let you head off to the after-party with Mr. Merit Scholar and the goddamn flower he gave you?" Avenant grabbed the corsage right off her wrist, crushing the purple carnation in his hand. His eyes glowed electric-blue. "Or were you just fucking with me?"

That did it. Belle's lips pressed together and she started around him.

He wasn't expecting her to stop arguing and walk away. "Where are you going?"

"I'm done with you, Avenant. Forever."

"What? No." He chased after her. "You don't mean that."

She kept going, wishing she could do or say something to really hurt him. To break him, like he was always trying to break her. But that was impossible, because he didn't care about anything. "I *do* mean it. You're not even worth fighting with anymore."

"Stop." Avenant blocked her path, his face pale. "Belle, no. You can't leave me."

"You're out of control! You just ruined my prom, my friendship with Peter, and my first corsage!"

"I know. *Shit.* I didn't mean it. The Beast was lashing out and I just lost it for a second."

"What?"

"Please." He seemed almost panicked. "I'll buy you a new corsage. A bigger one. I *want* to. I can buy you whatever you ask for. Flowers, jewelry, books, horses. Name it and it's yours."

"I don't want anything from *you*."

He flinched.

Belle glared up at him. "If you weren't the prince, no one in this entire kingdom would put up with you. They're just afraid of you. You're not going to bully me like you do the others..."

"I'm sorry." He interrupted simply.

She hesitated. Avenant had never apologized before and it took the wind from her sails. "You are?"

"Yes. I shouldn't have touched your corsage. I just *hated* seeing it."

She eyed him suspiciously. "Are you sorry about wrecking my date, too?"

"Fuck no." His expression darkened. "Peter will be lucky to live to graduation."

That was the Avenant she knew and loathed. "Leave him *alone*."

"Give me a reason."

"I won't give you *anything*."

"No kidding. You sure don't give me a *chance*." He seethed. "*That's* what makes me crazy. You give that pasty son of a bitch a chance and not me. Why?"

"What are you talking about? I have given you plenty of chances to be a Good person and you can't do it. You show me again and again that you never think of anyone but yourself."

"That's not true."

"You're Bad all the way through, Avenant."

"That's not *true*." His voice cracked. "I swear, it's not."

"Name one person you care about, then. *One*."

His gaze sharpened. "You." He moved closer to her, his body brushing against hers. "I care about you, Belle. More than anything else in this world."

She drew in a gasp at his words and at the feel of him. It was like that day in the pool, only better. She automatically shifted closer, feeling the hard ridge of him brush her stomach and... liking it. Her nipples tightened into points and her blood thickened. She tried to think of something to say and came up empty. All she could focus on was the blue of his eyes as they met hers.

She stared up at him in a trance.

Avenant's breathing got harsher when she didn't push him away. "You don't *ever* have to be afraid of me." He whispered. The electric glow was back in his eyes, but it was no longer angry. "I will give you everything I have and more. Gladly. I'll hand over the whole kingdom if you ask. I can become a Merit Scholar. I can even try to be a knight in shining armor." He leaned down, his lips brushing over hers. "Just give me a chance, Bella. You have no idea how I long for you."

Oh God.

She bit back a whimper as his mouth slowly coaxed hers to open. She'd never been kissed before. Reading love stories from the time she could sound out the words had turned her into a romantic. She'd always had big expectations for her first kiss. Epic plans for its splendor. No boy had ever seemed up to matching her imagination. And she'd certainly never pictured *Avenant* in her dreams. At least, not that she'd ever admitted to herself. He was always so mean to her and Bad and selfish. But this...

Desire washed over her and her toes curled.

This was what she'd been waiting for.

"Please, my love." He breathed against her lips and she knew what he wanted.

Belle gathered her confidence and kissed him back. It was insane, but she kissed him back.

Avenant gave a growl of approval at her hesitant response. He maneuvered her backwards so she was trapped between the gym wall and his body, his fingers tangling in her hair. The careful work of the stylist was ruined and she didn't care. Belle's arms wrapped around his neck, lost in the heat of it.

Avenant's hands shook with need. His mouth carefully caressed hers, even as the strength of his grasp had her flattened against the cinderblocks. He touched her like he expected her to slip away and, at the same time, like she was precious to him. The combination of power and gentleness was intoxicating. Belle softened against him, granting him even deeper access. He was always so cold, but now she felt him melting. Giving. Avenant's whole body leaned into her embrace, his restless cruelty tamed. He wasn't trying to ravish. The Beast of the Northlands wanted to be tender with her and Belle was completely under his spell.

This was *who* she'd been waiting for.

When the kiss finally ended, Avenant seemed as mesmerized as she felt. "You are the most beautiful thing I've ever seen." His thumb brushed her cheekbone like she was made of crystal. "You always have been."

"And you've always been a liar." She glanced away from his intense eyes, feeling befuddled and not knowing what to say. "Really, I should look a lot better, given how much this outfit cost."

Her parents hated budgets and had flawless taste when it came to clothing. Prom was one of the few occasions when she deferred to their wishes and let them dress her up as fancily as they wished. God knew, she had no sense of style.

She'd wanted to look pretty... but she was suddenly very sure it hadn't been to impress her date. Like so much else in her life, it had all been about Avenant.

Belle hesitated, trying to make sense of this.

"I love this dress, even if you did wear it for another guy." Avenant's palm came up to cup her breast through the yellow silk. "But, it is definitely *not* what makes you beautiful, Bella."

No one had ever touched her like that before and it felt... amazing. She'd always been embarrassed by her breasts. They were too small, but, when he touched them, she could feel them swell with desire. Shocked, her gaze flew back to his and she saw his mouth curve.

Since she was never inclined to give Avenant the benefit of the doubt, she didn't stop to think he was smiling because of her astonished reaction. Instead, her mind instantly went to a dark place.

He was tricking her.

He was *laughing* at her.

Of *course* he was. It was the only thing that made sense. Why else would Avenant be there with her, when he could have anyone? He was out for revenge. She'd done everything in her power to make sure he wasn't elected prom king and now he was trying to get back at her. Or it could've been because she'd been named valedictorian over him. Or because of a thousand other things. Their battles were endless and this fake seduction was just a new tactic.

Belle shoved him away. "No." She shook her head, trying to clear it. "I'm not falling for this, you bastard."

Avenant seemed surprised. "Belle..." He reached out his hand and she swatted it away.

"Don't." She warned.

"But..."

"What are you really up to? Are you videotaping this or something?" She looked around for cameras.

"No!"

"Well, whatever you're plotting, it's not going to work."

"God*damn* it!" He looked like he was going to explode, no doubt angry that she was spoiling his newest plot to humiliate her. His voice got darker and he didn't seem to notice. "This is real. You can deny it if you want, but you feel it, too. We're *real*. That's what's scaring you."

She began fixing her dress, trying to hide the tremors in her limbs. "I can't believe I almost bought your bullshit. I can't *believe* I let you kiss me against a wall. The punch bowl really is spiked."

"Don't walk away from me. Not when we are so *close*."

"Close to *what?* You doing something else to ruin my night?"

"You're supposed to be with me!" He roared. "It's supposed to be this way. Why can't you see that?" He scraped a hand through his hair, dislodging his stupid paper crown. "Why won't you just surrender? Do you get off on torturing me? Is that it?"

"How in the hell have you turned yourself into the injured party here?"

"I've been the injured party since we were kids. You never thought I was Good enough to be your friend, but we're *going* to be a lot more than that. It's inevitable."

"No."

"*Yes*." He was more worked up than she'd ever seen him, blue eyes glowing with rage. "*I'm* your True Love! Not Peter. Not anyone else. *Me*."

Belle's mind whirled, her mouth parting in shock. "What?"

"It's true and you know it. You *have* to know it, Belle."

"No." She didn't trust him. She never had,

because he gave her no reason to. "I don't believe you."

"Take your clothes off and I'll prove it to you, then." He shot back furiously. Good folk always knew their True Love when they had sex. "Why the hell would I lie about this?"

"So you can set me up, obviously! So, you can get me into bed and then laugh your ass off when it's over."

"You think I'm thrilled about it? That I wouldn't walk out there and find someone less aggravating if I could?" He flung a wild gesture towards the prom on the other side of the bleachers and all the large-busted girls who idolized him. "You think I can't have *anyone* I choose?"

Belle's temper reached its flashpoint. "Well, you can't have *me*. You could beg me on your knees, I *still* wouldn't be yours." She shouted. "You're playing some new game to try and screw with me. Only it won't work, because I see right through you. I see how cold you are inside. You wouldn't know your True Love if you sat on her, because you aren't capable of feeling anything real."

"Oh, I'm feeling a lot of things, right now."

Belle shook her head. "You can't win this. You know that, so just give up the ploy." She met his eyes. "It will always and forever be *no*, Avenant."

Avenant glanced away, his face going tight. For once, he didn't have anything snarky to say. He knew his scheme had been busted and that she'd won the round.

Feeling vindicated, even if her body was still aching, Belle marched past him. "You'd better not tell anyone about this either. It never happened."

"I've already forgotten it and *you*. I'm going back to my very limber prom queen and you can go back to being the third wheel on Jill and Peter's date."

As always, he sounded completely confident in his

own superiority. Untouched and unaffected by her. But when she glanced at him over her shoulder, Avenant wasn't heading towards the dance floor. He was alone, leaning against the wall with his face tilted back and his eyes squeezed shut in defeat.

Like he was broken.

Chapter Eleven

Rosabella Aria Ashman: As soon as I started looking into the finances of the kingdom, I knew there was a problem. I don't know why I was even surprised that Avenant was behind it. He's always got some trick up his sleeve. Look at him over there plotting.

Defense: Ms. Ashman, my client is handcuffed to a chair and surrounded by armed guards. Surely you're not so paranoid that you think he's up to something right *now*

Rosabella Aria Ashman: Of course he's up to something! He's breathing, isn't he?

Testimony of Ms. Rosabella Aria Ashman- *The People of the Northlands v. Prince Avenant*

Belle let out a gasp as Avenant's lips met hers. It was unfair that he was so beautiful. That he tasted so good. That he felt so warm. All the clear and rational reasons why she should stay away from him faded away when he touched her.

"Goddamn it." She whimpered as his teeth grazed her lower lip. "How do you keep doing this to me?"

"It's you who does it to *me*. You always have." He lifted a palm to touch her cheek and Belle saw his palm was bleeding.

"Are you alright?" She caught hold of his hand and turned it to survey the damage. "You're hurt." The jagged thorns of the rosebushes had torn long gashes into his flesh. He'd cut his skin to ribbons coming to find her. Belle lifted her eyes to his. "You should've been more careful. For all we know these plants are poisonous."

"When you're out of my sight, all I care about is having you beside me, again. This?" He lifted his wrist and made a rueful face at the scratches. "This is one of the *least* crazy things I've done to be with you." He dipped his head to find her mouth, again. "I want you so much it makes me insane."

Belle felt herself falling under his spell. It was always like that when the Beast showed her his softer side. When Avenant stopped snarking at her and became tender, she felt almost spellbound.

And very, very aroused.

The kiss got deeper. More passionate. Avenant took everything she offered and demanded more. His body pressed against hers and she instinctively rocked against his erection. Belle's whole system was screaming for him. The last time he'd done this to her was right before he was sent off to jail and the memory of it still left her waking up panting for him. It was such a bad idea to let this happen, again.

Belle tried to think. "What about your True Love?" She asked, coming up for air.

"This has been brewing between us since that day in the pool. Longer than that." His breathing was harsh. "We're never going to move forward until we deal with it."

Belle's body felt like it was on fire. "You think we should sleep together?" She translated, wanting to make sure they were on the same page. "Really?"

"This is our moment." His voice was dark and hypnotic. "Sooner or later, it had to happen. We both knew that."

She managed a scoff. "Because you're just so irresistible, I suppose."

"Because you and I are inevitable."

Belle stared at him, wanting to be convinced.

"We're alone. Maybe we'll die in here, Bella. This could be it for us. Our last chance."

"That's a good line, but I'm not ready to have end-of-the-world sex just yet. I'm pretty sure we'll live to see tomorrow."

Avenant's eyes narrowed, quickly switching to a different strategy. "We'll make a deal, okay? We'll do it one time." He held up a finger. "One. We'll just face this physical pull, while we're both calm and rational about it. Once it's over, things will be a lot simpler between us. It'll be one less point of tension."

That argument was more persuasive. "One time?"

"And then we won't ever have to mention all this, again. We'll know we got the hardest part over with." He nodded. "It's really the most logical plan. I think we both see that." He began shedding his clothes as if it had all been decided. "It's going to be such a relief, don't you think?" He shrugged his chest plate aside.

God, she wanted him. This was nuts, but she wanted him. "Hang on..." She began desperately.

Avenant kept going. "If we escape this maze, I know that you have a happily-ever-after planned with some knight in shining armor. That's why we have to get this out of our system, now. Even your True Love would want you to do this. I'm sure of it." His voice was utterly certain. "He'd want you to have everything clear in your head."

Belle's eyebrows compressed. "You think so?"

"I *know* so." He pulled off his shoes. "So do you have any special preference on where this happens?" He looked around the clearing for a suitable spot.

Belle felt dazed. "No, but..."

He cut her off, again. "Because, I have an idea of what I'd like to try."

She managed to swallow as his shirt hit the ground. This was exactly why Good girls always wanted to date the Baddest guy in school. Because he could talk you into doing just what you desperately wanted to do. "Do we have to be naked?" She asked softly.

The question was tantamount to an agreement and they both knew it.

Avenant's eyes blazed, lighting up with that amazing, erotic electricity. "Yes. Very, very naked." His pants came off next and she found herself transfixed by the hard length of him. His body was so beautiful.

All her insecurities rushed in. "It would still work if I stayed mostly dressed." She got out. "I mean, the point is to just get it over with. We're scratching an itch. Why do we need to complicate things?"

"Because I've waited a long time to see the itch I'm scratching." Stepping forward, he began unbuttoning her blouse. Apparently, he was in a hurry, now that she was sort of going along with his crazy plan.

"But..." Belle bit back a whimper as he removed her top, his palms brushing over her breasts as he peeled off the fabric. Her insecurities from high school came flooding back. "What if you don't like what you see?"

He frowned like he didn't understand. "Why wouldn't I like it?"

"Because I'm not as pretty as you are, obviously." She could feel the heat of his hands through her bra and her nipples beaded. Belle had always hated how small her breasts were, but they were incredibly sensitive. Especially around him. This wasn't going to be like the last time. "I don't want you making fun of me, again."

"What are you talking about?"

The more she thought about it, the more determined Belle became. "The bra stays." She decided firmly. She wasn't being completely naked in front of a man who'd probably been with two supermodels at a time. "Otherwise, I'm calling this whole thing off."

Avenant studied her, weighing her resolve. "You can't be serious." He decided.

Belle's lips firmed and she started to pull away.

He capitulated so fast it was almost funny. "Alright." He said in something close to panic. "Yes. Fine. Keep it on."

"Really?" Belle was a little shocked it had been that easy. She was instantly suspicious. "Why are you being so accommodating?"

He blew out a breath. "Because, I'm desperate and you're holding all the cards. Insane or not, we'll do this however you want. You're in control."

"Oh." Her gaze slipped down to his straining erection and realized he would've agreed to anything, at the moment. Her confidence came rushing back. It wasn't a trick. Avenant wanted her. "Well, okay. I guess we can do this, then." She unlaced her shoes, toeing them off. "How did you want to…? You know…"

"Come here." His voice went darker as he extended a hand to her. "I'll show you."

Belle debated the wisdom of letting him direct this part. "Alright." She edged closer to him. Avenant probably knew what he was doing, at least. "Just don't laugh."

"I'll try not to." He watched her with a hooded gaze.

She cleared her throat, stopping in front of him. "Okay, let's get this… *Oh!*"

Avenant grabbed her arm and guided her

backwards until she hit the stone wall. He loomed over her, pinning her there…. And she suddenly knew what he wanted.

"Really?" She whispered nervously. "Is it a good idea to complicate this?"

"It's the best fucking idea I've ever had." His hand unfastened her pants, stripping them off of her. Before Belle could adjust to the idea that she was naked from the waist down, Avenant's hand brushed against her damp flesh, testing her readiness. Her head went back as he slipped a finger inside of her. God, his touch always felt so damn *Good*.

"Beautiful." He murmured.

Avenant adjusted her leg so it was at his hip, giving him total access. Vulnerability hit her and she whimpered. The Beast could do anything to her… and she liked it. Belle automatically looked away from his face, even as her body wept with pleasure at his invasion. She rocked against his palm and she knew she was rapidly losing control of this situation.

"I'm getting all the way inside of you." He leaned closer to her, his lips grazing her neck. "Just like I told you I would the last time. You're going to give me everything, Bella."

See? That didn't sound like she was in charge, but still her body was screaming for more. For years, she'd been fantasizing about this. About him. She was seventeen again and Avenant had her pinned up against the wall of the gym. Then and now, the man overwhelmed her. What was she doing?

"Avenant? Are you sure about this?"

"Only you would ask me that." He kissed her throat, even as his fingers slowly explored. "God, I have waited so damn long." Apparently, he was willing to wait some more, because the man was taking his time. "Just let me touch you."

She had to get this experiment back on track. Belle's hand came up to grip his shoulder, her fingers digging into his skin. "We don't have to make this quite so... leisurely."

"You in a rush?"

"It feels complicated." She said desperately. "You're trying to get what I denied you at prom and this is supposed to be *quick*. That was the plan." Why did Avenant always get her so muddled?

"I don't remember saying I'd be quick."

"You implied it." The longer he took, the more mixed-up her emotions became. This would be so much easier if it was just physical. If she didn't feel so much. "Once it's over, I won't be so," she swallowed, "confused."

"You're right. I'll make it clearer for you." His finger vanished and then the hard length of him was at her entrance. "Here's the simple truth, my love: You didn't deny me at prom." Avenant smiled. "You just postponed the inevitable."

Belle gave a long cry of pleasure as he eased into her. It was sooooo sloooow, like he wanted both of them to experience every millimeter of his possession. It felt so right. It felt *too* right. Panicked, Belle's gaze flashed to his and she realized that he'd been waiting for that.

Electric-blue eyes caught hers and held fast. "Luckily, I'm very patient when it comes to my True Love."

Belle gaped at him. "Wha...? Oh *God*."

She instinctively went up on tiptoe to accommodate his final push home, unable to even speak as he filled her to bursting. Then, he just stood there so she could feel him. All of him. So she'd know it was true.

Good folk always knew when they had sex with their True Love, but Bad folk knew even sooner than that. Avenant had led her to this point, because he'd already figured out what she was suddenly realizing.

They were True Loves.

Belle squeezed her eyes shut.

Goddamn it, maybe she'd always known that. Who else would her True Love be but Avenant? The very thought of him marrying another woman had made her crazy. No other man had ever fascinated her like this one did. Fate had tied them together, right from the beginning.

It had always been Belle and Avenant.

But that didn't mean she'd surrender like this. He had *totally* tricked her into it. He hadn't planned to make love once and then never mention it again. That had been a lie so he could trigger the bond. This whole time, he'd been setting her up!

"Told ya so." Avenant whispered. "At prom, I *told* you what this really was, didn't I?"

"You son of a bitch. You think you're going to beat me?"

"I think I just *did*." He began moving in unhurried thrusts that left her seeing stars. "It took a while, but I've finally claimed my prize." He smiled, relishing his victory. "You can't get rid of me and you know it."

Belle's body undulated against his, instinctively trying to pull him deeper. She glowered at him, her mind and body on two separate paths. "It's not going to work." She snapped in irritation, even as her fingernails dug into his back. "You don't really want me. You just think it's all a game."

"Certainly *feels* like I want you." Avenant nuzzled her temple. "Feels like you want me, too." His teeth nipped her ear. "You can't fight the inevitable, my love. You're mine."

Belle hated him. Absolutely *hated* him. Except... *Jesus,* he was good at this. Her eyes squeezed shut. "Harder." She needed it just a little harder. "You might as well finish this before I kill you."

Avenant chuckled at that. "Christ, how I've longed for you." His pace increased like he just couldn't help himself.

Oh *God*. Her mouth parted in wonder as he sped up. *That* was what she needed to come and he knew it. That powerful penetration right at her core. Her orgasm loomed and it would just make him even smugger. She tried to focus, but it was getting more and more difficult. "Even if I'm your True Love, I'm *not* 'yours,' you know."

Except, she was.

God*damn* it.

"We'll see about that." He lifted her other leg, so it was wrapped around him and he was supporting all of her weight. "Right now, I have what I want. Or at least, I'm getting there fast." His perfect face was tight with passion. "Can we take the bra off, now? I need to see more of you."

"*No*." She panted. "You're lucky... I'm not making you... stop altogether."

"I *knew* you were going to be bitchy about this."

Belle gave up arguing for the moment. It was too hard to concentrate. Her thighs tightened on his body, so close now. "Please, Avenant." The words escaped without her meaning them to. She'd always known it would be like this between them.

"Tell me what you need." He braced one hand on the wall, somehow achieving an even deeper angle. "You want it harder?" Avenant teased her with one forceful thrust and Belle gasped. He liked that reaction. "I think I was right about you in the courthouse, Bella. I don't think you're Good, at all." He bent his head to whisper in her ear. "I think you like it when I do Bad things to your pretty little body."

She almost exploded just from his words. "Please." She moaned, right on the edge.

"I think you like coming for a beast. Don't you?"

She gave a jerky nod.

"And you're all hot and ready for it." He sounded sooooo solicitous, but she knew better. "You're just aching for that little push." His eyes glinted. "Ask nicely and maybe I'll help you out."

"Bastard." Her forehead fell to his shoulder. "Give me the climax and then get smirky."

"Give me a reason." He sounded strained. "Why should I let you come when you won't even take all your clothes off?"

"Because…" She tried to think, but it was hard. *He* was hard and Bad and it felt so right. She gave a languid sigh and forgot what they'd been talking about.

He shifted, hitting a new spot. "Give me a reason, Bella."

She bit her lower lip and tried not to beg. "So you can laugh at me?"

"I swear to God, I won't laugh." He met her eyes. "Please, my love."

She gave up and just went with the truth. "Because, this is the way I always imagined it should've ended on prom night. Except, you weren't being such a total asshole in my dreams." She'd deal with the ramifications of that admission later. Right now, it was impossible to care about his gloating. She was so *close*. "God, I can't even tell you how many times I've imagined this."

Avenant's mouth curved. "Feel free to try. I want to hear every twisted idea in your head."

"I knew you'd laugh."

"Believe me, I'm not laughing." He pounded into her, his voice getting desperate. "Christ, it's my fantasy, too, Belle. That's why it *had* to be this way the first time. I've spent years jacking-off to that memory and now I get to finish it for real."

His rough words and the increased friction had her eyes going wide.

"I knew you were my True Love, even back then." He continued relentlessly. "You've always belonged to me. If you hadn't panicked, I would have had you that night." Electric eyes burned into hers. "But, I have you now and I'm never letting you go." He slammed into her, harder than ever before. "*Never.*"

Belle exploded.

She vaguely processed Avenant's shout of triumph as he found his own release. It sounded like the roar of a beast. Then, all she could do was hold on as waves of pleasure wracked her. She clung to him, shaking and sobbing his name. It was exactly the way it was supposed to be between True Loves. Intense and insane and *incredible.* How else would it ever feel with Avenant?

When Belle finally recovered, she was still wrapped in his arms. He was cradling her against him and looking more arrogant than he'd ever looked, which was quite a feat considering the size of his ego. She slowly raised her eyes to his, wary of what came next.

...With good reason.

He kissed her cheek. "I win." He said simply.

Goddamn it.

Chapter Twelve

The Beast didn't have a *true* royal palate, because he's nothing but an animal. I was the royal baker and Avenant said I was insubordinate, because I refused to only make chocolate desserts. After he fired me, I sat in the corner for weeks, eating pies to console myself. I'd eaten two-hundred and sixty of them, when the paramedics found me.

He's why I contracted plum poisoning.

Testimony of Mr. Jack Horner- *The People of the Northlands v. Prince Avenant*

His True Love was curled up beside him, safe and warm.

Avenant inhaled deeply, breathing in the scent of her hair. He'd longed for this moment forever. Belle had spent the night cradled in his arms, like they'd been made to fit together. Which they had been. He'd always known that. After so many years of waiting, Belle was finally right where she belonged. And she wasn't getting away.

Inside, the Beast was satiated, purring contentedly with their prize. It had been screaming at Avenant to claim her for longer than either of them could remember. At last, Belle was securely in its clutches. She didn't want to be his True Love. She'd never love him. She didn't even like him. But, short of killing him --which, granted, was always a possibility-- there was no way she could undo their connection, now.

He'd won.

So why didn't it feel like it?

Avenant tightened his hold on Belle, uneasy despite the fact he had what he'd thought he wanted.

He'd believed that being True Loves would be enough. He'd tricked her into having sex with him, because, once he was inside of her, she'd know the truth. He'd lied and told her it would only be once. He'd pushed her farther than she'd ever go on her own. He'd completely manipulated her in order to get his own way. It had been cheating, but he didn't care. It had *worked*.

Except, it hadn't.

Belle still hadn't surrendered. Without that, she could just... leave.

She made a soft sound and he realized he was gripping her too tightly. Avenant eased back, but she was already half-awake. Belle shifted in his grasp, her stunning eyes blinking like she had no idea where she was. He could see her sleepy confusion. Then, she looked up at his face and the most amazing thing happened...

Belle forgot she hated him.

For one drowsy moment, she forgot their war and smiled as if seeing him reassured her. "Hi." Belle murmured, turning towards him. She cuddled into his embrace, drifting off again like she instinctively felt safe with him beside her.

If Avenant had been standing, it would've dropped him to his knees.

He was beaten. Christ, he'd been beaten since kindergarten. It was a good thing her eyes were closed, otherwise Belle would've seen how far gone he was. How completely and totally at her mercy. Avenant would do whatever she asked, if only she'd stay with him. He'd hand over his kingdom, his heart, his soul... *anything.*

He *had* to make her surrender before she figured that out.

Using their bond was the best way to accomplish

that, so obviously it was his next move. Avenant's hand slipped down, easing between her legs. Jesus, she was the softest thing he'd ever felt. Belle opened to his touch, the liquid warmth coating his fingers. She gave a hum of pleasure and Avenant's mouth curved. He'd gotten through eight months in prison fantasizing about that sound.

He pressed his lips to her temple, guiding her towards release. Getting her used to his touch. She was always responsive and, once True Loves slept together, the need between them grew even stronger. It only took a moment to have her right on the edge. Belle bit down on her lower lip and Avenant pressed even deeper. Belle liked it a little bit hard, which was just fucking adorable. He squeezed another finger into her tight channel and felt her body clench.

She realized what he was doing a second before she came. Her eyes popped open, but it was too late to stop the inevitable. He kept his gaze locked on hers as he stroked her to completion.

"*Ohhhhh.*" It was whimpering moan and then she rippled around his hand.

Before she had a chance to regain her senses and shove him away, Avenant rolled her on top of him. She made a helpless sound that almost sent him over the edge. Dazed, she let him position her knees on either side of his hips and thrust home. Belle's mouth parted, her eyes squeezing shut as a second climax tore through her.

Avenant's teeth ground together at the sensation. The Beast gave a growl of pure lust. "Ride, my love." He gripped her waist, guiding her up and down. She was still shivering from the orgasm, intensifying the sensation. "That's the way." His head went back as Belle braced her hands on his chest and found her rhythm. Yeah... this wasn't going to last long.

"Oh God." Belle arched in desire. Dark hair fell like a veil around her pale skin as she moved. "*Avenant.*"

Avenant smiled in wonder at the sound of his name on her lips. It was beautiful. She was beautiful. He would never, ever get enough of this woman.

His palms came up to cup her pretty little breasts through the lace of her bra. He wanted to see them. To suck her hard nipples into his mouth. From the time he'd figured out girls were different than boys he'd been fascinated with Belle's delicate curves. He tried to unfasten the damn bra, but she swatted him away. Not wanting to push his luck, he gave up and let the annoying scrap of fabric stay in place. He had so much else to focus on.

Inside his head, the Beast was fighting for control.

Avenant's jaw clenched as Belle rocked against his body, somehow keeping the monster down. He wanted this to last forever, but she was so damn *soft*. Christ, as many times as he'd dreamed of her, he'd never imagined how *soft* she'd really feel around him. It was a miracle he was still conscious.

When Belle convulsed for a third time, Avenant couldn't hold on any longer. Grasping her hips, he slammed into her as deep as he could go. Belle cried out his name again and Avenant erupted. His eyes nearly crossed as he came long and hard within her hot depths. She milked him dry and it was goddamn *beautiful.* The Beast and Avenant roared at the same instant, two sounds becoming one in his head. For one perfect second, he felt... whole.

Belle collapsed onto him, her forehead on his shoulder. She was struggling for breath, tremors still traveling through her body and into his. It was like touching magic. Everyone said sex was more meaningful between True Loves, but he'd never understood it until now.

Still panting, Avenant buried his face in her hair and kissed the top of her head. "That's why people die for their True Loves." He whispered.

"Funny you should say that, because I'm ready to beat you to death." Belle lifted her head to glare at him. "You're like a blond, smug Satan." She jerked away from him and he instantly felt the loss of her warmth. "I can't believe this!" She grabbed for her clothes and jumped to her feet. "*Shit*. I can't *believe* you did this to me!"

He stacked his hands behind his head. "Three times *is* pretty unbelievable."

"Shut-up!" She tugged her pants on, which was a crime against nature. "We're undoing this, you understand me? We can go to a wizard and break the True Love bond. There's a whole legal process to dissolve disastrous matchups like this."

Avenant made a regretful "tsk" of a sound. "I don't think that will work. I've lost my faith in the legal system, I'm afraid."

"No, it'll work." She insisted. "It's not complicated. We just have to sign a sacred scroll to make all this go away."

"We'd both have to *agree* to dissolve the bond, though." He reminded her. "And historically speaking, when's the last time we've agreed on *anything*?"

Belle stared at him, realization dawning.

Avenant slowly smirked. So did the Beast.

"You're not going to sign the scroll, are you?" She sounded stunned. "You're really not."

"No." He sat up, keeping his eyes on her. "I'm really not."

She swallowed. "You want to win so badly that you'd trap us like this?"

He wanted her so badly that he'd do *anything*. Anything, at all. "Evil princes keep innocent girls trapped all the time. Don't you watch the news? It's kind of our thing. Usually, it's in a tower or something, but..."

Belle cut him off. "I won't let you get away with this!"

"Get away with what?" He shrugged. "I'm not the one who made us True Loves. I haven't done anything except be happy with the whims of fate."

She threw a shoe at him. "You're not happy, Avenant! You don't even like me!"

"Trust me. I've spent my morning liking you *a lot*."

"That's just the connection between us. Sex is always explosive between True Loves. Everyone knows that." She glowered at him. "But what about the rest of it? We can't stand each other. Do you really want to spend the rest of your life bickering with me?"

God yes.

Probably best not to tell her that, though.

Belle kept going. "I remember you telling me at prom that you'd pick someone else if you could. Well, you *can*. You can sign the scroll and be done with me forever."

Avenant hesitated, because she had a point. About the prom thing, anyway. When she'd refused to even consider the possibility of being with him, he'd said all kinds of crazy shit. The Beast had been going wild and Avenant had been just as out of control. His heart had shattered into so many pieces that night that it still hadn't healed.

"I shouldn't have told you that. It isn't true." He

admitted. "I will *never* be done with you, Bella. I will *never* marry another woman. And you will *never* talk me into giving up our bond, so you might as well save your energy. Accept that we're True Loves." He met her eyes. "It's why the Icen Throne didn't melt when you usurped me. You're my rightful Princess."

Her lips pressed together. "I'm not marrying you." She decided. "We might be True Loves, but I'm *still* not tied to you."

"I know." It was why he needed her to surrender. This would never be settled until she gave him *everything*.

"I mean it." Belle insisted. "You were right back at prom. You should go marry some vapid princess and I can go be with," she faltered, searching for a name, "somebody I'm important to." She finished decisively, waving a hand to encompass the entire world. "And you have no say in it, because we are *not* bound."

"Go ahead. Date whomever you like."

That brought her up short. "...Really?"

"Absolutely." Avenant reached for his clothes. "I haven't killed anyone in weeks. I miss the faces people make when their windpipes freeze over. It's always good for a laugh."

Belle's eyes narrowed. "You wouldn't dare."

Avenant arched a brow. She knew him better than that. "No one takes what's mine. I always play gentle with you, but I have limits. If you touch another man, I will solidify the blood in his veins. I promise you."

"I'm *not* yours!"

"Tell it to fate, my love." Belle's temper was blazing out of control, so he tried to think of something that might calm her down. When she was angry, it was impossible to predict what she'd do and he liked all his body parts connected. "It's not all Bad news, you know.

I've got a castle and some really expensive horses. When we get married, community property gives you half."

She wasn't appeased. "I'm going to find Excalibur." Belle said tightly. "I am going to claim the kingdom. And then I'm going to use my power to dissolve the True Love bond *without* your consent and banish you to Wonderland."

Avenant frowned. Sending him to the WUB Club had been one thing, but Wonderland was a pit of anarchy and weirdness. "Let's not say things we don't mean, alright?"

"Like what? Like I wish a house would fall on your head? Like I think you deserve to be pelted with poison apples? Like a giant should mill your bones to make his bread? Because, I mean *all* of that."

"Do giants still do their own bone milling? I think it's all been outsourced, now."

She heaved her other shoe at him and it collided with his shoulder. This could've been going better. Of course, it could've been going *worse*, too. At least, she hadn't blackened his eye this time. When she'd slugged him in that pool, it had fucking hurt. The girl packed a wallop.

"Bella..."

"Shut-up. I'm not speaking to you!"

"...people spend their whole lives looking for their True Love." Avenant finished, ignoring her interruption. "It's what we're all hoping to find. Don't you want that?"

"Of course I want it. But, not with *you*."

Avenant had anticipated that response, but the rejection still felt like a knife in the chest. He looked down at the ground, too resigned to even be angry. "And you wonder why I had to trick you into this." He muttered. "You would never give me a chance, otherwise. If it were up to you, I'd be alone forever."

"It's not my fault you're sneaky and manipulative and cold!"

"It's not my fault, either." He snapped. "It's part of being Bad. I can't become some knight in shining armor, no matter what either of us might want." When he was in college, Avenant had actually tried to join the Knight Academy to impress her, but his father had laughed at the idea and blocked his entrance. Beasts weren't welcomed in the hallowed halls. "Bad people do Bad things. It's who I am."

Belle's lips thinned. "I think Scarlett's right. I think Good and Bad are just labels. I think you choose to be an amoral jackass. I've seen moments when you've been as Good as anyone. You saved my life yesterday, without even thinking about it."

"That's different." What he'd do for Belle was *completely* different than what he could manage for anyone else in the world. She was the only Good part of him.

"It's *not* different." She jabbed a finger at his chest. "You're not some crazed animal. You *choose* to be Bad, Avenant. You choose it so often, you think it's your nature."

"It *is* my nature. I'm Bad all the way through. You've said so yourself."

"Well, explain why I should ever accept you as my True Love, then?" She crossed her arms across her chest. "Why would I want someone who's wholly Bad?"

Avenant had no ready answer for that. Why *should* Belle want him? Nobody could want a beast. His mind raced for a plausible argument to trick her into this.

"You're the one who created this mess." She pressed when he remained silent. "You must have some idea as to why it's a good plan for me to be with you, when you can't even be nice."

Goddamn it. What was he supposed to say? Whatever it was, he needed to think of it fast. Belle was right on the edge of walking away. And without Belle, he might as well be locked in that cell, again.

Avenant went with the obvious sales pitch. "I told you, I have a castle and..."

"So help me, do *not* mention those horses, again! I don't even ride, you idiot. Tell me a real reason I should give you a chance."

He was forever asking Belle to give him a reason. Having the tables turned was disconcerting. "A reason you should be with me?" He echoed. "Because... I can take care of you better than anyone else could." That was true. No other man would guard her half as ferociously.

She snorted. "I don't need somebody to take care of me. I just need somebody who needs me back."

God, the woman really did drive him insane. "Who the fuck could need you more than I do? Look at me! Everyone hates me, I'm barely holding it together in this tiny little space, and I've just escaped from a mental institution! Obviously, I'm a very needful guy."

"But..."

He cut her off. "Why would I even be doing this if I didn't need you? Don't you think there are easier ways to get a woman into bed? I'm lost in a goddamn tomb, because it was the only way I could get *you*."

Belle frowned at him, still not convinced.

Avenant scraped a hand through his hair. "And it's not that I don't *want* to be nice, it's that I don't know *how*." He belatedly admitted. "My parents weren't exactly role models on how it works. They hated everyone. Especially me."

Belle blinked at him in surprise. Avenant had never said anything like that to her before. He'd never said anything like that to *anyone* before. Talking about his parents made him *think* about his parents and he never wanted to think about those assholes, again.

Avenant cleared his throat and glanced away. He didn't like feeling so exposed. "Look, I know you're not happy about this. Why would you be? But, I can't help what I am. The Beast is inside of me and it won't go away. Believe me, I've investigated every spell and potion you can imagine trying to get rid of it."

"Inside of you?" She repeated, looking as confused as he felt. "You mean literally?"

"Yes!" Avenant nodded. "So, if you want a logical reason why you should accept me as your True Love, this is it: Without you in my life, the Beast will take control and people will suffer. I promise you. You are all that anchors me. You care about the Northlands. You're a better ruler than I ever was. You should stick around to make sure the Beast doesn't flatten the whole kingdom."

"You think this thing inside of you is another whole... being?"

"Of course it is. I know you've seen flashes of it. Its eyes glow and its voice gets darker. It's a monster I have to keep chained. My parents knew I was an animal at heart. It's why they were so hard on me." He couldn't believe he was defending the fuckers. "They wanted me to have discipline."

"That's ridiculous. You can instill discipline without torturing a child."

"The doctors didn't think so. They told my parents to keep me locked up as much as possible. But it wasn't the cages that kept me in control. It was knowing that *you* were out there. It's always been you." He shook his head. "The Beast and I both know you're ours. We're not going to give up our True Love. You can call it selfish, but it's just our nature. We need you."

Belle hesitated, looking skeptical. "How could there be an actual monster inside of you? Two separate beings in one body? I've never heard of anything like that happening before."

"I don't know, but it's there."

"What would happen if you let it loose?"

Avenant frowned. "Something Bad."

"You've never tried unchaining it to find out?"

"No!" Was she kidding? "Pieces of it come out, but never all at once. All my life the doctors have said it would be a disaster to lose control over it. My parents would beat me whenever they saw even a flash of it. I wouldn't…"

Belle cut him off. "You're better than your parents, Avenant." Most of her anger seemed to fade. "And you can be much better than they gave you credit for --Better than you give *yourself* credit for-- if you try. If that Beast *is* in you, I don't think it's all Bad."

Avenant had no idea what to say to something so… idiotic.

Belle was brilliant. Truly brilliant. How could she possibly say something so dumb? "You really believe that?" He asked after a long moment.

"Yes." Her voice was firm. "I *have* seen flashes of him and he isn't some crazed monster. He's never tried to harm me, even when you and I were arguing. I don't think the Beast is the problem, I think *you* are.

The Beast preened under her words, wanting to get closer to her. It hated it when Belle was upset, usually blaming Avenant for their disagreements. Avenant wasn't surprised that somehow he was the villain in Belle's mind, too. The two of them were the biggest headaches in his life, so of course they'd be on the same side.

"You *like* pushing people away, Avenant." Belle continued. "You don't want to be close to anyone. I spent my whole childhood being ignored and not fitting in with my family. I won't do that again."

Avenant had always disliked Belle's flighty, self-involved parents. They hadn't known what to do with their oddball daughter, so they'd ignored her. It was one of the reasons he and Belle had forged such a strange bond. The two of them had been the kids whose parents didn't care enough to walk them to school, or put their drawings on the fridge, or tuck them in at night. Underneath everything, their isolation had always linked them.

"You say you need me," she swept her hair behind her ears, "but I've reached out to you again and again and you were a total asshole."

"I just wanted you to pay attention."

"You just wanted to be an asshole." She jabbed a finger at him. "I won't be True Loves with someone who's cold to me. If there's a chance in a million of this working, you need to let me in. You need to be honest and unguarded and *not* an asshole."

Belle wanted him to surrender.

No, no, no, no, no. Avenant actually shook his head at the idea. He wasn't doing that. *She* had to be the one to give in. Anything else would be failure. It would be *weakness*. Belle wouldn't want him if he broke down and told her everything that was in his heart. She would laugh at him. The only way this would work is if he *won*. If he showed her he was strong. Then, she'd looked at him and just... know.

The labyrinth began to move again and cut off his

frantic thoughts.

Belle scrambled backwards to watch the shrubbery reposition itself. A new pathway opened up, which meant they were no longer trapped. Unfortunately the new passage led directly to Lancelot.

…And Lancelot's latest victim.

The knight was standing over another body. It looked like a gremlin. The sharp angles of its face were still locked in an expression of terror. Avenant hadn't really considered his cousin a prime suspect for the murders that kept cropping-up in the labyrinth, but there was no arguing with the evidence. Lancelot was literally ankle-deep in blood.

Avenant wasn't sure whether to be pleased or not.

Either way he didn't have much choice. Not with his True Love standing right there, defenseless and small. Avenant got to his feet, reaching for Belle's arm. "Stay behind me, while I go kill this idiot."

"Hang on now, I didn't do this." Lancelot proclaimed loudly, gesturing to the body. "He was already in pieces when I got here. You've gotta believe me."

"I believe you." Avenant didn't believe him.

"I'm telling you, I'm innocent! Lancelot insisted. "I would never do something this Bad. This is the work of a monster." He glanced at Belle as if realization had suddenly dawned. "*He* did it!" He pointed at Avenant. "Of course, he did. I should've known. He's trying to set me up!"

Belle shoved her way in front of Avenant. "That's a lie. Avenant was with me the entire night."

Avenant snorted. "Don't bother, Bella. He's just trying to deflect the blame so he can steal the Icen

Throne. They don't like to crown potential murderers. Believe me, I know."

They ignored him.

"Avenant's evil!" Lancelot snapped. "He probably used evil trickery to sneak away and evilly slaughter this poor gremlin while your back was turned."

"He didn't sneak anywhere. He was right beside me."

Lancelot gasped in overacted horror. "He was *beside* you? You slept with the Beast? What kind of floozy would...?" He stopped short as Avenant stepped forward. "Wait." Lancelot backed away as if braced for a blizzard to freeze him solid at any moment. Maybe the guy wasn't such a lack-wit, after all. "Let's be reasonable."

"You think beasts give a shit about reasonable?"

"Belle, talk to him! You're the only one he ever listens to."

"My True Love isn't your biggest fan." Avenant snarled. "Aside from the fact that you're a chauvinistic dickhead, you're trying to steal the kingdom from her, *too*."

"I just want what's mine! I didn't..." Lancelot broke off, an amazed expression on his face. "Hold on. She's your True Love? *You* get a True Love?"

"Belle's mine." Avenant confirmed. "And neither of us likes you."

"Avenant?" Belle grabbed hold of his arm, dragging him to a stop before he could take more than two steps towards Lancelot. "Don't."

The woman and her soft heart drove him insane. She always had endless compassion for everyone except him. "Why shouldn't I destroy him?" Avenant demanded. "Give me a reason."

"Because he's your cousin. Because it would be wrong to kill someone for killing someone if he didn't actually kill anyone. Because he's a jackass, but I don't think he deserves to die for it."

"Exactly!" Lancelot agreed with a vigorous nod. "Geez, anybody Good would know all that, Avenant. Even a woman. This is why it's only right that *I* be in charge of the kingdom."

"Shut-up." Belle said absently, her attention still on Avenant. "And finally... because I'm pretty sure that's a rabbit hole, right in front of you." She pointed to a shimmering spot on the ground. "If you fall into it, there's no telling where you'll end up."

Avenant's eyebrows soared, catching sight of the mirrored pool. It was only about a foot wide, but it was far more dangerous than even the minotaur had been. Rabbit holes were dimensional vortexes that made black holes seem predictable. They led to places you certainly didn't want to go and which you probably couldn't get back from.

He glanced down at Belle, confused as to why she'd just saved him from toppling through the looking-glass surface. Given her mood, it seemed more likely that she'd shove him in.

"I hate you with a festering passion." She said softly. "But, I don't want you lost forever somewhere in space and time. I think I might miss you. A little."

Avenant's mouth curved, realizing that was the sweetest thing Belle had ever said to him.

Lancelot used their momentary distraction to take off in the opposite direction. "You'll never defeat me, Beast! I'll claim this kingdom for all the Good men of the realm!" He ran down the path, the hedges shifting behind him so no one could follow.

Not that Avenant even cared enough to bother chasing after him. Instead, he stared down at the rabbit hole. His own face gazed back at him. He'd always hated mirrors. All he saw was his father. Logically, he recognized the fact that he was handsome, but what difference did it make? It certainly never got him what he wanted. Belle would choose a Good man over an attractive one, any day. Beneath the surface, she knew he was…

His head tilted, a new thought occurring to him. "Read that journal entry, again."

Belle quickly backtracked to grab her knapsack, following his logic. She got the book out and flipped to the entry he meant. "A prince must have faith in those around him and not in a mirror." She read. "Otherwise, he will be lost in the darkness for all time." She looked up from the page. "You think Adam means the rabbit hole? You think we're supposed to go through?"

"Only one way to find out."

Chapter Thirteen

His parents knew Avenant was Bad all the way through.
It was why they detested the very sight of him.
Many nights I was dragged from the cupboard and lit up, so his mother could read to him about his ancestors.
She hoped that if he heard about the royal line, he'd try to live up to their example.
Or at least not to be such a total disgrace.

Testimony of the Palace's Talking Candlestick- *The People of the Northlands v. Prince Avenant*

Five Years Ago

"The woman is making a goddamn fool of you!" Vincent, Prince of the Northlands threw the newspaper at his son and heir. "She outsmarts you at every fucking turn and you do *nothing* to stop her. How do you think that makes us look?"

Avenant didn't even bother to duck as the day's headlines rained down. He could read them as they drifted around him, the typeface three inches tall:

Belle Bests Beast!

She'd singlehandedly stopped Avenant from strip mining the Great North Mountains. Her environmental appeals and legal tactics had scuttled the project for good. Millions in gold would be lost so that Belle could protect the homeland of some rabbits and owls. The minerals would stay trapped beneath the rocks, the wildlife would frolic, and Belle would win.

And his father would kill him.

Avenant eyed Vincent, prepared for a fight. His

father was the one who'd wanted the mining deal to go through, even though he'd made sure Avenant was the face of the project. He might despise the fact that his only child was Bad, but he knew how to use it to his advantage. All the family's unpopular actions were blamed on Avenant. Strong-arming uncooperative teddy bear shop owners... Jailing people for picking the royal roses... Seizing orphanages so the land could be used for lucrative property deals... Everything that would necessitate threats or extortion or heartless greed. Vincent liked to keep his hands clean with the citizens, wearing a façade of princely nobility.

But, within the castle walls, the mask fell and he was free to be his cruel self.

"Were you even trying to defeat her or were you thinking with your cock, again?" He demanded nastily.

"I was trying." Avenant said. Belle had just out-maneuvered him. "I didn't anticipate her getting the funding for those ridiculous commercials with the crying chipmunks."

The public hadn't liked the idea of making the chubby little rodents extinct. Especially not when Belle got done editing videos of the fuzzy bastards frolicking to mournful music. Then, she showed some photos of what their homes would look like after the bulldozers came through and rows of little chipmunk graves and hearts broke throughout the land.

The woman played hardball.

"You're an impotent moron." Vincent leaned forward in the Icen Throne, looking so much like his son that Avenant hated his own reflection. "That girl is *laughing* at you. The whole kingdom is laughing at you. And you stand there like the failure you are."

Avenant didn't respond to the insults. He was

used to his father's hatred and scorn. It had been heaped on him every day of his life. This was just the warm-up to the real reason he'd called Avenant into the throne room. Vincent wouldn't have summoned him for a private audience unless there was something far bigger brewing.

Something to do with Belle.

His father wasn't an idiot. Over the years, he'd watched Avenant interact with the girl. Vincent knew that Avenant enjoyed Belle's antics. Even when he lost, Avenant loved that they were *playing*. He loved the fact she'd ruined his father's plans. He loved that she fought back against people who could crush her. He loved that she wasn't afraid of him.

Not that she had reason to be. Belle could've set him on fire and Avenant wouldn't have harmed her. He put up a front, but anyone paying attention would've seen the truth.

And Vincent was always paying attention.

"That do-Gooding commoner is your True Love." It wasn't a question. "You get her under control or I *will*."

Avenant stared at his father and felt the Beast stir. "No." He said quietly. "You won't."

Vincent didn't like being contradicted. "None of this would be happening if you weren't so weak." He snapped. "When her parents died, they were so in debt you could've *owned* that girl. Instead, you ensured she kept everything. The house and the lands. Then, you secretly set it up so she'd have backing for that fucking bookshop. You think I don't know that was you? You even closed the library to help her with sales." He snorted. "At least *that* idea showed some business sense. But, of course, you screwed it up and gave her a *new* library the minute she got in your face about it."

"She sued us to have it reopened, remember?

How could I stop the judge from ruling in her favor?"

"You could've bribed the prick."

"I tried. She bribed him more."

"With the money *you* made sure she had!" Vincent shook his head in disgust. "The point is, you should've used Belle's misery to your advantage. That was your opportunity to bring her to heel." His hand fisted. "To *break* her."

"I don't want her broken."

Belle had been far too close to shattering when her parents died in a carriage accident the year before. Avenant had done everything he could think of to shore her up, but he'd felt helpless in the face of her grief. For the first time, Belle had seemed fragile to him. Of *course* he'd covered her parents' debts. He couldn't let her lose her home on top of everything else. He would've done anything to make her feel like herself, again.

Even if it meant giving her new reasons to hate him.

She'd been furious when he won everything she owned in that auction and then handed it back to her. For the first time in weeks, she'd been shouting at him and it had been like old times. Belle had eventually bounced back, more bitchy than ever. Over the past months, she'd been twice the foe she'd been before. Tougher. On the offensive. Harder to predict. Every day, she seemed to wake-up and devote all her energy towards scheming against him.

Avenant was so delighted he couldn't stop smiling.

Belle's attention was fixed on him and he'd never been happier.

"If you don't break her, she'll break you. That's the only way you get ahead in this world. You have to crush the competition and take what's yours. Otherwise, you'll just look weak. Is that what you want? The woman to think you're a pussy?"

Avenant's jaw ticked.

"Rosabella Aria Ashman is Good." Vincent reminded him smugly. "Do you think she'll *ever* willingly have you? Prince or not, you're a beast and the whole kingdom knows it. If you ever plan on owning the girl, you'd better start thinking like a man."

His father thought of everything in terms of ownership. It was no wonder his mother had jumped off the highest turret in the castle when Avenant turned eighteen. She'd no doubt been looking for an escape. His parents were a classic example of what happened when people married for position instead of True Love. They cared for nothing but power and it had rotted them from the inside out.

Listening to Vincent talk about love was like trusting a fish to give you rock climbing tips.

"I know what I'm doing with Belle." Avenant told him shortly. Sooner or later, she'd surrender. It was inevitable.

Vincent scoffed. "If you know what you're doing, why isn't she here in the castle, pregnant with my grandchildren? Providing me with an heir I could actually be proud of. Why is she living in the village, organizing fucking protests against us?"

"She's not ready."

"Not ready?" Vincent repeated incredulously. "She hates you, you twat. And who can blame her? She's probably down there screwing every man in the village, hoping to find a True Love who isn't a dickless monster."

The Beast snarled. So did Avenant. "Belle is *my* True Love. No one else's." He ground out. "Deep down, she knows it..."

Vincent cut him off. "Good folk don't know their True Loves until they've bedded them. That's what you need to do. Fuck the girl. *Now*."

Avenant blinked. "She's not ready." He repeated. Even the Beast knew that.

"Who cares? Hold her down and take what's yours. Once you're inside of her, she'll know who she belongs to. They'll be no more of her meddling in my business plans." He waved a hand at the newspaper.

Avenant couldn't believe what he was hearing. "You want me to rape my True Love?"

"I want you to stop being a failure." Vincent jabbed a finger at him. "Show that woman you won't be beaten and she'll respect you for it."

"Even if that were true, how can I show her I'm a winner by hurting her? She'll never care about me if I do something so horrible to..."

Vincent cut him off. "She'll never care about you, *anyway*. But, if you take her hard enough, at least she'll fear you. It's about as much as you can hope for. Force her and she'll submit."

"You're insane." Avenant knew the words would just piss his father off more, but he couldn't stop them. He'd endured Vincent's punishments and sadistic commands all his life, but *this*.... Not even Avenant had ever considered something like *this* and he was a goddamn villain. He gaped at his father, seeing the man for the first time. "You're *fucking insane*."

"And you're Bad. Stop trying to pretend otherwise and go do what needs to be done."

Vincent knew nothing of Bad folk. By and large, they were fanatically obsessed with their True Loves. No matter how evil, they treasured what was theirs. They protected it. It was their primary drive. A threat to their True Love was a declaration of war.

Rage filled Avenant, feeding the Beast. "'That woman,' as you call her," he gestured in the direction of Belle's house with a desperate swing of his arm, "is my goddamn *wife*." Even if it wasn't official yet, Belle was his one and only bride. She had been from the moment he saw her coloring with crayons at the kindergarten table. "Do you think I'd *ever* harm her?"

"If you're going to be all weepy about it, you can tie her down with pretty silk ropes and hand her a pillow." Vincent sneered without a drop of compassion. "Just so she knows who she belongs to when it's over. I've had it with that bitch making me a joke in my own kingdom." He arched a blond brow. "Either you handle her *education* or I'll have my men do it. I have them standing by to pay her stupid bookshop a visit."

The Beast surged forward. It happened so fast, Avenant almost lost control of the chains. As it was, the monster was less confined than he'd ever been. It prowled towards the man who'd targeted Belle, wanting blood.

...And Avenant let it.

Vincent leapt to his feet, seeing the change come over his son. "What are you doing? That *thing* is getting loose..." He trailed off with a yelp of panic as Avenant seized him by the front of his suit and hauled him closer.

"If you threaten my princess again, I'll stake you to the front gate with an icicle through your heart." He said, meaning every frosty word. "Belle Ashman belongs to me." He paused, making sure his father saw the Beast's cold rage. "Actually, she belongs to *us*." For once, he didn't even bother to try and contain the monster. It felt liberating. "Understand?"

Vincent looked up at him with pure hatred, but he gave a curt nod.

"That's what I thought." Avenant dropped Vincent back onto the throne. In that moment, the man stopped being his father. Stopped being his prince. He was just the son of a bitch who'd planned to harm Belle. "Nobody touches what's mine. Remember that, because you don't want to see my Bad side."

"You think I'm scared of you?" Vincent spat out.

"I *know* you are." Avenant had known it from childhood. His parents were repelled and fearful. The citizens of the Northlands were cowed and bitter. There was only one woman in the world who'd ever showed him any warmth. Who treated him like a person. The only woman who mattered to him. And *no one* was going to hurt her. "You're right to be afraid of me, too, because there is nothing I wouldn't do to keep my True Love safe. *Nothing.*"

"She'll never love you." Vincent spat as Avenant turned away. "No matter what you do, she'll always see you as the monster you are."

Deep down, he knew his father was right, but Avenant refused to react to the bitter words. "Just stay away from Belle or I'll inherit this kingdom far sooner than you have planned. I promise you."

"Underneath, you're nothing but a mindless animal." Vincent called as Avenant stormed out. "Nobody could *ever* want a beast."

Chapter Fourteen

Avenant said I was trespassing and tore down the wall with me on it.
I fell to the ground and it took weeks to put me back together again.
You can still see the cracks.
Now, just hearing his name triggers post-traumatic stress.

Testimony of Mr. Humpty Dumpty - *The People of the Northlands v. Prince Avenant*

Belle hated this idea.

She'd pretty much hated every idea Avenant ever had, but this one was probably his worst. "What if this passage is one way and you can't get back through?"

"Then, you won't have to worry about being stuck with me as a True Love anymore." He sat down on the edge of the vortex and dangled his legs into the hole. They vanished beneath the mirrored surface, giving no clue as to what might be on the other side. "Good news. My feet haven't been bitten off, yet. Whatever's down there, it's probably not sharks."

"That's not funny." She warily gazed into the reflective pool. "We should do this another way. I should be the one to go. We'll keep the cord between us attached. Then, you can pull me back up."

He shot her a sideways look. "You'd trust me to do that?"

"Yes." She met his eyes. "I know you won't let me go." Avenant would never let her fall. She believed it without hesitation.

Avenant studied her for a beat. "If something goes wrong, I trust you to pull me back up, too." He finally decided. "So, I'll go through and you stay on this end, ready to yank on the rope."

"I weigh less than you do. I'm not strong enough to haul you back. We don't even know if the cord will hold you." She gestured to the thin filament tying them together. "My way makes more sense."

"No."

"I'll just look around and see if it's safe. Ten seconds and you can pull me topside."

"No." He wasn't even considering the idea. "Stay here. I'll be back in a minute."

"You're an idiot. You just *have* to disagree with me, even when you know I'm right. This is why we lost the sixth grade scavenger hunt. I told you we should look for the pink flower first, but you were so damn sure you knew better."

Avenant was getting annoyed. "Trying to find the orange mailbox made more sense. There *had* to be more pink flowers than orange mailboxes."

"Except there *weren't* and we came in second." She arched a brow. "This time, why don't you be smart and listen to me?"

"You're not going through that fucking hole, Belle! Give it up." He sounded deadly serious.

Thank God she didn't have to listen to a word he said.

Belle flicked him off and stepped back through the rabbit hole. She heard his bellowed curse, but there wasn't anything he could do.

Belle tumbled into the abyss. Everything around her was blackness. She didn't see a floor beneath her or walls surrounding her or anything else. It wasn't just an absence of light. It was an absence of *anything*. The string connecting her to Avenant unraveled as she fell deeper into the hole, finally reaching the end of the spool. It jolted her to a stop so fast that Belle flipped upside down.

"Shit!" She could see the vortex glimmering far overhead and nothing else. Belle spiraled her arms, trying to right herself. The knapsack slung over her shoulder slid forward to bang against the back of her head. Her phone fell out of the front pocket and she didn't hear it hit the ground. Whatever she was dangling over was too deep.

Goddamn it, she *hated* heights.

She definitely should have let Avenant do this.

Using her legs, Belle managed to use the cord to drag herself upright. It wasn't particularly graceful, but at least she wasn't poised to drop headfirst into oblivion, anymore. Somehow she got the pack unzipped in the dark and found the flashlight inside. Belle scanned the beam around and saw...

...nothing.

Just as she'd suspected, there was nothing to see. "Hello?" She called and her voice echoed off into the void.

Yeah, she really, really hated this.

Belle swallowed hard. There was no way to tell what was underneath of her. This pit might go on forever or maybe the bottom was only three feet down. If Avenant didn't pull her out, she'd be stuck in the blackness with no idea how far this abyss went. Panic started pounding in her head. She looked up again, her hand tightening on the cord. Maybe she should try climbing...

Avenant started hauling her towards the surface before she could even finish the thought.

Belle smiled in relief. He was going to get her out of there. Thank God. She'd known this plan would work.

No way could she have lifted him as easily as he was lifting her. She was right and he was wrong, as usual. The sooner he realized that, the happier their relationship would be.

She still couldn't believe she was even thinking about Avenant and the word "relationship" in the same sentence, but what the hell else could she do?

They were True Loves.

The reality of it hit Belle fully and she felt kind of dizzy as she accepted the truth. Avenant wasn't going to sign a scroll to dissolve their bond. And angry as she was, Belle wasn't certain she wanted to, either. Having a True Love was like winning a huge prize. The biggest. Giving that up without even trying seemed like quitting. She'd never been a quitter.

Not when there was a chance of having something… amazing.

"You're a reckless fucking idiot!" Avenant raged as she cleared the top of the hole. "What the hell where you thinking?" He grabbed hold of her arm and dragged her back to solid ground. "What if the cord had snapped, huh? Did you even consider…?"

Belle cut him off. "Do you want to hear what's down there or not?"

"I don't give a shit what's down there!" He scanned her face and body, looking for injuries. "Every decision you make is emotional, you know that? When you're mad, you don't think more than two goddamn seconds into the future."

"Because you're such a calm and logical guy, right?"

"I try to be. You make it hard, though. You always have." He ran a hand over her hair, his voice still dark. "Are you okay?" His thumb brushed the curve of her cheek. "Are you *sure* you weren't hurt?"

It was impossible to be mad when he was so gentle with her. "I'm sure." Belle hesitated. "I knew you weren't going to abandon me, but it was still pretty damn reassuring to feel you lifting me skyward. I don't like heights."

Gentle or not, he was pissed. "Well, I didn't really have much of a choice, did I?"

"Nope. Not now that I've ruined you for other women."

Blue eyes slammed into hers like he couldn't believe she'd just said that.

Belle couldn't believe it either. The words had just sort of popped out. As much as she'd surprised herself with that comment, though, it was nothing compared to Avenant's astonishment. It occurred to her that she'd never teased him before. Given his perpetual snarkiness, she was willing to bet that *no one* teased him. He hadn't even looked so shocked when she'd had him arrested.

She bit down on her lower lip, trying not to smile.

"You ruined me for other women long ago." Avenant's mouth slowly tilted up at one corner. "More importantly, there's no way I'll let you die before I see you topless."

Belle wrinkled her nose. "You not going to become fixated on my breasts, are you?"

"*Become* fixated? I've been fixated for quite some time."

"There's nothing to be fixated *with*. You've felt them. I'm not exactly round as a tuffet." She made a face. "You're just going to be disappointed."

"You're insane."

She rolled her eyes. "Can we focus on you pulling

me from the rabbit hole, please? I was thanking you. Just say 'you're welcome' and let's move on."

He dipped his forehead to briefly rest against hers. "You're welcome, my love."

God, he was handsome. What woman wouldn't take a chance on him? The man was like one of those carnivorous flowers that grew extra beautiful in order to lure bugs closer and devour them. You knew it was dangerous, but you were just so dazzled by all the amazingness that you forgot common sense.

Belle cleared her throat. "Good. Right. So anyway, getting back on track, there is nothing down there." They were still sitting on the edge of the rabbit hole and she gestured to it. "Not that I can see, anyway. It's a dark chasm."

"A chasm?"

"Of the possibly bottomless variety."

"Great."

"I think it's a leap of faith thing. We can't see the bottom, we just have to trust that it's there."

"Great." Avenant repeated with a sigh. "Because, I'm so eager to take things on faith." He frowned in consideration, thinking for a long moment. "Any ideas on our next move? Maybe we just need a longer rope."

"I don't think that..."

The gunshot caught her completely by surprise.

Belle gave a panicked cry as the bullet ricocheted off the stone wall and hit Avenant. The momentum of the projectile knocked him backward right through the vortex. "*No!*" Belle grabbed for him, but he disappeared through the hole.

Her head instinctively snapped around to see who'd fired at them and came face-to-face with

Bluebeard. Resplendent in his citrus-colored finery and brandishing a revolver, he stood at the edge of the pathway. His turquoise beard was studded with leaves, as if he'd been struggling through the plants all night.

"Are you out of your mind?!" She screamed.

"You think I'll let that bastard kill me like he did the others?" He shrieked back. "I *know* the Beast is behind it! No one else could take down so many people."

Belle didn't get a chance to offer a retort. The cord connecting her to Avenant pulled tight, yanking her forward. He must have reached the end of the line. Her fingers dug into the ground, trying to hold on, but it didn't work. Belle was dragged towards the edge of the rabbit hole.

Shit!

The clip on her belt wasn't going to hold his weight for long and there was no way she could pull him back up. She either had to disconnect from Avenant or follow him down.

And she *really* hated heights.

"Hey, is that a rabbit hole?" Bluebeard asked, apparently just noticing Avenant had disappeared into a mirrored abyss. "Don't go through that thing, girlie. Those things will kill you."

Belle fixed him with a deadly look. "You'd better hope I die in it, you son of a bitch. If I climb out, you're gonna be real unhappy to see me."

With that, she dropped back into the vortex.

Belle wasn't really afraid of *heights*, so much as she was afraid of *falling.* Now, for the second time in ten minutes, she was careening into darkness. Belle tumbled down for so long she wondered if the rabbit hole had a bottom at all. Maybe it went on forever. Maybe it was an endless shaft of black, empty space and she'd just keep falling until she died. She couldn't work up much concern about that, right now. As terrified as she was about splatting into goo on impact, she had an even bigger problem.

"Avenant?" Belle called, trying to see him below her. "Are you okay?"

No answer.

The bullet looked like it had hit his shoulder. Did people die from getting shot in the shoulder? She wasn't sure. Why wasn't she sure? All the books she read and she didn't know anything about anatomy. What if he bled to death before she even…?

Belle splashed down in water.

It was icy cold and so deep she nearly drowned reaching the surface. She swam upward, her lungs screaming for oxygen. When she finally made it to the top, she was panting for breath and still in complete darkness. Deep as it was, the water had a fast moving current and she was dragged along.

"Avenant!" Belle shouted, not sure where he was or if he could even hear her. "*Avenant!*" They were still tethered together and she quickly began yanking on the rope. "Answer me, goddamn it!"

The cord led her to Avenant, floating face down in the river.

"*No!*" Belle flipped him over, trying to locate a pulse. She didn't feel anything. Panic became terror. "No, no, *no*. You're not going anywhere, you son of a bitch." She held his head above the rapids, willing him to breathe. "This is *not* how it's supposed to go! You're supposed to stay with me!" All her life, it had been Belle and Avenant. They were connected. He *knew* that. He couldn't just leave her. "*Please*, open your eyes. Please… *Shit!*"

She didn't find land. *It* found *her*.

Belle thudded into an outcropping of rocks hard enough to see stars. She shifted at the last moment, so she took the impact instead of Avenant, jarring every bone in her body. Christ, but she hated this labyrinth.

"Avenant, hold on!" Belle managed to drag herself onto the stones and then lugged him up beside her. Her eyes were beginning to adjust to the darkness and she could see that he'd hit his head on something. Dropping to her knees, she began doing CPR the best she could. She'd only ever seen it done in movies, but the basics of it seemed simple enough. If he would just cooperate, this would work. Except it wasn't working. Why the hell did he always have to make everything so difficult? Why couldn't he just start breathing and...?

Avenant came to with a watery gasp. He was swearing and coughing and *alive*.

He was alive.

Belle sat back, sobbing like she might never stop.

"Fuck." Avenant quickly took stock and ran a hand through his wet hair. "Belle, are you alright?"

"No! You were dead, you asshole!"

"I was?"

"*Yes.*"

He blinked, seeing she was furious. "Well, it wasn't on purpose..."

"How could you do that to me?" She raged, cutting him off. The relief and anger were making her an emotional basket-case. "How could you abandon me like that?"

"I didn't. I *wouldn't*." His voice softened and he reached out to pull her into his arms. "Don't cry, my love. I'm here."

Belle let out a shaky sigh, leaning against his

chest. She was being ridiculous. She knew that, but she couldn't stop. "If you didn't come back, I'd be alone." She whispered. It didn't matter how many other people she knew, Avenant was the one who really mattered. Without him, she'd have nobody. "You can't do that to me. You can't leave me all alone."

"I will *always* come back for you." His voice was warm in her ear. "You should know that, Bella. Nothing in this world or the next would keep me from you for long." He kissed the side of her head. "You are my True Love in every possible way."

Belle swallowed and lifted her eyes to his. "Are you alright?" He was the one who'd been shot and she was the one in tears. "How badly are you hurt?" She pulled back to examine his arm. Her heart stopped as she saw blood staining the white fabric of his shirt.

"It's alright." He glanced down at the wound. "The bullet just grazed me. I think I whacked my head of the side of the rabbit hole. That was what knocked me out."

"Bluebeard shot you."

"I noticed. Remind me to freeze him to death, someday." He looked around the dark cavern. "So this is that bottomless chasm you were talking about, huh?"

"Turns out it has a bottom, after all."

"Yes and I'm thrilled to be sitting in the middle of it." He didn't sound thrilled. "You see what leaps of faith get you?"

"At least we're alive." Belle stood up. "And, if we're reading the journal right, this is the way to Excalibur, so we're still on track."

He gave a sigh. "You couldn't have just pulled me back up to the jungle level?"

"You were too heavy."

He glanced at her with sharp eyes. "So, I dragged you down here?" He surmised.

"No. I came after you."

Avenant regarded her silently for so long Belle began to feel self-conscious. "Well, you followed me when the ice floor cracked." She reminded him. "You think I'd just let you go when you were in trouble?"

"I think it's lucky that you really are my True Love." He sounded utterly serious. "I could never give you up, Belle. If you belonged to some knight in shining armor, I'd have to steal you for myself and this would be a lot more complicated."

"Oh please. You'd love kidnapping me away from a knight in shining armor." Belle busied herself wringing out her clothes. "The poor guy's ice-cubed body would probably be pictured on your Christmas card, with a Santa hat and a merry holiday warning."

"You believe I could defeat a knight?"

Belle blinked at his surprised tone. "Avenant, you could defeat anyone." Growing up, she'd always admired knights and their heroic exploits, but they were *nothing* compared to the Beast. "There's nobody in the world who could ever beat you."

"You could." He said quietly, getting to his feet. "You could break me right in half if I let you."

"I wouldn't..."

"I know you wouldn't." Avenant interrupted, his voice going firm. "Because, I'm not going to *let* you. I'm going to get that damn sword, Belle." Determination filled every word. "I'm *going* to win. I have to. True Love or not, you won't beat me."

"Winning is that important to you?"

"The prize is that important to me." He took the sodden backpack from her and slung it over his uninjured shoulder. "Come on. Let's get out of here before we drown."

"You *did* drown." Belle reminded him testily. "I saved you, although at the moment I'm wondering why I bothered."

"So am I." Avenant started up the steep embankment of rocks. "In case you hadn't noticed, it just postponed the inevitable." He gestured around them. "There isn't a way out of here."

Belle snorted. "What else is new?"

Chapter Fifteen

Prosecution: Come now, Prince Avenant. You know why you're here. Wouldn't you agree that you have mercilessly oppressed the Good citizens of the Northlands since you took the Icen Throne?

Prince Avenant: Only the annoying ones.

Prosecution: Sir, it's a well-documented fact that you've tortured *everyone* in this kingdom.

Prince Avenant: Which simply proves this kingdom is filled with annoying people.
I mean, just look around this room. …Or in a mirror.

Testimony of Prince Avenant- *The People of the Northlands vs. Prince Avenant*

"Soggy marshmallows make a terrible breakfast."
"Why do you think I've chosen to go hungry?" Avenant finally got the fire going and sat down across from her. The flames would give away their position if anyone else got this far into the maze. He knew that, but he didn't care. Belle needed to get warm and he was pissed enough to take on anyone who got in his way. His arm hurt, his lungs burned, and his skull felt like it had been pounded with a brick. "This is not how I pictured our honeymoon, you know."
"Funny. It's *exactly* how I pictured our honeymoon. It's a cold day in hell."
"Very witty."
This level of labyrinth seemed to be nothing but water and stone and darkness. The river roared in front of them, behind them stood a solid rock wall, and all that was in between was a narrow dirt ledge. They'd made it

to the small piece of dry land, but there was no way off of it. The only path was the one forged by the rapids and the water was moving too fast to get back in that torrent. Avenant had no idea how they were going to get out of there.

This contest of valor thing was more complicated than the stories let on.

Avenant sighed. "Grandpa Adam was a real dick, you know that?"

"It runs in the family." Belle sifted through the wet backpack. "Seriously, I'm starving. If we're stranded here, we might as well take a break and eat. Do we have any chocolate? We could make s'mores."

Avenant was briefly interested in a new chocolate dish. "What's a s'more?"

"You don't know what a s'more is?" Belle sounded shocked. "Geez, you really need to get out more. It's a toasted marshmallow, a square of chocolate, and two graham crackers sandwiched together. Kids make them on campouts."

"I never went camping as a child." He muttered. Not unless you counted sleeping on the floor of his closet, wishing he had food.

"Me neither." She admitted. "But, we're kind of camping now. Better late than never."

Avenant glanced at her. The flickering light of the flames cast dancing shadows over her perfect face. "We're not late." He said with absolute certainty. "Everything is working out just like it's supposed to. It's inevitable."

Belle gave him a small smile. "You really believe in destiny, don't you?"

"Of course."

"I never noticed before, but you're kind of a

romantic."

That was the most ludicrous thing she'd ever said. "I'm not a romantic. I'm a fatalist."

"No, you're not. You're too arrogant to accept the idea that you aren't in control of your own fate. Not unless you think it's all going to work out in your favor." She shook her head. "I think you believe in destiny because, deep down, you want to believe in happily-ever-afters."

Avenant rolled his eyes. "You sound like Scarlett. Bad folk don't get happily-ever-afters. We just take what we want. I know you and I are inevitable, because I *want* you and I'll do whatever it takes to *have* you. That's not sentimentality. It's survival."

"If you say so, Prince of Denial." She ate another mushy marshmallow. "What *I* want figures in there someplace, though. And I want someone who's emotionally available."

He slanted her a glare. "I'm emotionally available."

"You outlawed Valentine's Day, Avenant."

"I had to. Someone else might've sent you flowers." Ever since he'd drawn her a picture of a rose in kindergarten, he'd wanted to be the only man to give her flowers. Seeing her wear Peter's corsage at prom had just about killed him.

"Why didn't *you* send me flowers?" Belle retorted. She clearly didn't even remember that stupid crayon scribble he'd given her. Why would she? "If you knew I was your True Love, why didn't you ask me out, or buy me jewelry, or do what a normal guy would do? Why did you have to be so cold?

The woman drove him insane. "Because you didn't want me! I tried to tell you the truth and you refused to hear it."

"You told me *once* when we were teenagers and in the middle of an argument. Why didn't you *really* tell me you were my True Love?"

Avenant was quiet for a long moment.

"I would've believed you, if you'd given me a chance." Belle insisted. "You didn't have to trick me."

"Even if you'd believed me, you wouldn't have slept with me and made it official. At best, you'd feel sorry for me. I *had* to maneuver you into it or you would've said no. I can deal with the fact that you don't love me, but I'd rather have your hate than your pity."

Belle stared at him.

Avenant dropped his eyes and decided to change the subject. "I think Lancelot may have been the one who sent those men to attack you in your bed." He told her. "It only makes sense. He needed me out of the way to claim the Icen Throne, but he's too ball-less to fight me himself. So, he set it up for you to overthrow me, thinking he'd then get the kingdom. Except the judge handed it over to you, instead."

Belle cleared her throat and gamely went along with the new topic. "Lancelot's a knight. He'd only trust other knights on a mission like that and I don't think those guys in my bedroom were knights."

Of *course*, she'd defend her precious squad of armored idiots. "Knights can be dickheads, just like everyone else."

"I know. But, they probably wouldn't make so much noise breaking into a house. They're trained to be stealthy."

"Sneaky." He corrected. "As in sneakily trying to steal my crown in the sneakiest way possible. By going after my True Love."

Belle still wasn't convinced. "Lancelot was pretty shocked up on the jungle level when you told him we were True Loves. I don't think he knew. He's not a good enough actor to pull off such genuine surprise." She paused. "Besides, Lancelot doesn't have anything against me. Or he *didn't* before I took over the Northlands. The more I think about it, the more I feel like there was a more personal reason for them targeting me in my home."

Avenant grunted. "We should kill him, just to be sure. If nothing else, he's definitely behind all the dead bodies we keep tripping over. Well, Lancelot or Bluebeard. We should kill them *both* and cover our bases."

"The two of them blamed *you* for the murders."

"Because they're both fucking liars." Avenant snapped. He instinctively defended himself, just in case she believed them. "You were with me, Belle. You know I didn't…"

She cut him off. "I'm not accusing you, for God's sake. I'm just saying that if *they* were the killers, they wouldn't assume *you* were the killer."

"They're morons. Who the hell knows what they assume." He arched a brow. "Or maybe they're just trying to set me up. It wouldn't be the first time."

"I still feel like we're missing something." Belle chewed on her marshmallow. "Anyway, we need to get out of here. That's the most important thing. No matter who's doing the killing, sooner or later, they're going to come after us and you've already been shot once today." She got Prince Adam's journal out again and flipped through the wet pages. "Damn it, some of the ink is running. I hope we can still read what your extremely-great-grandfather says about the third level of this maze."

"Oh me, too. It's sure to be riveting." Avenant made a face. "The man's idea of princely behavior was abysmal. First it was the crap about helpfulness..."

"And when we helped Lancelot, we found our way to level two, didn't we?"

"...Then the 'looking within' crap..."

"And we went through a mirrored rabbit hole. It was talking about seeing passed our reflections. Even you recognized that."

"...Now, I'm sure we'll have to hold hands and sing *Kumbaya* or something equally *un*regal."

"Well, we *are* camping." She pointed out distractedly. "Besides, you need to step out of your 'regal' box every once in a while. Maybe it'll help you thaw out a bit."

He snorted at that idea. A prince had to maintain a standard of aloof splendor at all times. Everyone knew that. Belle ran the kingdom like it was some bleeding heart charity ward, instead of with the proper amount of authority. It was why she made a brilliant ruler and also an easy target. The citizens loved her, but they knew that they could take advantage of her softness. All this talk about "emotional availability" meant nothing compared to strength. He'd never seen his father so much as smile and that man had ruled for forty-five years.

...Of course his father had been a total jackass.

Avenant frowned.

"Here we go." Belle exclaimed excitedly. "Good, the page isn't all washed away. The entry for this level is," she hesitated, "actually it's pretty short."

"Short is good." Avenant wasn't the biggest fan of Adam's proselyting, so the less of it the better.

"It says, 'To be the true ruler that his kingdom deserves, a prince must find his balance.'" Belle wrinkled her nose in irritation. "That's it. What do you think it means?"

"We probably have to walk on a tightrope. And fight dragons. Quests always have dragons at the end."

She slammed the book shut at his glib tone. "You know, you're taking this all very lightly. That sword is the only thing that will get you the Northlands back. I'd think you'd be a *little* more concerned about the fact that we're stranded on this rock and no closer to finding it."

Avenant shrugged. "Maybe it's just my romantic faith in destiny, but I'm not worried about someone else claiming Excalibur."

"Maybe you know something that I don't." She retorted. "This whole time, you've been smirking your 'I've got a trump card' smirk, so you might as well just tell me what's going on. You knew going into this labyrinth that you were the only one who could win, didn't you?"

"I have no idea what you're talking about."

"Bullshit. The contest of valor was *your* idea and you wouldn't have risked..."

"Rosabella Aria Ashman." The minotaur called out, interrupting her. "I never expected you to make it this far. How very interesting you've turned out to be."

Yeah... that didn't sound ominous, at all.

"Knoss?" Belle turned to scan the darkness with a happy smile, like she completely trusted that asshole not to be an asshole. "Hey, is this the water you were talking about?"

Avenant got to his feet and grabbed her arm. "Get away from the fire." He tugged Belle deeper into the shadows, keeping her behind him. The woman never had enough sense to be afraid of beasts.

Knoss chuckled, the sound coming from all directions. "I've lived in this labyrinth all my life, Prince.

Do you really think I can't find you?"

Avenant closed his eyes for a beat. When he opened them again, he was seeing with the Beast's vision. The monster could see far better than Avenant. The blackness was suddenly alive with shapes and movement. He could see the details of the rocks and the scrubby twigs he'd used to feed the fire and the damp curls of Belle's hair.

He also saw a certain horned bastard.

Knoss had somehow found his way onto the thin ledge and was standing there with his huge arms crossed over his huge chest. The Beast snarled in Avenant's head, wanting to get free. It didn't like the minotaur being so close to Belle.

Avenant fought it back. He'd spent his entire life keeping the Beast caged and he wasn't about to let it lose. Especially not in front of his True Love. He was having enough trouble convincing Belle to give him a chance without showing her that he was really an animal.

"Knoss isn't going to hurt us." Belle assured Avenant. Because, she and the minotaur were apparently best friends, now. "He's here to help."

The Beast and Avenant both glared at her. "Why the hell would you think that?"

"Because he *said* he was, remember? He said if we made it to the water, he'd find us. Obviously, he's going to help us get across it."

"Cross it to *where?* Look over across the river. It's just another wall of stone over there."

"The labyrinth doesn't care what you see." Knoss reported, stepping into the firelight. "Its purpose is to show you what you *don't*."

"God, you really just said that." Avenant was so damn sick of all the quasi-philosophical bullshit about the maze. They even had *him* half-convinced it possessed some kind of awareness about their actions. "Fine. Tell me, what I *don't* see, then. I'd like to get out of this pit sometime before July."

"You cancelled July, too." Belle reminded him.

"You canceled July?" Knoss arched a brow. "Why the fuck did you cancel July?"

"The entire month annoyed me." Avenant had been slightly drunk and very pissed when he'd made that edict. Belle's birthday was in July and she hadn't invited him to yet another one of her parties. Obviously, it hadn't been his finest moment.

Belle rolled her eyes and looked back at Knoss. "Just ignore him." She advised. "All the calendar manufactures did. Right now, we need to find the sword and you need to help us."

"Do I?"

"If you ever want to get out of this maze you do. Once we have Excalibur, you'll be free. We have to be getting close, right?"

"Geographically." Knoss allowed. "But, given the number of dead bodies I've been finding in my labyrinth, I doubt you're going to make it. You people seem to be faring poorly on this quest. If I were you, I'd quit while I was still breathing."

"We can't quit." Belle told him firmly. "Do you know who's been killing all the contestants? If we stop them, everyone will be safer."

"Whoever it is, they've had help navigating the labyrinth." He lifted a shoulder in a shrug. "Probably from one of my kind. Not every minotaur loves the idea of freedom. Many prefer to stay here, rather than risk the unknown."

"I'm sure *some* people can relate to that." Belle

sent Avenant a pointed look.

Avenant gave a scoff. "Please don't compare me with these... beings."

Knoss arched a brow at Belle. "Are you sure you wish to seek Excalibur with this man? What do you plan to do if you find the sword? Give it to him? Fight him for it?"

Avenant's jaw ticked, knowing Knoss was right. Strategically, it made more sense for Belle to go on alone. Only one of them could win this contest and now was the perfect opportunity for her to take the lead. The minotaur would help her and happily leave Avenant behind. She could make it to Excalibur while he was still trying to forge the rapids.

Goddamn it.

He *couldn't* lose this. The only way to show Belle that he was strong and worthy was to get that fucking sword, so that's what Avenant was going to do no matter how many minotaurs he had to decapitate.

He slanted deadly glare at Knoss, sizing up his foe. "I'll kill you before I let you take her." He warned and he heard the Beast's darkness rumble in his voice.

Knoss smirked at him. "Try it, boy. Your monster is nothing compared to mine."

"Both of you stop." Belle pushed herself between them. "I'm not abandoning Avenant on this rock, so the whole argument is pointless. He and I have a deal. We're going to get to the end of this contest together and *then* we're going to see who claims the sword. I'm not about to change the rules."

"In your place, he would change them." Knoss nodded at Avenant. "You're close enough to the finish line that he'd leave you behind and try to make it on his own."

"He wouldn't leave me." Belle sounded very sure of that.

So sure that even Avenant blinked at her.

Knoss gave a scoff. "Of course he'd leave you. You're an interesting girl, but he's a beast. Why wouldn't he choose the most selfish path?"

"Simple. He hasn't seen me topless, yet." Belle nodded. "We had a whole discussion about it. Apparently, he's fixated."

Knoss and Avenant both stared at her.

"Oh." Knoss said. "You're right, then. He wouldn't leave you." He glanced back at Avenant. "Not even you seem that stupid."

Avenant barely heard him. God, he would never get used to Belle's teasing comments. He felt himself gaping at her, amazed that she was sort of flirting with him.

She gave him a slow smile.

Avenant shook his spinning head and turned back to Knoss. "Just show us the way out of here, before I toss you in that river." He ordered. "We're staying together."

Knoss studied Belle for a moment longer. "You aren't going to reconsider, are you?"

"Nope."

"So be it." He shrugged, absolving himself of any liability. "When you hit rock bottom, the only direction is up." He pointed to some barely perceptible handholds in the sheer wall. "And up. And up."

Avenant's eyes followed the makeshift ladder up, and up, and up… and then finally to what looked like the world's ricketiest suspension bridge spanning the gorge downstream. "Oh you've got to be kidding me."

Belle sighed. "I suddenly wish we'd gotten that dragon."

Chapter Sixteen

Everyone knows the Beast killed his father.
We should never have allowed him to claim the Icen Throne, but we were all too scared to oppose him.
When I protested that a Bad folk couldn't inherit a kingdom, Avenant threatened to smush me with a water spout.

Testimony of Mr. Itsy Bitsy Spider- *The People of the Northlands v. Prince Avenant*

Three Years Ago

His father was dead.

Avenant still couldn't fully process it. Vincent's cold hatred had been such a constant that he didn't know how to navigate his life without it. Ever since Avenant had attacked Vincent in the throne room, their relationship had been worse than ever. They barely spoke, most of their communication reduced to chilling glares and pointed insults. He kept expecting his father to pop up and ridicule him for falling for this elaborate hoax.

Although not even Vincent could've faked an explosion that big.

His father had died touring an oil platform. If he'd read any of Belle's environmental pamphlets, he would've known it was operating with fourteen different code violations, but Vincent had never been very interested in other people's opinions. He'd allowed the drillers to cut corners and pocketed their bribes and look where it got him...

Blown into so many pieces that his whole body fit in a freezer bag.

Rumors abounded that Avenant had "helped" with the accident, but, in truth, he hadn't been involved in his father's death. He just didn't mourn for the man. Just like he hadn't mourned for his mother. He'd never felt close to them or anyone else in his family. Pretending otherwise was pointless.

All his life he'd heard stories about his proud lineage, but they'd been impersonal lessons instead of tales designed to span generations. His parents didn't care if he felt a bond with them or understood any of his ancestors. They just wanted to make sure he didn't disgrace them. They'd both made their choices and none of their choices ever involved loving him.

It would be weakness to care for people who'd shown him nothing but disgust.

At his father's funeral, he was dry-eyed and distant. He heard the whispers, noting his lack of emotion. Witnessed the glances of disapproval as he didn't give a eulogy lying about what a wonderful dad and prince Vincent had been. Saw them all waiting for the Icen Throne to melt underneath him. So far, it hadn't, much to their dismay. Avenant seized control of the kingdom before anyone could stop him. Nobody was strong enough to take what was his, so fuck them all.

Avenant had no illusions about his citizens. They were never going to accept him as their ruler. They saw him as a beast. Why even try reaching out to them when it was hopeless? Better to reject them, before they rejected him. Better to make them fear him, right from the start. All the people who avoided his gaze or cringed away were going to know real terror. He was going to make sure this kingdom never forgot who was in charge.

Bad or not, he controlled the Northlands and everybody in it.

Avenant was the last one in the graveyard, stoically watching the coffin be lowered into the ground. His parents were gone. He was free. Except he didn't feel free. He didn't feel anything.

He sensed Belle before he saw her. It was always like that. The Beast detected her presence and started pacing, trying to get closer to her warmth. Avenant slowly turned his head as she came up next to him, taking in her somber outfit.

"Black isn't your color." He decided. She was too bright for the stark shade. Too full of life. She didn't belong in this graveyard, paying respects to a man who'd wanted her raped. She belonged in the brilliant yellow sunlight.

Belle ignored his opinion. "I'm sorry about your father." She said quietly. "I know how hard it is to lose your parents."

"I'm twenty-seven. Hardly an orphan."

"You feel like an orphan no matter how old you are." Her chocolate gaze stared up at him. "Give yourself a chance to grieve."

He snorted at that idea. "I didn't even like my parents."

"I don't think it matters. They were still your parents." Belle chewed her lower lip. "Do you need anything?"

She was the first person to ask him that. Everyone else knew better. He rolled his eyes and told himself not to be touched. She wasn't asking because she cared about him. The woman was just pitifully *Good*. As much as he hated to admit it, Vincent had been right. Belle would never love him. Not in the way he longed for. She couldn't.

He was a beast.

"I'm Prince of the Northlands, now." He reminded her flatly. "My word is law. Didn't you hear all the whining from the lawyers, before I arrested them? Everything I need is one royal decree away."

"I wasn't asking the Prince of the Northlands. I was asking Avenant."

Shit.

Just like that, his defenses crumbled. Before he felt nothing; now he felt far too much. Avenant's lips pressed together, not trusting himself to speak for a long moment. If he did, he'd break down. "I'm fine." He said shortly. "Go home. You've done your duty and sucked up to the new monarch."

"That's not why I came and you know it."

"Then why did you come?" He flashed her a glare. "To bitch at me about how I'm becoming a dictator?" Avenant already knew Belle was going to oppose his rule at every turn. He had absolute power, now. He could have her killed fifty different ways, but she never seemed to notice. She just kept fighting. He didn't understand how she could be so blind to the fact that she was outmatched.

Or how she kept fucking *winning*.

"Well, you *are* becoming a dictator." She began. "You used the funeral to stage a coup…"

Avenant cut her off. "I don't need to hear about how I've oppressed puppies or littered in a school zone, alright? I already have kids sending me crayon hate mail about my evilness."

"You cancelled Mother Goose's TV show! What do you expect?"

"Those damn puppets were annoying me. They were singing some so-called 'rhyming' song about how your True Love is your best friend, till the end, it just depends, on your Good *inten*...sions. And that doesn't rhyme, at all." Also, it was a total lie. He was getting pissed off just thinking about it. "That squawking bitch was rotting the brain of every child in my kingdom and I needed to stop her."

"Mother Goose helps preschoolers learn to read. Don't you want an educated populace?"

"No. I want them beaten down and toiling."

"You're impossible. I don't know why I even bother."

"Look, I'm sure you have a list of a thousand things I've done wrong, so far. But, right now, I just want..." Avenant trailed off because he had no idea what he wanted, aside from Belle to stay with him. The thought of going back to that empty castle triggered his claustrophobia, making him want to wrench at his tie and suck in oxygen.

He should have ordered some kind of reception. He hadn't wanted the normal array of sycophantic people around, pretending to care. But, at least they'd be *something*. He didn't want to be alone. Why was he always alone?

Belle's annoyance seemed to fade as she gazed up at him. "We can talk about your insane power grab later." She assured him quietly. "I'm sorry. I'm not here to continue our war. I promise. Today, we should just focus on getting you through this."

"Oh great. Do we get to share our feelings?"

"If you'd like." Belle offered. "It would probably be really good for you."

"I don't have any feelings."

"I'm sure you'd like to think that's true." She muttered. "Look, you should come home with me. I can make you dinner. You probably haven't eaten."

"I have cooks." He refused to give into temptation. "I can eat anything I want, anytime I want." She was inviting him because she felt sorry for him and he couldn't stand that. It was worse than even her scorn. "I don't need you or your pity."

God, how he needed her.

Belle was quiet for a long moment. "Do you want to be alone?"

"Yes."

No!

Belle let out a sigh and turned to go. "Okay."

Goddamn it, why didn't she ignore what he said and stay? It wasn't like she'd ever listened to him before. The Beast was roaring in his head, screaming that he was an idiot. Avenant didn't need the monster to tell him what he already knew, but he couldn't stop himself from pushing Belle away. If he didn't, she'd see how weak he was. He wanted to beg her not to leave. He wanted to tell her every feeling inside of him. He just wanted to cling to her warmth.

But, the last time he'd tried opening up to her, she'd almost broken him. He didn't even blame her for not wanting him. Not really. His father had been right. Nobody could ever want a beast. Avenant had been an idiot to approach Belle at the prom. The way to victory wasn't with begging, it was through strength.

He was going to run the Northlands with an iron fist. He'd show Belle that he could win against all the people who hated him. That he wasn't one of her pathetic charity cases. That he was strong. Then, she'd look at him and just... know.

She'd finally *surrender*.

Belle took a step, hesitated, and then turned back to him. "You don't always have to be so cold, you know.

It's okay to have emotions. No one will think less of you if you let go."

"Bad things will happen if I let go."

"Maybe. But, what will happen if you keep hanging on so tightly?"

Avenant shot her a frown. "Exactly the same thing that's been happening all my life."

"Exactly." Belle gave him a sad smile and walked away.

Chapter Seventeen

Don't trust a beast.
E-I-E-I-O

Testimony of Old MacDonald- *The People of the Northlands vs. Prince Avenant*

"I feel like you're looking at my behind. Are you looking at my behind?"

"Absolutely, I am."

Belle stopped climbing and glowered down at him.

"What? You said you wanted me to be honest." Avenant sounded like she was the one being unreasonable. "You have an incredible ass. Of course I'm going to look at it. It's certainly better than staring down at the ground, isn't it?"

Belle sighed in frustration. "Why don't we switch places and I'll sexually objectify *you*, for a while."

It wasn't that she minded his ogling exactly, but her nerves were frayed and he was a convenient target. She really hated heights. A lot. Falling through the rabbit hole had been scary enough, but this was freaking her out. It took everything in her to put one hand in front of the other.

Don't look down. Don't look down. Don't look down.

"I would love for you to do all kinds of sexual things to me, Bella." His hand gripped her ankle, helping her find a foothold. "But, I need to be back here to make sure you don't fall. You can't see as well as I can."

Damn it, it was hard to argue with him when he was being logical. Belle made a face and kept climbing up the stone wall. They were ten stories in the air, with nothing but jagged rocks beneath them. Knoss had better be right about the bridge.

"Explain to me again why you can see in the dark and I can't." She instructed. She needed to concentrate on something besides her impending pancaking into two-dimensionality.

"The Beast." Avenant said shortly.

She could tell by his tone that he didn't want to talk about it. That just encouraged her to press harder. If they were going to make this True Love thing work, he was going to have to open up. Even if she had to use force. "So *you* can see better or the *Beast* can see better?" She asked, wanting to understand.

"Both of us. I can see through his eyes."

Belle considered that for a moment. "Maybe you're just seeing through *your* eyes."

"What?"

"Maybe there isn't a 'both' of you. Maybe there's just *one* of you. Maybe what you think is a Beast is just a part of you that you're trying to repress."

"That's insane."

"Is it? You're not someone particularly in touch with your feelings." Belle dug her fingers into the next handhold and dragged herself up another few inches. *Don't look down. Don't look down. Don't look down.* "I think you try to wall up huge parts of yourself and maybe the Beast is just one of those parts."

"It's a physical change, Belle. It's not all in my head."

"So? Wolves physically change. They turn from people into…"

He cut her off, sounding affronted. "First you compare me to minotaurs and now *wolves?*"

"Oh for God sake. I'm not saying…" She broke off with a cry as gravel moved beneath her hand. Belle slid backwards, trying to find purchase. For one heart stopping second, she thought she was going to fall. She looked down into the darkness and swore she could see it rushing up to meet…

Instantly, Avenant's palm was there to steady her. Belle released a relieved breath, her pulse pounding in her ears. It was okay. Avenant was right behind her, keeping her safe.

"Thank you." She got out.

"You're welcome, my love."

She loved it when he called her that. The man was a total jerk, but she might just be adapting to having him around. "Anyway, I'm not saying you're a wolf." She continued, resuming the climb. *Don't look down. Don't look down. Don't look down.* "Not that there's anything *wrong* with being a wolf, Mr. Judgmental."

He gave a snort. "You clearly haven't spent much time with Marrok."

Belle disregarded that. "I'm just saying that wolves go through physical changes, but they're still who they are."

"Yeah, they're still wolves." Avenant snarked. "I'm not a wolf. *They're* refugees from the zoo and *I'm* a prince."

God, he really was a snob. "Just take a second and think about the maybes. *Maybe* you shouldn't try so hard to keep this 'Beast' part of you separate. *Maybe* if you let it loose, you'll find that it isn't so Bad. *Maybe* you're claustrophobia and emotional frigidity comes from boxing up huge parts of yourself. *Maybe* you have to accept all the aspects of yourself if you're going to be whole."

"*Maybe* I'd sooner jump off the rocks than think about those maybes."

She really wished he wouldn't talk about jumping. "Just *try to* think about it, then."

He gave an unconvinced grunt. "You're almost to the top. How about you focus on reaching it and I'll focus on your cute little posterior and we'll skip the psychoanalysis."

Belle made a face. "You can never just admit when I'm right." She heaved her way onto the summit and then turned to help him up. "Are you okay?" She asked when they were both standing on solid ground. "Did the climb hurt your shoulder?"

Avenant frowned at her as she checked the makeshift bandaged she'd fashioned for him earlier. "You shouldn't show any weakness." He lectured in a particularly lecture-y tone. "You worry about my bullet scratch or waste your time trying to find the Good side of the Beast, when you *should've* left me behind and had Knoss show you this path on your own. You won't win unless you're strong."

"I'll bear that in mind." Belle assured him dryly. "How's your shoulder?"

He let out a sigh that suggested he was the sane one in their relationship. "It's fine."

"Good." Belle moved on to check the gash on his temple. "How's your head?"

"You're so fucking soft." For once, it didn't sound like a complaint. Instead, Avenant gave her a small smile, as if he found her amazing. "Even when I know I should try and change you... I would *never* want you to change."

"Of course you wouldn't." She arched a brow.

"Because you think you're going to beat me. But, you *won't*. I'm not going to lie down and just let you win."

"I don't want you to let me win." He adjusted the backpack over his arm and shook his head. "That won't get me what I'm after."

"It would get you the sword. What else is there?"

Avenant rolled his eyes and headed in the direction of the bridge. "What do you *think?* I want you to give me a chance. I told you that. This contest is just a means to an end."

She had no idea how his mind worked sometimes. "So, you really did all this to convince me we were True Loves?"

"*Yes.*"

"What if someone else gets to Excalibur first? Did you even think of that?"

He scoffed at that idea. "No one else will free that sword."

"What if they *do?* Or what if *I* do? What if you lose the Northlands because you were so determined to maneuver me into bed?"

Avenant gave an unconcerned shrug. "Then, I'll figure out a way to get it back."

"What if you can't?" She hurried to catch up with him. "You say I make emotional choices, but it doesn't seem like you've been acting so rationally, either."

And that gave her more hope than anything else he'd done.

Belle needed to be important to the man she married. She needed to be the most vital part of his world. Growing up, her parents had forgotten to set a place for her at dinner countless times, because she just wasn't important enough to remember. They once went on a weeklong vacation and didn't notice that they'd left her at home. If she'd blinked out of existence, they probably would've just felt guilty relief that she wasn't around to embarrass them at cocktail parties and then never thought of her again. Belle couldn't spend the rest of her life as the overlooked guest in her own family. She *wouldn't*.

The more she thought about it, though, the more it seemed like Avenant had just put his crown on the line to try and win her over. If Avenant did something so stupid, then he couldn't possibly be cold all the way through. This True Love bond must matter to him. That meant maybe *Belle* could matter to him. She just had to encourage him to drop some of his walls and realize that emotions weren't so scary, after all.

Since she already knew what she felt for the jerk, the least he could do was reciprocate. She just needed to show him how.

Belle took a chance. "Would you have left me behind to go for the sword alone?" They'd agreed to end their partnership when they were close to the finish line, after all. "Do you want to play every man for himself?"

Avenant's jaw ticked. "No." The word was quiet. "I want to win with you beside me."

"And I'm *going* to win with you beside *me*." She assured him sweetly. "That way you can clap in awe."

He gave a snort. "I love it when you're a bitch."

Belle smiled at that. "The point is, I think we should stick together right to the end." She saw the quick flash of relief on his face and kept going. "In fact, I'll consider a permanent truce."

That caught him off guard. "What do you mean?"

"I mean, we could extend our partnership after we get out of here. Working together is a hell of a lot better than constantly fighting, don't you think? We're certainly accomplishing a lot more pooling our resources then we were battling each other."

Avenant mulled that over like he was looking for traps. "You want to be... friends?" He translated, apparently braced for her to start laughing or something.

Belle had no clue why he was wary about the idea. "Would that be so terrible? If we can't even be friends, I don't see how you expect us to be True Loves. It's the only way I..."

"I *want* to be friends with you." He interrupted. "I always have. You're the one who never thought I was Good enough."

"That's ridiculous." Except, she could see he actually thought it was true. "How in the world could you think *I* was the one keeping us from being friends, Avenant?" The man was insane. "Actually --you know what?-- it doesn't even matter." She waved a hand. "Let's just start over and... *start over*."

"Start over?" He still looked suspicious.

"Yeah. Watch." Belle quickened her step so she was beside him and held out a palm. "Hi. I'm Rosabella Aria Ashman. I own a bookstore and sometimes run the Northlands. Who are you, handsome stranger?"

His eyes met hers and something warm moved in their arctic depths. "I'm Avenant." He murmured, his hand clasping hers. "I'm a prince and an ex-convict and your True Love."

"My True Love? Wow. Nice to meet you. I'm sure glad you just *told* me, instead of doing something sneaky and underhanded to get your own way."

"Well, I'm a nice guy."

"That's good news, because I have a thing for nice guys." She made an exaggerated expression of surprise. "Hey, we should be friends."

"First impression of me and I strike you as friendly?"

"I guess it's your cheery personality. What do you say?"

Avenant's mouth curved. "I say, you've *always* been my best friend, Belle. From the time we were kids, I've been waiting for you to let me show you that." He paused. "Even though we just met."

The man was irresistible, damn it. "Funny. I feel the same way." She drawled out. "We should probably try to build off that."

"Well, I certainly support the idea of you seducing me, if you're considering a 'friends with benefits' thing."

"No, I was thinking more like dinner or…"

"Oh, come on." He interrupted with a quick grin. "Give seduction a shot. I dare you."

She glanced at him from the corner of her eye. Belle couldn't refuse a dare, especially not a teasing one. It was about time he lightened up a little bit. "Alright." She arched an exaggerated brow and cleared her throat. "So… you come here often?" She tried.

He got extra credit for keeping a perfectly straight face. "All the time. I like the atmosphere of this pit. The mold invigorates my lungs."

"Prince, ex-convict, True Love and wiseass." She nodded like a world-weary femme fatal. "It's a tricky combination, but I can handle it."

"Even though I'm not a knight in shining armor?"

She shrugged. "That knight thing was kind of a phase I was going through. I like my men a little more beastly, now."

His gaze glowed electric-blue for a moment and Belle knew the Beast liked her, too. "How do you feel about sleeping with beastly men on the first date?" His voice was darker than before.

"My seduction technique was that successful, huh?"

"Oh, you wouldn't *believe* how easy I am."

Belle was delighted that he was being playful and cooperating with the new game. "Good. Let's win the kingdom. Then, we can get naked, again." She told him cheerily.

Avenant blinked. "Wait... For real?"

"What can I say? You've seduced me, too. It was the being *nice* part."

He seemed stunned by how simple that had been. "That was being nice? And it actually *worked?* Jesus, that's all you want from me?"

"I want you to be warm to me and have fun with me and be *open* with me. It's not rocket science, doofus."

Avenant lapsed into thoughtful silence. He was *trying* to figure out what she wanted, which was really at least half of what she wanted. "I can do all that." He said after a long moment. "We'll make a deal. I can be... open and you try to accept me as your True Love. Okay?"

"Okay." Belle said and began to believe that their insane relationship might actually succeed.

"Okay." He looked like he'd just placed a huge bet on a longshot. "You need to be patient with me, though, because I'm probably going to fuck up a lot." He warned. "You can't just give up on me."

"Believe me, I'm used to being patient with you." She said dryly. "*And* with you fucking up."

That seemed to reassure him. "God, I *really* love it when you're a bitch." He glanced down at her when they reached the suspension bridge. "So, would you feel safer going across first or second, my love?"

"I'd feel safer staying right here on solid rock."

Belle took in the rickety planks he expected her to walk across and shook her head. The gorge over the river seemed endless. "What if Knoss is wrong and there isn't anything over there?"

"Then I get to live my dream and finally kill him." Avenant started across the bridge. "Come on. I won't let you fall. You won't get away from me that easily."

It was pathetic, but that actually comforted her a little. Belle edged out onto the bridge after him. The makeshift structure swayed with each step, sending the boards bouncing up and then sinking back down. She squeezed her eyes shut at the sickening sensation and slowly pressed onward. No way was she going to give Avenant the satisfaction of running.

Don't look down. Don't look down. Don't look down.

With her eyes shut, Belle's other senses were heightened and, after a moment, she caught a whiff of something strange. Unlike the damp scent of the cavern, this was sharp and acidic and oddly familiar... And completely out of place in the labyrinth.

Belle opened her eyes and looked around. "Do you think another contestant could've made it this far?"

"Not unless they cheated." Avenant frowned. "Why?"

"I smell something weird." She glanced at him. "Knoss said that the other minotaurs might be working with the murderer. Maybe they passed this way recently or..."

"I didn't say the *other* minotaurs." Knoss's voice interjected from behind her. "I simply said one of my kind was aiding in the kills."

Oh shit... Belle slowly turned to look at him, already knowing that Avenant would never let her live this down. Knoss was poised at the entrance of the bridge, blocking their retreat.

"I *knew* you shouldn't have tried to befriend a beast." Avenant had the audacity to sound pleased. "I told you so, Bella."

Belle ignored his provocations, her eyes on Knoss. "You're the one killing people?" She guessed gloomily.

"No. I'm merely helping him stop the others, before I stop him, as well."

"Who's *he?*"

"I don't know his name." Knoss shrugged. "I never even thought to ask. My only goal is to punish all those who quest for Excalibur and he was eager to help."

"Why?" It didn't make any sense. "Finding it would set you free."

"I don't want to be 'free.'" He mocked as if the word itself was tainted. "I *like* the labyrinth. All my life, I've been inside these walls. Why would I want to leave?"

"Because all your life you've been inside these walls?" She snarked. "Maybe you're scared to take a risk, but isn't it worse to stay trapped in here forever?"

"I'm not trapped!" He shouted back. "I'm just staying where everything's safe and familiar. Outside, I'd be ridiculed and mocked."

"You don't know that. You haven't even tried."

"I don't want to try!" He raged. "This is my *home*. It's my duty to preserve what Prince Adam created. To protect the sword and all who dwell within these walls."

Belle flashed Avenant a glare, blaming him for his idiot ancestor.

"Don't look at me. I'm on the record as saying Adam is a drunken lunatic, remember?"

"I'm sorry it had to come to this Rosabella Aria

Ashman." Knoss shook his head, getting his anger under control. "I knew you would get farther than the others, but I had hoped you'd see reason and turn back when you saw this bridge. I was praying that wouldn't attempt to cross it." Knoss sighed. "It's too bad you wouldn't quit. I didn't want to kill you. You really are an interesting girl."

"And you really are an asshole." Avenant retorted, edging forward so he was in front of Belle. "She wanted to give you the benefit of the doubt, but there's rarely a point with monsters, is there?"

Knoss glowered at him. "On the other hand, I don't regret killing *you*, at all." He stepped out onto the bridge, the wobbly structure sagging under his sheer mass. "Let's not make this harder than it needs to be. There's no way you can stop what's about to happen, Prince. You may think you're a beast, but you're no match for me."

"You've never met my Beast."

Belle glanced up at Avenant, a brilliant idea occurring to her. "Introduce them." She prompted in a quiet tone. "Unchain the Beast."

"What?" Avenant sent her an amazed look. "*No*. Are you crazy?"

"You were thinking about doing it the last time he almost ripped us apart, weren't you?

"Yeah, but..."

"Well, if there was ever a time to drop those walls, this is it."

He shook his head. "I don't even know if I *can*. I've never tried to let go before."

"So try *now*." She hissed back. "Unless you can think of another way to stop the gigantic, horned maniac from slaughtering us."

Knoss was immune to magic, ten feet tall, and

determined to bathe in their blood. They might be able to reach the other side of the bridge before he tore their heads off, but then what? The minotaur knew the labyrinth better than they did. He *would* catch them. There weren't a lot of options here.

"*Fuck*." Avenant said and she heard the frustration in his tone. "I *can't*, Belle. You don't understand. I can't do it."

"You haven't even tried. Did you hear what I just told him? Because the same applies to you. Don't stay trapped, because you're too afraid of what's outside the cage."

He looked hunted. "I'll think of something else. I *will*. Just give me a second."

"We don't have a second!"

"Are you seriously going to argue with me, right now? *Seriously?*"

Knoss gave a snort at their bickering. "Jesus, you two really are True Loves, aren't you? I suspected as much." He actually smiled. "Well, it's fitting that you die together, then." Gripping the sides of the bridge with his hands, he used his powers to set the whole thing on fire. Flames began flickering along the thick ropes. In a matter of moments they would burn away and send Belle and Avenant careening onto the rocks below. At this angle, they wouldn't hit the water. They'd smash into jagged stones.

Belle tried not to hyperventilate. Her head snapped around, instinctively trying to gauge the distance to the opposite side of the ravine. Too far. They weren't going to make it.

"Good-bye, Rosabella Aria Ashman." Knoss called, heading back to solid ground. "You were a worthy contender for the sword, but you..." He slammed into a wall of ice.

Belle's eyebrows soared. Avenant had used his powers to seal off the exit, trapping the minotaur on the bridge with them. "What are you doing? He'll just melt it."

"Trust me and hold on."

"Trust you?" She repeated skeptically. "You wouldn't say that unless you were about to do something crazy." But, her fingers automatically wrapped around the rope railing, because she *did* trust Avenant. She was clearly losing her mind.

"You holding on or not?" He prompted, his attention still on Knoss.

"I'm holding on." Belle swept her hair behind her ear with her free hand and braced herself. "Commence with the Badness."

Avenant shot her a slight grin. "This being friends thing is working for me."

"Foolish prince." Knoss fixed him with a snide look, the fire growing between them. "You know I'll burn right through your pitiful snowdrift."

"Sure you will." Avenant smirked. "But, how much weight do you think this bridge can hold?"

Knoss's eyes went wide as Avenant dumped several tons of frost onto the rotted planks. The ropes behind the minotaur snapped, sending all three of them swinging across the gorge. It was now only connected by the posts on the far side, so it acted like a huge jungle vine.

Belle let out a shriek of panic, her fingers tightening on the railing as the bridge slammed into the wall. The force of the impact drove the air from her lungs and spun her around, nearly making her lose her grip. Pure terror shot through her.

Don't look down. Don't look down. Don't look down.

"Belle!"

She looked down.

She heard Avenant call her name and the dizzy sensation in her stomach meant nothing in comparison. "What?" She shouted back, hating heights and minotaurs and *him*. But, Jesus, she was glad to see that he was safe.

"Are you okay?"

"Do I *look* okay? *This* is why I should never, ever trust you!"

He gave her a smile that made her want to pelt him with loose rocks. "Except you just did, my love."

"Oh, shut-up."

Peering through the darkness and smoke, Belle realized that she and Avenant were now dangling above flames. He was holding on several yards below her, his elbow hooked through one of the floor planks. Further down, the fire burned. She could see Knoss hanging onto the very bottom, struggling to heave his massive body upward. But, he was too big and the flames were spreading too fast.

"Start climbing, Bella." Avenant ordered. "We have to get out of here."

"He's going to fall." She whispered, her gaze on Knoss.

"No shit. Unless you want us to join him, you'd better move it."

Belle moved it. She started climbing up the wooden planks like a ladder, headed for the top. Her whole body was shaking, but she forced herself to move faster. Avenant was right behind her. If she didn't get off the bridge, neither would he and she *had* to get him off the bridge. The jackass was vital to her.

"You'll never have what you seek, Prince!" Knoss shrieked. "You don't know how to surrender and that's the real test of this labyrinth. You won't win, because you're too afraid of losing..." His final taunted ended in a yell of terror and fury.

The fire ate through the ropes, breaking the bottom section of the bridge free of its moorings. Knoss's arms helplessly spiraled, searching for something to hold onto and finding nothing but air. He went tumbling onto the black rocks below, his scream abruptly silenced.

Not even a minotaur could survive a fall like that.

"Go!" Avenant shouted when Belle just stared down in horror. "We have to keep going!"

Belle gave her head a clearing shake and forced her hands to move. He was right. They had to keep going. It was the only way they were going to get out of the labyrinth alive.

Chapter Eighteen

I was such a merry old soul before Avenant came along.
Then he confiscated my favorite bowl, said my pipe was a controlled
substance, and indicted my fiddlers three for tax evasion.
Did he care when I cried? No. Because, a beast could never care for
anything but himself.

Testimony of Old King Cole - *The People of the Northlands v. Prince Avenant*

The good news was this section of the maze had enough light that Avenant could see the cave surrounding him without the Beast's eyes.

The bad news was it was still a cave.

He let out an annoyed sigh. He wanted out of this whole labyrinth. More importantly, he wanted *Belle* out of it. Avenant had started this misadventure to win his True Love, but he'd never imagined that his plan would endanger her. Christ, he'd never do *anything* to put Belle at risk. ...Except, he'd dragged her down here and now there was someone trying to kill them. It was his fault that she'd been trapped on a burning bridge and fallen through a rabbit hole and been attacked by a psychotic minotaur. Everything that happened was all on him.

"Belle?"

"Yeah?"

"I'm sorry."

This final passage was carved from dense rocks that glowed with magic. The two of them were making their way down a stone hallway so cramped that he had to duck down to avoid knocking his head on the ceiling.

She turned to give him a surprised look. "Sorry

for what?"

"When I suggested the contest of valor, I didn't expect it to get so screwed up."

Belle snorted. "Well, there *were* easier ways to convince me you were my True Love, that's for sure. But, I forgive you." She hesitated. "They say True Love conquers all, you know. Do you believe that?"

His heart flipped. "Yes." He said simply. "Do you?"

"...I think so."

The quiet words were closer than he ever imagined being to his prize. Belle wasn't trying to get rid of him, anymore. She was willing to give their relationship a chance.

It still wasn't enough, though. She wouldn't fully accept him unless he showed her he could be open. Whatever the hell that meant.

"About the labyrinth." Avenant cleared his throat and pushed past his emotional comfort zone. For Belle, he would do anything. Even... share. "I should've handled everything better." He tried, edging his way through the minefield of "feelings." "Obviously, I had no idea there would be people in here trying to kill you."

"I don't blame you for Knoss." Belle sounded surprised. "You're the one who saved me from him, Avenant." She shook her head. "If anyone's to blame, it was me. I was the one who said we should trust him. I didn't expect that asshole to be a villain."

"Of course you didn't. You're Good all the way through." Avenant found her softness endearing, but it did leave her vulnerable to the monsters of the world. "I'm the only man you've ever noticed is a villain."

Belle's eyes flicked to his. "You're the only man I've ever noticed, *at all*."

Avenant's brain experienced a full system shutdown. That happened every time she said something even remotely flirtatious. He lost the ability to think and became a gaping moron.

Belle didn't seem to mind. She gave him a small grin. "Listen, we can do *anything*, so long as we're working together." She nodded earnestly. "I'm really starting to believe that. I'm not worried about any more minotaurs trying to kill us or the labyrinth swallowing us up. As bad as things are, we're going to be okay so long as we stick together."

Avenant automatically hid how deeply her words touched him... Although, he wasn't quite sure anymore *why* he should hide it. Belle had just said something amazing to him. Wouldn't it make more sense to say something nice back to her?

His father wouldn't have thought so. Vincent would've said it was weakness to even consider this "openness" thing. But, what had that bastard ever done right in his whole life? Nothing. What had being cold and rigid gotten him? Certainly not happiness. Avenant didn't want his father's miserable life in an empty castle.

He wanted Belle.

Shit, had he been completely wrongheaded about this whole "strength" thing?

Belle was oblivious to his silent revelation. "And I *know* we'll stop whoever's murdering the other contestants." She concluded confidently.

"I still say it's probably Lancelot." Avenant muttered, trying to rally his scattered thoughts.

"How could it be Lancelot? Knoss beat him to a pulp earlier. Hardly the actions of two people on the same nefarious team. And then there was the weird smell on the bridge...."

"Lancelot smells." Avenant agreed with a nod.

"That's not what I mean and you know it."

Avenant shrugged. Lancelot's armor-y stench was the last thing he wanted to talk about. "Anyway, the point is, I didn't mean to get you into this mess." He continued, wanting to get the conversation back on track. "The contest of valor was my idea and it sucked." He paused, remembering the incredible feel of her body against his... and how she said they could be friends... and every smile she'd shined his way. "Well, not *all* of it sucked. A lot of it was mind-blowingly successful and turned out to be the best plan I ever had." He admitted. "But, I'm sorry about dragging you through the parts with the river and the fireballs and the dead bodies."

"Thanks. That's really touching."

"The stories skimmed over a lot of the messier aspects of the labyrinth," he finished, ignoring her dry interruption, "so I apologize for not anticipating how rough it would be on you."

There.

It had been like swallowing straight pins, but he'd been very open. Belle would see that he was *trying* to be nice and appreciate his sharingness or whatever. Avenant let out a relieved breath, pleased with himself for struggling through that horrible ordeal. He didn't have to be like his father. If he could prove that to her, she'd...

"What stories?" Belle asked, interrupting his silent back-patting and latching onto his slip.

Fuck.

That would be the one part of his speech that she paid attention to. The woman and her high IQ drove him insane.

"I grew-up hearing stories about my ancestors and Adam was one of the perennial favorites." Avenant chose his words carefully. "Drunken lunatics are great object lessons in the perils of Bad behavior."

Brown eyes narrowed. "Wait, how much did you know about this labyrinth before we came in?"

He hesitated. "Not much. I knew Adam had built it and," he cleared his throat, "I knew some stuff about the sword."

"*What* stuff about the sword?"

Damn it, she was going to keep pushing. Why couldn't she see he was *trying*? Why did Belle have to rip everything down and leave him totally exposed? Why couldn't she just realize the truth without him having to be so... truthful?

"Avenant?" She prompted in a serious tone."

"I don't want to lose." He heard himself say.

"Neither do I, dummy."

"No, I mean I *can't* lose. I'm trying to be what you need. But, if I lose, you're not going to want me and I can't let you go."

Belle frowned at him in confusion. "Avenant, finding the sword isn't going to affect my feelings for you."

"It will." When he had Excalibur, she'd look at him and just... know. He had to believe that.

"No, it *won't*." Belle gave her head a mystified shake. "We play this game, going back-and-forth, but it's just a *game*. Winning has nothing to do with our relationship. The only thing I care about is how you feel."

"How I feel?" He squinted at her, trying to understand what she meant by that lunacy. "How I feel about *you*, you mean?"

"Yes! What else?"

"But, you *know* how I feel." *Everyone* knew how he felt. It was the worst kept secret in the Four

Kingdoms. Why were they even talking about something so obvious? Was this some kind of trick? Did she want him to say it out loud so she could laugh at him?

"No, I really *don't* know how you feel. Am I important to you or just...?" Her voice trailed off, her eyes falling on something over his shoulder. "Oh." She whispered.

Avenant turned and saw the sword.

The chamber had obviously been carved to designate the end of the quest. Huge goddesses surrounded the room, holding laurels and trumpets. At the center sat ceremonial black rock with a blade suck halfway in, just like an illustration from a storybook. The grip was made of gold and decorated in raised snowflakes. The pommel was studded with a cabochon sapphire the size of a golf ball. A shaft of light glinted off the polished steel, highlighting the engraved word "Excalibur." It was a weapon fit for a prince.

Avenant stared at it, a sinking feeling in his gut.

"I didn't expect it to be so beautiful." Belle said quietly. But, she didn't lunge for the sword.

Neither did Avenant. He didn't have to. He was about to win. This was the moment... Except, it didn't seem like it would be winning, at all.

Belle tore her eyes away from the sword and looked up at him. "So now what?" She asked.

Avenant cleared his throat. "I don't know."

All the times he'd pictured his victory, he hadn't envisioned the moment quite like this. He thought he'd feel triumphant. He thought he'd relish the look on Belle's face as he claimed the sword and she realized he was worthy. Instead, he felt like he was about to fail the only test that mattered.

From out of nowhere, he thought of Knoss' final

words.

You won't win, because you're too afraid of losing.

"Well, wanna play rock-paper-scissors for it?" Belle suggested lightly, but he heard the tension in her voice. She didn't know what to do either. Neither one of them wanted to give in... But, one of them was going to have to.

And it was going to be him.

"Shit." Avenant whispered in defeat. All this work. All the effort. All the planning. Finally, he'd reached the end and he couldn't go through with it.

He was going to surrender first. He suddenly knew it was inevitable. Beating Belle wasn't the answer. That stupid minotaur had actually been right. There was only one way to really win and it was through losing. If he ripped that sword right out from under her, Belle would never be his.

Avenant pinched the bridge of his nose and sighed with extreme frustration. "You're not going to be able to pull the sword free."

Belle blinked at him. "What?"

Avenant took a deep breath and started tearing down all his walls. "Whoever frees Excalibur gets the kingdom. Adam set it up as a test, right?"

"Riiiiight." She drew out the word, watching him with deep suspicion.

"So would one of my ancestors really create a test that lets some *other* family rule? Adam was a drunken lunatic, but he wasn't stupid." He lifted a shoulder in a shrug. "Excalibur is enspelled."

Belle's lips parted in outrage. "You're saying the contest of valor is rigged? You've been cheating this whole time?"

"No!" Avenant instantly denied. Then, he paused to consider it. "Well... sort of."

"*Sort of?*"

"I was *sort of* cheating." He allowed. "Adam wanted to ensure his line would always retain control, so he created a failsafe. The sword will only come loose for someone with royal blood."

"So that's why you've been so smug since we got in here." She shook her head. "I *knew* you were up to something."

"I wasn't *smug*. I was *confident*."

"Because, you're the only person with royal blood who could complete this maze? What about Lancelot?"

"You really think that moron's going to get this far?" Avenant rolled his eyes. "Please."

"You're unbelievable." Belle brooded for a long moment. "If your plan was to use this failsafe to your advantage, why are you telling me about it? Why don't you just walk over there and win?"

"The whole point of this contest is to protect the family." He shrugged. "And you're my family, Belle."

She studied him from the corner of her eye and made a face. "That's the only *possible* answer that could've gotten you out of the doghouse."

Despite everything, his mouth curved.

"Don't look so pleased with yourself. You still haven't won this damn thing."

"I don't care about winning the sword. I care about winning *you.*" Avenant told her honestly. Being open was like ripping off a bandage. Once you got going, you might as well get it all over with fast. "I thought if I won the game, you'd surrender. But, that's not what I want, anymore."

"It's not?"

"No." He scraped a hand through his hair and made his choice. There *was* no choice. Belle was the only prize he'd ever cared about winning. "Fuck it. You can have the Icen Throne." He decided. "I forfeit."

Belle's eyes went wide. "What?" She sputtered. "No! Avenant, *no*. The kingdom's always been yours. I've only been fighting you for it to... *fight* you for it. It's just part of the game."

"The game's over. I'll pull the sword free and *you* can claim it, Belle."

"You don't mean that."

"I *do*." Avenant was after something far more important and he could only have victory if he was unafraid of losing. Unafraid of being laughed at. Unafraid of emotions. The farther he went beyond the walls, the easier it got to say the words. "I'm sorry I let this get so far. I just wanted to win, so you'd see I wasn't weak."

She squinted at that logic. "That doesn't make any sense."

"I know." It sounded nuts even to him, now that he stopped to think about it. His idiot father had been dead for years and he was still screwing up his life. "Getting a sword might prove that I'm strong, but I don't think it's what you want. You need to see I can be *more* than strong. That I can be *worthy*." He took a deep breath. "So, I'll surrender everything --the Northlands, my pride, this whole fucking contest-- if I can just have *you*."

Belle stepped closer to him, looking dazed. "You'll surrender the game?" She whispered. "I'm really that important to you?"

How could she even ask that? "There's *nothing* I wouldn't surrender for you, Belle. You're the most important part of me. Every thought in my head is about you."

Chocolate eyes glistened with tears. "Really?"

"Really." Avenant touched her cheek. "I am insanely in love with you, you idiot."

A huge grin spread across her face. "You love me?"

"Of course." It shocked him that she needed to hear the words. Three vision-impaired mice could've seen that he was head over heels for this woman. "I don't remember a day of my life when I haven't loved you. You shared your crayons with me in kindergarten and I was a goner."

Belle swallowed. "Okay." She announced and stopped directly in front of him. "You win."

Avenant's brows drew together at the unexpected response to his declaration. "I'm not trying to win. I just told you that."

"Well, I'm declaring you the winner, anyway. Now that I think about it, whichever of us surrendered first was bound to win. Now, you get to hold it over my head forever that you took the leap of faith before I did."

Avenant's heart rate increased. That actually sounded promising.

"Of course, there's one little problem with your romantic plan." She pointed out, ruining the moment. "If I got the sword, wouldn't you be Prince of the Northlands, *anyway?*"

"Only if we were married." He focused on securing total victory. "Speaking of which, I want to get married."

"That's a coincidence." Brown eyes sparkled. "To me or to my new kingdom?"

"The Northlands has nothing to do with this." He groused, even though he knew she wasn't serious. "I just *gave* you the kingdom, didn't I? If that's what I wanted, I would just keep it."

"See? *Already* you're holding it over my head."

He ignored her teasing and pressed onward. "I know you don't love me back. I'm not asking for the impossible. Nobody would ever want a Beast. But, if you'll marry me, I can make you happy. I promise."

"Hang on." Belle stopped smiling. "I wouldn't marry someone I didn't love." She seemed confused by the very idea. She must have seen his disappointment, because she frowned. "What are you talking about, Avenant? Do you honestly not understand how I feel about you? I think I've been telling you since the fourth grade spelling bee."

"But, I can change." He assured her desperately. "You said yourself we could be friends, now. If you would just give me a chance…" Avenant stopped mid-word, the Beast's instincts firing up. "Someone's coming."

Belle's head whipped around to the chamber's entrance. "Great. Perfect timing." She blew out an irritated breath. "Just kill whoever it is, because I want to continue…" She trailed off when Lancelot appeared. "Crap." She muttered, her gaze fixed on the gun. "I didn't expect that asshole to be a villain, either."

Chapter Nineteen

Monkey: I'm not saying that Prince Avenant was the one who bumped him off. Folks were always chasing Weasel, so it coulda been *anybody* who wanted to shut him up. But, that night, Weasel and me were at the Mulberry Bush Saloon and I thought it was all in fun. Then, a couple of bullets came through the front window and *POP!* goes Weasel.

Defense: Objection! Your honor, we've established that Prince Avenant has an alibi for that whole evening. He didn't even know this Weasel person or any of his gangster friends. Why is my client being blamed for *every* crime in the kingdom? Is this a trial or a witch hunt?

Testimony of Mr. Monkey- *The People of the Northlands vs. Prince Avenant*

Eight Months Ago

Life plus a century.

When the wizard had slammed his gavel down and delivered Avenant's sentence, Belle's stomach had dropped to her shoes. She'd never thought it would be so harsh. It wasn't what she wanted, at all.

"Wait!" She'd surged to her feet, disregarding the gaping onlookers. "That isn't right. Avenant isn't really a criminal. Well, technically he *is,* but he shouldn't have to spend the rest of his life in jail for it. He can be rehabilitated. He can be saved."

Avenant had turned to stare at her, his expression unreadable. They had him handcuffed, a magic inhibitor on his ankle so he couldn't use his powers to freeze them all. Not that he'd done that, even when he'd had the chance. When Belle showed up in his castle with her rebels, he could have attacked her. He could have struck her down and won. Instead, he'd slowly held up his hands. Rather than harm her, he'd let her arrest him.

She had no idea why, but she knew it was important.

"Avenant deserves a second chance." Belle had told the judge, even as he ordered her to be quiet. She couldn't stop. She was the one who'd set this into motion and, now that she had her victory, it felt worse than defeat. "Maybe he could do community service or something, instead." She'd suggested desperately. "Avenant could learn to be a better ruler. He just needs some help."

"If we let him out, he'll only come after the kingdom, again." Lancelot had snapped from his seat in the front row. "This is the only way to keep the Northlands safe. We even gave him a trial, which is more than most Bad folk get. He's guilty and he deserves to rot in a cell like any other monster."

Belle had ignored him. "Sending Avenant to prison forever is such a waste. He's so *smart*. So gifted. If he tried, he could be a real prince. I *know* he could."

"He's Bad." Lancelot had proclaimed righteously. "No one Bad could ever lead a kingdom. These lands must be kept safe for the Good people of the Northlands. As their new prince, I will…"

"Rosabella Aria Ashman is in charge of the kingdom, now." The wizard had interrupted. "She was the one who dethroned the Beast. She now takes his crown, under the law."

"I don't want to be ruler." Belle had shaken her head. "Hang on. That's not what this was about. I just wanted to beat him."

Avenant's jaw had ticked.

"What?" Lancelot had been stunned by the

judge's proclamation. "That's impossible! *I'm* the prince, now. Everyone knows that!" The wizard started rattling off legalese to justify his decision, but Avenant's cousin wasn't listening. "*I* am next in line to be prince, not some *woman*. I'll fight this in every court in the land!"

The wizard hadn't cared. He'd made his ruling and nothing they said would sway him. In retrospect, Avenant's family really shouldn't have confiscated the man's summerhouse and turned it into a putting green twenty years before. The judge had swept into his chambers with a self-satisfied swirl of his robes. Lancelot had stomped out of the courtroom in a rage, the musty smell of armor wax wafting after him. Guards had yanked Avenant to his feet, ready to transport him to the Wicked, Ugly and Bad Mental Health Treatment Center and Maximum Security Prison.

...Belle had hightailed it to the ladies room.

She'd been standing there for ten minutes, still trying to work things out in her mind. She braced her hands on the sink and tried to figure out her next move. Avenant was going to jail.

There was suddenly a huge void in the center of her chest. Avenant was the most important person in her life. She hated him, but everything she did was because of that bastard. Belle woke-up in the morning with new ideas to fight him on. She spent her evenings planning vengeance for his evil tricks. She dreamed about him every single night. As mad as she was, the thought of never seeing Avenant again was...

The door to the restroom slammed open and she knew who it was without even looking.

Belle lifted her head and met Avenant's eyes in the mirror. "Don't." She said quietly, suspecting that this was going to get messy. "We have enough problems."

He answered by securing the lock and silently stalking closer to her.

Belle swallowed as Avenant came up behind her, his gaze on hers. "You should escape." She told him. "I won't try to stop you." He must have already gotten away from his guards if he was in here with her. The handcuffs were gone, too. There was time for him to slip away. "Or maybe I could get you a pardon."

He had a better idea. Avenant grasped her arm and turned her around to face him. His body crowded hers against the counter, pressing her legs apart with his knee.

She stared up at him, breathing hard. But, it wasn't from fear. "They're going to find you in about five minutes. This is insane, even for you. You're about to be taken off to jail. Get out while you can."

He ignored that and knelt down before her.

Belle's eyes widened as he pushed up the hem of her practical suit. "What are you doing?" She blurted out, even though it seemed obvious when he yanked off her underwear. She became so wet, so fast there was no way he didn't notice.

"I'm having my last meal." His voice was an erotic rasp.

"You can't." Frantic, she glanced towards the door and said the first thing that came to mind. "We're in a public building." There were a thousand *other* reasons why this was a Bad plan, but it was hard to concentrate on specifics when new sensations were bombarding her. The heat of his breath against her core had her heart racing. "Avenant, you can't do this." She automatically tried to close her legs, but his head was in the way.

Avenant kept going, tugging her skirt to her waist and baring her to his gaze. At prom, he'd been so tender.

Now, he was just determined. "You're not locking me in a cell before I taste you. No way in hell."

Belle struggled to think. Everything was going too fast. "People are out there!"

"Call them in to help you, then. Tell them to save you from the Beast." His lips slid higher and Belle stopped trying to shove him away. Instead, she felt her thighs instinctively shift forward to give him a better angle. "Beautiful." Avenant leaned in to kiss her inner thigh. "It's not fair that you're always so fucking beautiful."

Belle bit back a whimper. "You should be smart and use this opportunity to go out the window or something instead of... *Oh*." His mouth sealed over her and Belle arched in desire. "Oh, *God*."

He growled against her and it just increased her rapture. Ever since prom she'd been fantasizing about him touching her again and this was better than she could've dreamed. His tongue was doing things Belle hadn't even read about in books. Her hand clenched in his hair, holding on for dear life. In an instant, she was on the verge of the biggest orgasm of her life.

"Please." Belle's hips undulated against the relentless suction of his lips. She was going to come right there in the courthouse bathroom. Come for a man who she almost completely detested, and who'd sent men to terrorize her, and was probably only doing this for revenge. She was going to come against his mouth in a matter of seconds, like her body had been starving for him. All of that should have been enough to make her stop, but she couldn't. It was the most incredible...

"Ms. Ashman?" One of the knights standing guard pounded on the door. "Are you alright in there?"

Belle froze.

Avenant lifted his gleaming gaze to hers. He

242

knew he had her and he was going to take full advantage of it. She could see satisfaction all over his smug face. His teeth grazed her ultrasensitive flesh and she jolted, trying not to cry out.

He smirked, kissing her deeper.

"I hate you." She hissed, even as she rocked against him. Jesus, what was she going to do? He wasn't going to stop and she *couldn't*. Her body was poised right on the brink. She was going to come for the Beast of the Northlands. It was inevitable.

"Ms. Ashman?"

"Y-y-yes?" She bit down on her lower lip and hoped her voice didn't sound as shaky as it seemed. Avenant licked her core and Belle's head went back, banging against the mirror. The overwhelming tightness gave way to small tingles and she knew she was about to...

Avenant eased back, because he was a sadist.

"You son of a *bitch*." She panted.

Avenant ignored that and started the whole process over.

"What did you say, ma'am?"

The guard was going to hear everything if this went on much longer. Belle squeezed her eyes shut, her system screaming for release. "Please." She whispered again, unsure if she was begging for Avenant to stop or to go on.

Avenant answered by spreading her legs wider and claiming even more territory. Belle let him. He could have anything, if only he gave her the climax that was looming. It shimmered in front of her eyes and she whimpered at how close it was.

The guard tried knocking, again. "Prince Avenant has escaped, ma'am. We're conducting a search."

"Ummm...." She couldn't even process the man's words. The tremors were beginning, again. Her body bowed in anticipation, her breath coming in pants.

"Ma'am, are you okay in there?"

"Just... give me a minute." Belle somehow managed to call. "Please." She whispered to Avenant. "If he gets in here, he'll see us."

"I don't care." His voice was deeper than usual, his eyes an electric-blue. Avenant kept driving her higher and she forgot about protesting.

Belle twisted in his grasp, trying to find relief. Everyone in the kingdom could've walked through the door and she would've been helpless to push him away. Not when she was right on the brink of something *amazing*.

"Unlock the door, ma'am!" The guard started trying to knock down the door. "You could be in danger."

"*I said give me a minute, goddamn it!*"

Avenant smiled. He loved it when she was bitchy. His fingers tightened on her hips, dragging her closer. His mouth ravished her harder and faster and Belle started begging.

"Please." She gasped, close to sobbing. "Please. Now. I need you, *now*."

His expression softened for a flicker of time. "Not as much as I need you, my love." Avenant found the tight knot of her desire and she lost the capacity to speak. He gently bit down and Belle exploded.

She dimly processed his large palm coming up to cover her mouth as her body went into total meltdown. Her shouts were captured against his fingers and her body opened up to him completely. Tremors shook her as Avenant drained every drop of pleasure from her, leaving her replete. When it was over, she sagged against the counter, still gripping his hair as he lapped the moisture from her skin.

For a timeless moment, it was all just... right.

"Why, Bella. I think maybe I was wrong about you. I think you might be a *Bad* little girl." Avenant said smugly and then he was standing up. Blue eyes met hers. "Next time, I'll be inside of you." His hand brushed against her swollen flesh. "I'm done being patient. Next time, I'll take *everything* that's mine."

The man was insufferable. He'd done this just to prove he could. Just to humiliate her. "There won't be a next time, because you're going to jail, idiot."

"You really think you'll ever get rid of me?" He loomed over her. "You think this plan of yours will work?" His thumb did something and another aftershock of desire rippled through her. "I dare you to keep me in that prison for long."

Belle's eyes narrowed at him, all thoughts of maybe giving him a pardon vanishing. "Let me go." She snarled.

Avenant's fingers obediently slipped from Belle's slick depths and he readjusted her skirt. "Beautiful." He popped his thumb into his mouth, sucking the taste of her off his skin. "Christ, I knew you'd be beautiful."

"Are you done?" She crossed her arms over her chest, refusing to be embarrassed.

"I'm just getting started. You're trying to lock me away for life plus a century and steal my kingdom. This game of ours just became winner-takes-all, Bella. And *I'm* going to be the winner."

Belle kept her eyes on his. "I found Prince Avenant." She raised her voice so the guard could hear her. "You can come and arrest him, again. He's served his purpose in here."

The door was finally smashed in and a dwarf SWAT team dragged Avenant away. He turned to watch Belle over his shoulder as they led him down the hall. He might've been the one in handcuffs, but she wasn't crazy enough to think the guards were in control. The Beast of the Northlands wouldn't be contained for long. Not by anyone.

"Are you okay, Belle?" Peter Piper came up beside her. "Did he hurt you?"

Peter had slimmed down over the years, but he still favored florid purple clothing. Belle suspected he liked the color because it contrasted with his otherwise bland existence. He'd put his childhood math skills to use and become an accountant, which seemed to be the entirety of his existence. Despite the fact that Avenant had blackballed him from all the best banking firms, Peter lived and breathed columns of computerized numbers. They were his world. In fact, he'd been the one who discovered the slush funds that Avenant set-up to hide the stolen money.

"I'm alright." Belle glanced at him and tried to ignore the strong smell of pickled peppers that emanated from his pours. Throughout this entire ordeal, Peter had been a supportive friend. She'd *nearly* forgiven him for the whole Jill fiasco. "Avenant wouldn't harm me."

"He sent men to attack you in your bed!" Peter put a commiserating hand on her shoulder. "You're lucky you weren't raped and murdered while you slept."

"I'm pretty sure I would've woken up for that." Belle kept her attention on Avenant as he was herded into the elevator at the end of the corridor.

His blue eyes stayed locked on hers, his jaw tightening as he watched Peter pat her arm.

For no reason at all, Belle shifted out from under

Peter's palm. It wasn't because Avenant was glaring at her. She wouldn't accept that. But she also didn't like the other man touching her, even in an innocent way. It didn't feel right. No one but Avenant ever felt right, damn it.

Avenant's mouth curved as if he could read her mind. "Good-bye, Bella." He paused meaningfully. "For now."

"For*ever*." She corrected in frustration.

"We'll see about that."

"Give it up." Peter scowled at Avenant from a safe distance. "Belle is finally free of you." Avenant didn't even look his way, so Peter tried again. "You're *never* coming back to the Northlands."

Avenant stayed focused on Belle, not even noticing the other man existed. "Think of me while I'm gone, my love." Avenant winked at her as the elevator doors slid shut. "I'll certainly be thinking of you."

It wasn't a particularly reassuring promise.

"You bastard, you're *never coming back!*" Peter bellowed as if Avenant could still hear him. Belle had never seen him so agitated. "After all you've done to ruin my life, I've finally made sure you've lost *everything!*"

Belle barely processed his ranting. Peter was wrong if he thought Avenant was beaten. The judges and the guards could try to keep him in a cage, but it wouldn't work. Avenant would be out of that prison within the year. Belle suddenly knew it. He'd somehow get free and come back for her. There wasn't a doubt in her mind.

The Beast would never quit.

Which was appalling news and she should report her suspicions to the police, so they could double the width of the bars on his windows. Except for one little problem. As mad as she was at him... As much as he deserved to be arrested... As terrible as it would be when he came back for revenge... Belle *still* found herself smiling in anticipation at the idea that she'd see him again, soon.

Crap.

She was completely in love with that jerk.

Chapter Twenty

That beast could *never* be a knight.

Testimony of Sir Lancelot- *The People of the Northlands v. Prince Avenant*

Peter Piper stood in the entrance to the cavern, a purple cloak around his shoulders and Lancelot held in front of him like a shield. "One move to freeze me with your powers, Beast, and I'll shoot your cousin." He warned jabbing the revolver into Lancelot's neck. "I mean it."

Avenant actually chuckled at that threat. "Granted, there aren't a lot of hostages I would give a shit about, but you've managed to pick the guy who ranks dead last on the 'Don't Care' list, Pete."

"You must help me, cousin!" Lancelot's words came out in a desperate jumble. "He found me up in the hedge maze. He dragged me down here. He has a magical mirror that..."

"Shut-up." Peter's wild expression focused on Avenant. "All you need to know is that I've killed everyone else who got in my way of finding the sword and I'll kill you, too. I *want* to kill you. But not before you watch me steal *everything* from you, the way you stole *everything* from me."

"Big words for a Merit Scholar." Avenant glanced over at Belle and arched a brow. "I'm guessing that smell on the bridge was pickled peppers, my love. I can't believe you went to prom with this reeking ass."

"That was *your* fault for not asking me yourself."

Belle whispered back at him, her gaze staying on Peter. As shocked as she was to see him, things were making a terrible sort of sense. "You've hated Avenant since twelfth grade." She shook her head, anger burning through her fear and surprise. "You're the one who set him up for the embezzlement, aren't you? You doctored the accounts, so he'd go to prison."

"He deserved everything I did to him and more!"

"You son of a *bitch*." Belle's temper flashed, furious that Avenant had been hurt and that she'd been tricked into helping it happen. She shoved her way forward, stabbing a finger at Peter. "*You're* the one who should've been locked-up. Avenant was completely innocent and you had him thrown in a cage!"

Avenant looked down at her, his mouth curving at one corner. "Did you just call me *completely innocent?*" He asked in delight. "God, I adore you."

"Can you concentrate, please?" She demanded. The man couldn't have looked less interested in the lunatic holding them at gunpoint. "Do you not understand what he's done? That he's threatening you, right now?"

"I have faith that my True Love will protect me."

Peter glowered at her. "So what if Avenant didn't really steal from the kingdom, Belle?" He waved a dismissive hand. "He's done plenty of other stuff. Especially to *me*."

"I barely even know who you are." Avenant scoffed.

"I *still* don't know who he is." Lancelot's eyes were huge and terrified.

Avenant's gaze flicked over to him. "That's the guy I'm going to kill for attacking Bella in her bed." He said mildly.

Belle gasped. She hadn't even considered that part, yet. "Jesus!" She shouted at Peter. "You're the one who framed Avenant for that, *too?* I'm going to *help* him kill you, you bastard."

"Also, he *attacked you in your bed.*" Avenant stressed.

"I would never hurt Belle." Peter sounded insulted. "Once I claim the Northlands, I'm going to make her my princess. I just hired those guys to scare her and teach her a lesson. I was trying to make her realize that you're evil."

Belle saw red. *"Except he didn't do anything!"*

"He fucking ruined my life!" Peter roared. "Avenant blocked me from accounting jobs. He made me a laughingstock in school. He paid off the judges at the Mathlete Olympics to make sure our squad didn't win the junior championships."

Belle sent Avenant a quick frown. "I *knew* you were behind that." She muttered.

He shrugged with no remorse. "Technically, I blackmailed them."

"The Beast drew a target on my back, because he sensed that you and I have a connection, Belle." Peter continued persuasively. "He couldn't stand the idea that you might want me more than him, so he set out to destroy me and ruin my chances with you."

"Well, you certainly *helped* to ruin them, when you ended our one and only date by making out with another girl." She retorted.

"Avenant paid Jill to come on to me! I was the victim."

She rolled her eyes. "He tied you up and forced you to kiss her when I went for punch?" She shook her head. "I don't think so. He might have been a jackass, but *you* were the one who swallowed his bait."

Avenant smirked, loving the fact that she was sticking up for him.

"You zip it." She ordered, even though he hadn't said anything.

His elegant palms went up in a gesture of innocence.

"Cousin, I'm begging you, stop this random commoner from assassinating me." Lancelot implored.

Everyone ignored him.

Peter wasn't willing to give up his campaign to win her over. "I'm telling you, it was *his* fault, Belle! It's *always* him. Can't you tell that he's *Bad*."

Avenant snorted. "You haven't *seen* Bad. You've been trying to steal my True Love for twenty years, you little twerp. You're lucky you still have full use of your limbs."

"You don't frighten me." Peter hissed at him. "The only things you care about are Belle and the Icen Throne. I've always known that. And I'm about to take them *both* from you."

"How?" Avenant arched a brow. "By shooting that imbecile Lancelot? Go ahead. I can't stand him."

"Hey!" Lancelot yelped.

Belle sighed. The knight might be annoying, but he didn't deserve to get slaughtered. "Avenant..." She let the word trail off meaningfully.

"Come on, Belle." Avenant urged. "This is win/win. Let Peter kill the moron and then I'll kill *him* and we'll all be happy."

"Lancelot's your cousin."

"But, he's such a *moron*."

Belle frowned in his direction.

"*Fine*." Avenant muttered. "We'll save the

moron from this terrible hostage situation." He rolled his eyes with world-weary confidence in his own abilities. "But, you have to admit that this is a *really* stupid plan, even for Pete. I'm going to just freeze him and go home."

Belle sort of agreed. How did Peter think he was going to stop the Beast of the Northlands? They had to be missing something.

"You don't even *understand* my plan, Beast." Peter shoved Lancelot forward, edging towards Excalibur. "But, you're about to. You're about to see which of us is truly worthy of the prize."

Avenant crossed his arms over his chest. "Tell me when I'm allowed to kill him, my love."

Belle ignored that. "Peter, I really wouldn't touch that sword if I were you." She warned. Adam hadn't gone to all this trouble without having some extra tricks up his sleeve. "I don't think you should..."

Peter touched the sword. He grabbed the hilt and tried to pull it free. Excalibur didn't move. Instead, he jerked back with a scream of pain and the smell of smoldering flesh. Belle cringed, seeing that the raised snowflake design was now scorched into the skin of his palm.

"You have to have royal blood." Lancelot said. "I told you that. The sword will burn anyone else."

Avenant's superior sneer dimmed a bit. His blue eyes flicked to Lancelot, looking vaguely concerned for the first time. Now, the only other person who could claim Excalibur was standing two feet from it. "You know about that royal blood thing?"

Belle flashed Avenant a sideways look. "I *told* you this was a risky idea. You never listen to me. If I wasn't here to keep you out of trouble, you'd be dead fifty times over."

"He's not supposed to know about Excalibur, Bella. It's supposed to be a family secret."

"I *am* family." Lancelot whined. "My dad used to tell me stories about the sword. He always said one day it would give us a chance to claim the Icen Throne. But I don't even *want* the kingdom anymore. I'm going to get Excalibur and give it to this guy and then he promises not to make me look in that mirror, again." He tried to crane his neck to look at Peter. "Right, Mr. Kidnapper?"

"Of course." Peter's voice oozed insincerity.

Lancelot gave a relieved smile.

Avenant made a face. "You suck at being a knight, you know that?"

Belle's eyes narrowed at Peter. Something was off about this. Lancelot had always been a dim-bulb, but he'd never been this much of a simpering coward. Peter had done something to him. "What mirror is he talking about?"

"*My* mirror." Peter pulled out a silver looking glass, still keeping the gun on Lancelot. Maybe he was too crazy to feel pain, because he kept monologuing despite the blistering wound on his hand. "I bought this from a witch. It cost me sixty magic beans, four bags of gold, and nine of the children I don't have yet, but it was worth it."

"Uh-huh." Belle said warily. It looked like the kind of ordinary accessory a woman would keep on her vanity, except its shiny surface glowed with magic. Things that glowed with magic rarely belonged in the hands of maniacs. "What does it do?"

"It shows people their inner selves, of course." Peter's eyes sparkled. "Lancelot looked into it and saw that deep down he's nothing but a spineless little follower."

"I am." Lancelot sobbed. "I'm so sorry, cousin."

Avenant sighed in annoyance.

Peter laughed. "You see?" He cried. "Do you think *I* could've defeated Pumpkin-Eater or Cleo? He was a cannibal and she was a mercenary, for crying out loud. Even that gremlin was too much for me, on my own. I'm just an accountant. No." He shook his head. "I simply showed them this mirror. When they saw their true reflections, it drove them mad. *That's* what killed them."

"You made them stab themselves?" Belle gasped.

"*I* didn't make them do anything." Peter gestured to the mirror. "It's *this*. Scarlett Wolf is right with all her preaching. No one's a hundred percent Good. Certainly, not the people in this contest. When I showed them they're Bad, they try to cut the darkness out, but it's impossible. It was a part of them. Just like it is for the Beast." He suddenly pushed Lancelot out of the way and held up the mirror to Avenant's beautiful face. "And now you'll see it, too!"

"*No!*" Belle screamed.

Inside the silver surface lurked a monster of frost and snow. Of pain and screaming and terror. Every cold nightmare imaginable lurked in its electric-blue eyes. Whatever lived inside of Avenant snapped free of its chains and transformed his patrician features into an icy mask.

The Beast was coming out.

Avenant stumbled back from his reflection in horror. "Belle, get away from me." He choked out, his whole body shaking. "I can't stop it. I'm going to..." He trailed off with an agonized groan, his expression stark.

He was changing right in front of her. His skin became cracked and frozen, his voice growing too dark and his body growing too big. She could see the edges of him straining at the seams and she knew he was fighting the Beast.

Only he couldn't.

Lancelot gave a high-pitched scream and collapsed. His helmet clanged against the ground, his big body splayed out in dead faint.

Peter chortled in triumph as Avenant's splintering form hit the wall. "This is even better than I imagined. He's physically changing! That thing is going to rip him apart from the inside!"

Belle knew he was right. Avenant's hands were clawing at his head, like he was trying to peel through the hardening ice. He was going to tear himself to pieces trying to hold the Beast back. Avenant wouldn't survive this... Not unless he stopped fighting it.

She ran for him. "Avenant, stop!"

He didn't hear her. Maybe he couldn't. The Beast was desperate to escape, its gaze darting around wildly. It couldn't focus on anything except its own panic and fury.

"*Avenant!*" She screamed.

"He's gone." Peter chortled. "Gone, gone, gone. Give it up, Belle. You're finally free of him. We all are."

She spared him a furious look. "I will kill you if anything happens to him!"

"You'll forget about the Beast soon enough." Peter promised. He dragged Lancelot closer to Excalibur, folding the knight's limp hand around the sword's hilt and trying to pull it free. "Once you and I are married, you'll see that this was all for the best."

He didn't even matter enough to punch. Not when Avenant needed her.

Belle edged closer to her True Love, afraid he might bolt from the room. The Beast gave a roar of warning as she drew near, fangs flashing. Belle ignored it. This man wasn't a threat to her, no matter what form he was in. "Avenant, look at me." She ordered. "*Look at me!* You and the Beast are the same person. He isn't Bad and neither are you. Accept him or this will break you both."

He didn't seem to hear her. His arctic exterior was fracturing right before her eyes. She could see the fissures and feel the blast of cold coming off of him. Avenant was going to kill himself if he didn't stop. The Beast was already free and he'd die before he was caged again.

No.

Belle's jaw firmed in determination. She would *not* lose this fight. "Avenant, I love you." She said simply.

The Beast started to roar out in savage ferocity, but her words had him hesitating.

Electric-blue eyes suddenly burned into hers.

Belle kept going. "I've been in love with you since the first day of kindergarten, too. You pilfered my brand new box of thirty-six crayons and you said '*I'm* the prince and *I* want these.' Then, I pushed you off your chair and you started crying."

The Beast tilted his head, studying her face with something like recognition. He remembered that day. Of course he did. He was Avenant.

"So, I told you we could share the crayons to get you to stop bawling." Belle continued. "And you ignored me all day. But, right before we went home, you drew a picture of a yellow rose and you shoved it at me as you ran out the door. And I knew right then you were going to be the most important person in my life." She gave him a small smile. "I looked at you and I just... knew."

He stared at her, hypnotized.

"I still have the drawing. I'll show it to you when we get home, if you just stay with me." She coaxed. "Stop fighting yourself and fight for *me*. Fight for our future." She waved a hand at Peter. "Are you really going to let that fucking idiot beat us?"

"I've already won." Peter insisted. "I have Excalibur, so I own the Northlands and you have to do what I say. I'm your prince and you're my princess and..." He tugged at the sword, but it didn't budge. "Goddamn it." He repositioned Lancelot's fingers and tried again. "What's wrong with this thing? This guy has royal blood, so it should be coming out."

"You didn't read the directions, you prick." Belle snapped, not even looking his way.

Peter's gaze cut over to her. "You *did* something, didn't you?" He accused wrathfully. "You did something so it wouldn't come free."

"Lancelot doesn't have what it takes to claim that sword and neither do you." She said smugly. "You will *never* steal our kingdom."

The Beast gave a low growl of pleasure at her words. Avenant always loved it when she was a bitch.

Peter didn't share that sentiment. "What have you done?" He futilely yanked on the hilt. "Tell me why this isn't working. It's supposed to *work!*"

Belle ignored him, all her focus trained on her True Love. Avenant was trying to regain control, but he was still battling with his two halves. It wasn't going to work unless he let go. "Don't try to chain the Beast, again." She ordered. "You can't shove him away, this time. Let him be free and find a balance between the two of... *shit!*" Her words ended with a cry of alarm as Peter grabbed her from behind.

"How do I get the sword out?!" He spun Belle

around and shook her hard enough to rattle her teeth. "Tell me!"

That was probably the stupidest thing he could've done.

Avenant and the Beast stopped struggling against each other and turned their attention to Peter. Belle barely saw him move, but suddenly she was free of Peter and her True Love had launched himself at the smaller man. The two combatants hit the opposite side of the cavern in an explosion of violence and screaming and fangs.

She cringed at the frenzy and headed forward. "Avenant, wait! Don't..."

The gunshots cut her off mid-word. Peter still had the revolver. He tried to shoot Avenant and missed, the bullets ricocheting off the rock walls as he desperately fired. The Beast wasn't impressed with his efforts. Bones cracked as he crushed Peter's wounded hand. Peter screeched in pain. The mirror fell, landing glass side up at their feet. He forced Peter's head down so he was looking right into it.

Peter's own reflection shined back at him.

He let out a bellow of pure terror at what he saw. No one who'd killed so many people wanted to peer inside themselves. The darkness began to consume him and Peter flailed backward in an uncoordinated scrambled. "No! No! *NOOOO!*"

The Beast let him go, satisfied that he'd won.

Peter was out of his mind with fear and panic. He blindly ran for the cavern's entrance, fumbling with the gun. "Don't make me see it! Don't let me see it! I don't want to see...!"

They all knew what was going to happen.

Belle flinched at the final gunshot. The mirror

had killed him, just as it had the others. But, it wouldn't take her husband.

"Avenant." She hurried to his side. He was still struggling, clawing at his skull, again. Both sides of him needed to calm down or he wasn't going to make it. There was only one way she could think of to break through to him *fast*. Belle unzipped her jacket and yanked open her shirt. "Focus on something else." She unclasped the front of her bra. "Focus on *me*."

The Beast started to jerk away from her... then his glowing blue eyes flickered to her breasts.

He blinked.

"I thought that would get your attention." Belle seized his wrist and brought it up to cover one of the soft globes. The frigid temperature of his skin had her nipple beading into an erotic point. She jolted, but kept talking. "You know me, don't you? Who am I?"

The Beast couldn't look away from her. His free hand came up to cover her other breast, his grip tightening. "Mine." It was an animalistic rasp.

He squeezed her flesh and she swallowed down a whimper of pleasure. Obviously, he wasn't as disappointed in her cup-size as she'd feared. "I'm yours." She agreed, pushing her small curves deeper into his palms. "I belong to both of you. To *all* of you. And you belong to me."

"Yours." He rumbled. She sensed the tension draining from him as he caressed her skin.

"Who am I, Avenant?" She asked again.

Awareness began to return. "Bella." He murmured in something like reverence.

She smiled, trying not to cry. "That's right." The Beast and Avenant were both looking at her, now. Just as she'd thought, they could be one in the same. They *were* one in the same. They just had to find a balance. "Please stop fighting yourself. I'm scared and I need you."

"Don't want to hurt you."

"The Beast is just another part of you, Avenant." She wrapped her arms around him. "You would never hurt me. But, if you destroy him, you destroy yourself. And if you destroy yourself, *that's* what will hurt me. You need to find a balance. For me. Please."

He swallowed, his forehead coming to rest on her shoulder. She could feel him shaking. "I'm sorry I'm Bad." He whispered.

She held him tight. "You *aren't*. At least, no more than anyone else is. If you were Bad all the way through, you wouldn't be able to hang on like this. You'd be like Peter or Cleo or Mr. Pumpkin-Eater and shatter into nothing. But, your Good side is stronger than the darkness."

"My Good side is you." His voice was beginning to sound normal again. "Everything I am is you." His grip on her got stronger. "I love you so much there aren't words."

"You'll just have to spend the rest of forever-after showing me, then."

Time passed and his skin grew warmer.

"Have I mentioned I hate mirrors?" Avenant finally muttered.

Belle pulled back to look at his face and smiled when she saw his normal features cautiously staring back her. "Good news. You're handsome, again."

"I'm a monster." Avenant sounded broken. "It's still inside of me, only now it's not caged. It's part of me."

"Luckily, I love all the parts of you."

He shook his head, looking morose. "Nobody would ever want a Beast."

"I do, dummy."

Avenant hadn't been expecting that easy response. "You... do?"

"Yep." She leaned forward to kiss him, feeling overwhelming happiness. "I think the Beast is probably the easiest facet of your personality to deal with, actually. I had him wrapped around my little finger in no time. Handsome-you took a lot longer to tame."

Avenant frowned. "You're insane." He told her, but his mouth was beginning to curve upward at one corner.

"Don't be jealous. I love you both."

He still didn't look convinced. "Why?"

"Because," she reached up to touch his face, "all the bits of me that are missing, *you* have. We fit together. Without you, I'm incomplete. You have to feel that way, too, right?"

"I do, but..."

"You're my best friend."

"And you're mine, except..."

"And we're True Loves, aren't we?"

"Yes! Only..."

She cut him off. "What's with all the qualifiers? You already said you'd marry me, Avenant. Are you trying to back out of that or something? Because, I should warn you, I know where to get a sword."

"No, of course I'm not backing out. I just want you to be sure."

"Good, because I want a big wedding as soon as possible. With a dress, and rings, and a cake..."

Avenant surrendered. "*Chocolate* cake." He said softly, his eyes tracing over her face.

"Chocolate cake." Belle agreed and gave him a quick kiss.

He swallowed. "I have longed for you my whole life. There is nothing in this world or any other that I want more than to be with you, Belle. But, are you sure you want to tie yourself to a Beast?"

She arched a brow. "Are you trying to be selfless? That's such a knight-in-shining-armor-y thing to do."

"Don't be too impressed. If you actually took me up on my offer and tried to forget about me, I'd just do something crazy to get your attention, again."

"I don't doubt it." She zipped up her coat. "I mean, that's probably why watching you turn into a Beast didn't bother me. I've seen you do *way* worse things."

"Like what?"

"You redrew the royal processional route so it went straight through my front yard. Every day. At six am."

He winced. "I forgot about that one."

"Really? It sure sticks out in my memory. Especially the trumpeters."

"Well, you know, you've done some underhanded stuff, too." He retorted. "When the palace released my authorized biography, you put it in the comedic fiction section of your bookstore."

"Oh, that's where it belonged and you know it."

"Then you had clowns come and do readings of the chapters in funny voices."

Belle tried not to laugh at that memory, but it was hard. The book had been nothing but a pack of poorly ghostwritten lies, but the clown readings proved very popular. "The part where you invented pancakes was just hilarious after we added the balloon animals." She gave a muffled snort when he glared at her. "Sorry."

"I *did* invent pancakes."

"If you say so, honey." Belle patted his arm.

"Come on. Let's go claim our kingdom." She headed for Excalibur, stepping over Lancelot's splayed body. "Hey, do you think your cousin will be okay?"

"He's fine." Avenant crushed the silver mirror with his shoe, careful not to look at it again. The blue glow of magic winked out, its power fading. "Hell, I don't even think enspelled-Lancelot was so different than normal whiny him, anyway." He moved to stand next to her, studying the sword. "So, are you ready to tell me why Peter couldn't pull this thing free, even though Lancelot has royal blood?"

Belle shrugged. "There may or may not have been a final page to Adam's journal." She explained. "It may or may not have mentioned that royal blood alone wasn't enough. I may or may not have memorized it and then ripped it out, so no one else could win."

"And you're just now telling me this?"

"Is it my fault no one in your family reads?"

"God, I love it when you're a bitch."

Belle glanced up at him and grinned. "Thank you for saying I could claim Excalibur, by the way. Before I understood the last passage, I thought *I* was going to be the one to get the sword and give it to you." She shook her head. "You totally would've beat me to it, though. I was standing there, trying to figure out what to do next, and you just *leapt*. As soon as you surrendered, I knew I'd lost the real game."

"Neither of us loses, so long as one of us wins." He assured her piously.

"Remember that next time I crush you at Scrabble."

He gave her a slight smile. "You were really going to give me the sword?"

"Sure. After I made you suffer." She shrugged.

"Turns out I'm madly in love with you, but I still like tormenting you a lot. As it is, though, I think we should rule together, don't you? I think it was always supposed to be that way." She paused. "Also, I'd throw you in jail again if you ever tried to get rid of me."

"You really have ruined me for every other woman in the world, my love."

"I know." She waved a hand at Excalibur. "Okay, let's do this. Put your hand on it."

Avenant did, automatically giving the hilt a yank. The blade stayed locked in the stone. He frowned. "Are you sure…?"

Belle laid her hand over his. "We have to do it together." She explained. "That's the clue on the final page of the journal. It took me awhile to figure out, but now I get it. I think Adam was trying to say that being a true ruler means caring about other people and needing them and trusting them. No one can do it alone." She tugged upward at the same time Avenant did and the sword slid free, resting in both their hands.

Avenant let out a long breath, staring down at it in amazement. "You did it, Bella."

"*We* did it."

"We did it." He agreed and bent down to kiss her. "What did Adam's last entry say?"

She shrugged. "What else? 'True Love conquers all.'"

Chapter Twenty-One

To be honest, I think Prince Avenant could be an okay guy, if he gave people a chance, ya know? If he made some friends. Maybe took himself a wife and had some kids.
It's no good to always be a cheese standing alone.

Testimony of Mr. Farmer in the Dell- - *The People of the Northlands vs. Prince Avenant*

One Year Later

When Avenant's son was born, the kingdom rejoiced.

Eventually.

Prince Adam was a beast, just like his father. His tantrums created snowstorms in his nursery, his tiny body transforming into an ice-creature when he was unhappy. It freaked out more than a few nannies, doctors and passersby.

But, once everyone got used to the electric-blue glow of his eyes and the occasional frozen skin during diaper changes and an unscheduled blizzard here and there, they began to notice the new prince was *adorable*. He was always smiling and he liked to hear stories and songs. He was curious and sweet and way too smart for his own good. Most of all, Adam wasn't locked away or feared by his parents. He was loved.

The Northlands soon realized that a monster who was treated with love, wasn't really a monster, at all.

Everywhere he went, the baby beast was the

most popular person in the room. And not *just* because he was usually the cutest. Adam spent his mornings sitting on Avenant's lap on the Icen Throne, while his father dealt with bureaucratic concerns. Belle would grab him up in the afternoon, carting Adam from meeting to meeting, while she oversaw the Northlands' social programs.

The kingdom had never been so prosperous. Individually as rulers, Belle may have been too soft and Avenant may have been too hard, but, working together, they were just right. With *both* of them in charge, forcing each other to compromise, thing seemed to find a natural balance. The citizens were deliriously happy and most of their gratitude was aimed at Adam, who was the new symbol of True Love conquering all.

The baby thought it was all his due.

So did his father.

"You're spoiling him rotten." Belle warned. She sat up in bed, watching in amusement as Avenant adjusted Adam's fuzzy snowman pajamas.

"His Auntie Letty's the one who bought him this outfit, not me." Avenant held his son to the mirror and smiled. He no longer hated seeing his own reflection, possibly because Adam's features were identical to his own. "He looks great in it, doesn't he?"

Adam grinned in toothless agreement.

"He looks great in everything," Belle conceded, "but that's not what I mean. You got him *another* horse today. He can't even sit up yet, let alone ride."

"He will, though. And in the meantime, he likes petting them."

"That doesn't mean he needs every horse in the kingdom."

Cradling Adam against his chest, Avenant headed

over to the bed. Above the headboard were Excalibur and a framed crayon drawing of a yellow rose. "Alright, alright. No more horses. For a while, anyway." He laid down next to Belle, tugging her closer with one arm and holding Adam with the other. "I just want our son to know he's important." He explained. "I want *you* to know it, too." He kissed the top of her head. "I love you both more than anything in the world."

"We *do* know it." She leaned against his shoulder and smiled in contentment. "You show us every day. I've never seen anyone work harder to be open with his feelings. But, there's only so much room in the stable. Why don't you buy Adam more books, instead?"

"Because, we already ran out of room in the library, my love."

Belle shot him a mock frown. "You can *never* have too many books, though." She studied his face for a moment. "Is something wrong? You look kind of troubled tonight."

Avenant sighed. "Our search parties finished combing the last of the labyrinth and there's still no sign of Esmeralda or Bluebeard." He admitted. "I'm more convinced than ever that they fell through some rabbit holes." No one cared about Bluebeard, but Esmeralda was a different story. All her friends were looking for her. "She could be anywhere." Avenant continued. "And time doesn't always pass the same way in those things, so she could be any *when*, too. It's going to be next to impossible to find her."

"Nothing's impossible." Belle refused to give up. The Cheshire cat seers in the Enchanted Forrest said that Ez was still alive, so everyone would keep searching for her. "We'll send men into the rabbit holes to look, next."

Avenant snorted. "Let's put Lancelot in charge of

searching vortexes, then. He's gung-ho to be useful and anything that sucks that asshole into a realm far, far away is fine with me."

She refused to be amused by his snarking. "I think it's nice that he wants to be friends with you." Ever since Avenant had saved him from Peter, Lancelot had been working hard to gain his cousin's approval. And to live down the weeklong period when he'd been a crying mess, waiting for the mirror's magic to leave his system. "He's not *so* terrible... for a chauvinistic, egotistical idiot. At least he's accepting you as the rightful prince, now"

"I'd still be happier with him in another dimension." Avenant decided. "And with Esmeralda back home."

Belle chewed her lower lip. "You know, maybe Ez will figure out a way to contact us. Or maybe she'll get back on her own. She has magic, so she's pretty resourceful."

"She's also insane. And a lot of people don't like witches."

"A lot of people don't like beasts, either. You won them over. I'm sure Esmeralda can, too. You were twice as unlikable as she is."

He snorted. "I love it when you're a bitch."

"You say the sweetest things." Belle reached over to tickle Adam's jaw. "Your daddy used to scare everybody, you know. They would run when they saw him coming. But, mommy tamed him and now he's just a big old marshmallow. People wave to him on the streets and he doesn't even have them deported for it."

"That only happened once. Most people are still satisfactorily intimidated by me."

"Daddy's deluding himself, isn't he?" Belle kept her attention on Adam. "No one even tries to depose him anymore. And I hear he's going to let Mother Goose have her TV show back." She made a "tsk" sound. "It's almost sad how Good he's becoming."

"Annoying or not, my princess insists those rhyming games of Mother Goose's are educational." Avenant muttered. "Even though they *clearly* don't rhyme and they don't have the right number of syllables and they're stupid."

"The point is to encourage children to think about interesting words."

"*Mother Goose's Story Time Fun Show* makes me think of *a lot* of interesting words." Avenant rolled his eyes. "But, from now on the children of the Northlands will get to suffer through that feathered harridan's irritating whimsy every weekday morning at ten." He arched a brow at her. "I hope you're happy."

"I am."

He considered that. "*How* happy?"

"Very happy." She purred. "I like being married to a nice guy."

Avenant nuzzled her hair. "Oh, I can be *extremely* nice. Believe me." He murmured. "Let's put the baby to bed and I'll show you."

She liked the sound of that. "Can we make it a game?" She never got tired of playing with this man.

"Which game?"

Belle fluttered her eyelashes.

"Again? You always want to play with the Beast. Why can't we ever pretend I'm a knight in shining armor?"

"Because I prefer a beast in shining armor, of course." She leaned closer to his ear and knew it would take less than two seconds to talk him into the fun. Avenant might grumble a little, but he liked letting the

Beast loose to ravage her. He'd finally begun to see the monster as a part of himself, tearing down the walls of its cage. "Please?" She breathed flirtatiously. "I dare you to do wicked things to me."

He let out a low groan, his mouth finding hers. Yeah, he loved this game. "God, you really are a Bad little girl, Bella."

"I know." She nipped his lower lip. "Face it, nobody else would put up with either one of us. I think it was inevitable that we were stuck together."

Avenant gave a slow grin. "Now who's the romantic who believes in destiny?"

"You're rubbing off on me, I guess." She swept her hair back behind her ears. "That reminds me, do you know what next Tuesday is?"

She felt him hesitate. "The fifteenth of ex-July."

"Which is?"

"Your birthday." He said with a resigned sigh.

"That's right." Belle nodded. "And I'm going to throw a party at my old house, just like I always do."

Silence.

"I'm going to invite Scarlett and Marrok and Jana and Benji and all the women from my book club and that nice troll from down the road and *maybe* Humpty Dumpty. He's really making a lot of strides in his PTSD treatments, I think. He barely hides from you at all, these days."

Avenant regarded her warily. "It matters if an egg likes me or not?"

"Well, I can't have a guest being scared of my husband all day, can I?" She shook her head. "It would be awkward for you if he started panicking that you were going to make him into an omelet or something. I want you to have a good time."

Blue eyes glowed. "You're inviting me to your birthday party?" He asked in relief. "Really?"

"Of course!" She gave him a smacking kiss. "I'm insanely in love with you, in case you haven't noticed. You're invited *everywhere* I go, because you're the one I have the most fun with." She touched his face. "It will always and forever be *you*, Avenant."

His lips curved, his gaze bright. "I won big when I got you for a True Love."

"And you didn't even have to cheat... Much."

"I would have done anything, if it meant having you." He kissed her temple. "So what do you want for your birthday? Name it and it's yours."

"No more horses." Belle warned. "I mean it."

"What about a pony?"

"What about a daughter?"

"Done."

He was serious. So was she.

Belle began mentally expanding the stable. A certain doting daddy was going to buy his little girl a whole herd of thoroughbreds. It was inevitable. She shook her head, crazy about this man. "Avenant, my parties were *always* about you." She told him, in case he still didn't understand that. "I only ever threw the damn things to *not* invite you and to get under your skin."

"It worked."

"Well, you're easy to tease." She arched a brow. "Hey, do you think Adam would like a waterslide?"

"Everyone likes waterslides. Even beasts." Avenant stroked her hair, his face going solemn. "Thank you, Bella." He whispered.

"It's just a silly party..."

"No." He interjected. "I mean *thank you*. You saved me. You made me whole. I would've been cold all the way through, without your warmth. Thank you for setting me free."

Belle smiled at the Beast of the Northlands. "You're welcome, my love."

Epilogue

Q is for queen.
Sometimes she's mean and makes a big scene.
But, sometimes she brings toys,
and noise,
and all kinds of joys.
Maybe this queen is not what she seems,
But, could be that she's,
just what you needs.

Mother Goose's Story Time Fun Show

It was all Avenant's fault. No one could dispute that.

Esmeralda had been trying to do the jackass a favor. She'd gone into the labyrinth to help him get his kingdom back and win his True Love and --okay fine-- maybe to steal herself some shiny treasure or something. Instead, she'd lost track of Avenant and Belle, been chased by a minotaur, and spent the whole night freezing in the ice corridors of the maze. She hadn't even found anything worth swiping.

To make matters worse, she'd accidently stepped in a rabbit hole and fallen through. For who knew how long, she'd been tumbling through empty space with no idea what waited for her on the other side of the darkness. It could be anything from dinosaurs to clowns to that stupid upside-down land.

It better not be that upside-down land. That place was so frigging annoying.

Luckily, being a witch meant that an endless free fall through a vortex was just a minor inconvenience.

Esmeralda had been careening downward for ages, but now she was finally getting close to touchdown. Below her, she could see light. Wherever it was coming from, it was sure to be better than all this boring *nothing*.

She hated being bored.

Esmeralda's powers slammed out, slowing her descent as she neared the bottom. If she'd had a broomstick, she could've tried flying out of the hole. As it was, though, all she could do was make sure she didn't leave a crater when she landed.

She crashed through the other end of the rabbit hole, dropping into the bright sunshine of a... garden party? Surrounding her were dozens of fancifully-shaped rose bushes and dozens of people in fancifully-shaped hats. She'd landed in the middle of a long table, piled high with frilly decorations. There were polka dot teapots and crust-less sandwiched and some kind of irritatingly chipper music playing from a tiny mouse orchestra situated on one end.

She'd been wrong. Even *nothing* was better than elevator music.

Esmeralda blinked, her eyes adjusting to the bright sunshine and the psychedelic array of neon patterns on everything. Even the grass was pink plaid. The only landmark she could see around her was a red and white checkerboard palace. This was definitely not the Four Kingdoms.

Damn Avenant.

Getting to her feet, Esmeralda brushed her hands together to remove shortbread crumbs. She'd landed on a plate of heart-shaped cookies all iced with the words "EAT ME." This whole creepy place could eat her.

"Alright, where the fuck am I?" Ez demanded, standing on the table and glaring down at the partiers.

A caterpillar the size of a person gaped at her. "Wonderland." He blurted out.

"Wonderland." An anthropomorphized hare agreed, sounding shell-shocked to see a green-skinned witch before him.

All around her, the other tea drinking idiots were nodding. Stupid hats swayed as their heads bobbed up and down, all agreeing that Ez was stuck in the ass-end of all kingdoms.

Esmeralda groaned, her palm coming up to slap against her forehead.

Even the upside-down realm would've been better than goddamn *Wonderland*. Not only was it hard as hell to escape once you got stuck here, but it was filled with all kinds of bizarre, annoying, and lawless bullshit guaranteed to piss people off.

Avenant was sooo going to pay for this.

"Perfect." Esmeralda headed down the length of the table, kicking the dainty china cups out of her way. "Somebody tell me the quickest way out of here." She ordered, porcelain and scones crunching under her boots. "I'm not in the mood for this crap."

A Cheshire cat pointed off towards a gigantic row of hedges. "You must brave the mysteries of the white rose labyrinth." She said, awe in her voice.

"Nah... I don't think so." No way was Esmeralda dealing with another stupid maze. "What's the *other* quickest way?"

"Through the castle." The caterpillar told her. "But, you'll never get passed the queen and her guards."

"Whatever." Esmeralda hopped of the edge of the table, trying not to stare too long at any one spot. The colors of the place burned her retinas. Witches had a pathological aversion to so much *cheery*. It was definitely time to go.

Some playing-card soldiers came barreling down the steps as she neared the checkered palace, their heart-shaped spears at the ready. "Halt!" One of them bellowed. "Halt in the name of her majesty!"

Esmeralda rolled her eyes and kept marching forward. "Boys, you don't want to mess with me today." She warned the two-dimensional goon squad. "I haven't eaten, my hair's a mess, and your doofy kingdom gives me a migraine."

They didn't take her *extremely* good advice. Instead, the morons charged. Their creepily thin bodies scissor-stepped their way towards her.

"Invader!" One shrieked. "Sound the alarm!"

"Protect Queen Alice!" Another called.

"Kill her!" Several more chanted in unison. "Kill the invader!"

Well, it wasn't like she hadn't warned them. Esmeralda raised a hand and let loose with her magic. Green lightening streaked across the plaid grass, shredding through the playing cards like they were made of paper. Which, come to think of it, they *were*. The "fight" was over in two seconds flat and Esmeralda didn't even have to slow her steps.

The deck of idiots probably didn't have enough forces left to make a passable hand of bridge.

Tea party guests, intact guards, and everyone else around ran for the pastel striped hills. Clearly, there weren't many witches in these nauseatingly colorful parts. She'd just scared the hell out of every Wonderlandian in a two mile radius.

Esmeralda smiled, her mood improving. It was like Auntie Hazel always said: "If you aren't having fun being a wicked witch, then you're doing it wrong."

"It's the Queen of Clubs!" Somebody shouted. "She's come to murder us all!"

Five minutes in this place and she'd already been promoted to queen? It was about *time* Ez got the respect she was due. Witches lived to inspire terror, but Esmeralda had always been kind of a screw-up. Most of her plots for world domination got laughed out of the Cauldron Society. No matter how hard she tried, evilness just didn't come naturally to her. It was a huge embarrassment. Things were suddenly looking up, though.

Too bad no one important was around to see it.

She headed up the curving steps of the palace, delighting in the fearful response of the citizenry. They hid behind furniture. They cowered in corners. Their eyes were wide and damp with horrified tears. Damn, if only she had a camera...

"Stop!" An oh-so-pretty girl in a blue dress stepped directly into Esmeralda's path. "I am Queen Alice," she pointed to her crown just in case Esmeralda had missed it, "and this is *my* kingdom, invader!"

"Really?" Esmeralda wasn't impressed. "You should seriously think about redecorating this joint, then. It's like a rainbow threw-up on your entire realm, blondie."

Alice jabbed a finger at her, her lips narrowing into a tight line. "I am placing you under arrest for Badness and witchcraft and disruption of a tea party and..."

"Oh, shut-up." Esmeralda waved a palm and turned the jabbering twit into a log. She'd been going for a *frog*, but a log would do. Not quite as classically evil, but still kind of scary.

Kind of.

She wrinkled her nose. Ever since she'd gotten out of the WUB Club, her spells only had a 50/50 success rate. It was getting to be a problem.

Luckily, it didn't take much magic to intimidate the nitwits of Wonderland. The ones who hadn't already passed out or run away goggled at the hunk of wood that used to be Alice. The diamond tiara was still perched on its branchy top... which was actually a little bit funny.

Not that anybody here had a sense of humor. She seriously needed to find a way home.

Esmeralda stomped over to pick up the crown and plopped it on her own head. At least she'd finally gotten to steal herself something sparkly. "Alright." She looked at the traumatized faces surrounding her and arched a brow. "Which way to the exit?"

If you enjoyed *Beast in Shining Armor*, be sure to read the next book in the "Kinda Fairytale" series *The Kingpin of Camelot*. Available now!

The Queen: Guinevere must save Camelot. Ever since Arthur died, the evil Scarecrow has been trying to marry her and gain the crown. If she and her daughter are going to survive his mad schemes, Gwen needs to find Merlyn's wand. *Fast*. Unfortunately, the only man strong enough to help her on her quest is Kingpin Midas, a flashy, uneducated mobster dealing with a curse. Gwen is a logical, rational woman, though, and she can draft one hell of a contract. She's pretty sure she can come up with an offer not even the kingdom's greatest villain can refuse.

The Kingpin: Anything Midas touches turns to gold. Literally. The curse has helped him to rule Camelot's underworld with an iron fist. He has more money and more power than anyone else in the kingdom. He's convinced there's nothing he can't buy. One look at Gwen and Midas knows that he's about to make his most brilliant purchase, yet. He's about to own the one woman in the world he would give *anything* to possess. All he has to do to claim her is somehow win a war against the smartest man in Camelot, hide his growing feelings from Gwen, deal with his overprotective bodyguard's paranoia about the queen's hidden motivations, and adjust to a five year old demanding bedtime stories from a gangster. Simple, right?

The Contract: Gwen's deal is simple: If Midas marries her, she'll make him King of Camelot. It's a fair bargain. Midas will keep her enemies away and she'll give him the respectability that money can't buy. She never expects Midas to agree so quickly. Or for their practical business arrangement to feel so… complicated. Midas isn't the tawdry, feral animal that Arthur railed against. He's a kind and gentle man, who clearly needs Gwen's help just as much as she needs his. In fact, the longer she's around Midas the more Gwen realizes that their "fake marriage" might be more real than she ever imagined.

Printed in Great Britain
by Amazon